Right to Know

A novel by

Edward Willett

This is a work of fiction. The characters, incidents and dialogues are products of the author's imagination and are not to be construed as real. Any resemblance to actual events or persons, living or dead, is entirely coincidental.

Cover Illustration: Dan O'Driscoll
Cover Design: Virginia O'Dine

Printed in Canada
Published by Bundoran Press Publishing House
www.bundoranpress.com

Library and Archives Canada Cataloguing in Publication

Willett, Edward, 1959-, author

Right to know / Edward Willett.

ISBN 978-0-9880674-5-5 (pbk.)

I. Title.

PS8595.I5424R54 2013 C813'.54 C2013-904966-5

This book is dedicated to Butler, Missouri, birthplace of two very influential people in my life: Robert A. Heinlein, and my mother, Nina Mae Spears.

Chapter One

Rick's Place was crowded when Art stepped through the door, Treena on his arm. But then, everything was crowded in Habitat Twenty: the apartments stacked from deck to skyplate, the four levels of tubewalks, and even the central park, consisting of little more than a few hundred square metres of scraggly grass and a fountain that hadn't worked in fifteen years. The only thing the habitat had going for it was the beer in Rick's Place—best beer on the ship, Art was convinced—and Treena, the busty blonde who'd contacted him earlier that day out of the blue with the provocative news that her name had come up in the Conception Draft, that his name was on the list of approved fathers, and that she much preferred to fulfill her reproductive duties through old-fashioned rather than technological means.

Art was more than willing, and had arranged to meet her. Now they threaded their way through the crowd, nobody paying them any attention. It was another reason he liked Rick's Place. He'd been going there often enough he was seen as a regular. Nobody cared that every evening his face was plastered on screens all over the ship, reading the shipday's news. In the mid-Habs and higher there were fancier places where he would have been treated as a celebrity. That could be nice, but sometimes he just wanted to be an ordinary guy interested in ordinary things…like beer.

And Treena.

A table had just opened up in the corner; he steered Treena

to it. "I'll get us some drinks," he said to her, and she smiled. Her nose crinkled adorably and her chest heaved in an interesting fashion, and although her blue eyes were rather vacant, they were certainly pretty. Art smiled back and turned to pick his way to the bar.

"Rick"—Art had never known if that was his real name or not—had just put a pint of red ale and a fizzy pink cocktail on the bar when Art's arm was suddenly seized in an iron-like grip and twisted behind him. He gasped in pain as he was frog-marched through the crowd, which scattered in front of him. His unseen assailant smashed him up against the faux-wood wall, right between the dartboards, and growled in his ear, "You've got your nerve coming here."

The words were carried on a puff of hot breath smelling of fresh beer and old garlic. "Who—" Art began, but got no farther before he was spun around and squeezed up against the wall by a massive arm across his chest, so tightly he could hardly breathe. He blinked at the face just inches from his own. "Pete?" he wheezed.

His best friend from childhood glowered at him. "This is a place for Shipborn, Stoddard. *Shipborn.*"

Art managed to get a breath despite the pressure on his lungs. Beyond Peter's florid face he saw two beefy guys in nondescript clothes, arms folded, grinning: friends of Peter's, obviously. The other patrons of Rick's Place watched with interest, but no apparent inclination to rescue him. The owner looked concerned, though. "You damage anything, you'll pay for it," he growled.

Art flicked his eyes back to Peter. "What are you talking about?" he wheezed. "I *am* Shipborn. You know that. You—" He had to stop as the pressure on his chest increased.

"You're a boot-licking jelly-spined mouthpiece for the bloody Council and Crew, that's what you are!" Peter bellowed. "And you aren't welcome here!"

"Look, Peter, why don't we sit down—I'll buy you a drink—"

"I don't drink with Council or Crew!" But Peter let go of him and stepped back. "Come on, Stoddard, we've put this off long enough. Let's settle it!"

Art took a couple of deep breaths and pressed the heel of his hand into his aching chest. "Settle *what*?" he said, honestly bewildered. He'd come in here, minding his own business, looking for a little relaxation after a hard day spent sweltering in the rain forest in Hab Six trying to get some decent video of dead fish, and now…

Over Pete's shoulder he saw Treena downing a drink he certainly hadn't bought for her, and talking to a tall young man in tight blue coveralls. He wore the gold star of an approved reproductive partner, just like Art. Art groaned and turned his attention back to his erstwhile friend. "Pete, what's this all about?"

"I see you," Pete said. "Every night. You in your nice suit. You in your fancy studio. Living up in Habitat Three. We played together as kids. I was every bit as good as you at everything. Better at most things. And you're up there," he pointed toward the ceiling, "and I'm down here." He waved his hand vaguely to encompass the bar and presumably the entire habitat. "And you know what they've got me doing? Scrubbing hydro tanks. *Robot* work." His fists clenched.

Art flushed, and fought to keep his temper. He didn't want a fight—not with anyone, but especially not with Peter. Peter was—had been—his best friend. As kids they'd once promised they'd be friends all their lives. "Look, Peter, you're right, it's not fair. I just got lucky, that's all. It could just as easily have been the other way around." *If your father were on the Council and could pull the strings necessary to get you a job like mine*, he thought, *instead of a crazy drunk who managed the impossible task of getting himself killed by a maintenance robot. And speaking of crazy drunks…* "Let me buy you a drink and we'll—"

"I don't want a drink! You think you can buy anything, don't you? You think you've got it all—fancy clothes, money—lots of money—and girls. Lots of girls. You always got a girl, Art." He glanced at Treena. She wasn't paying any attention to them;

she only had eyes for the tall young man, who had now folded himself into the seat Art should have already been occupying, beer in hand.

Art felt a surge of anger at the sight. *This has gone on long enough*. He didn't try to keep the contempt out of his voice. "Would you like me to find you a girl, Pete? Is that what you need?"

Peter's face darkened even more. "I don't need anything from you, *Mister* Stoddard," he said as distinctly as alcohol would let him. "Except the pleasure of smashing your pretty face in. We'll see how much good you are to the Council after—"

"So go ahead! Smash my face in. And then what happens to you? It won't be hydro tanks any more. It will be sewage tanks. Or prison."

"You can't scare me!" But Peter's eyes narrowed, and behind him, his two friends exchanged worried looks.

"I am the Information Dissemination Specialist: Civilian," Art said coldly. "*You* are a…what? Manual Laborer, Fourth Class? A 'make-work jerk'?" It was a term of contempt, and Art made sure his voice dripped with it. "Just which do you think is of more importance to the workings of the ship, old *friend*?"

"You little *shit*!" Peter lunged at him, but his friends grabbed his arms and held him back.

"He's not worth it, Pete," one said urgently. "You heard him. You touch him and he'll have the 'keeps on you. He's practically Crew!"

Art had not moved and he said nothing, but his anger drained away and his stomach churned as he looked at Peter's rage-twisted face; then Peter shoved his companions away, straightened and turned his back contemptuously on Art. Art glanced around the room. No one would meet his eyes; even Rick turned away and busied himself with mixing drinks. The juke started cranking out the latest syrupy synthotune.

Art went back to the long faux-oak bar, where the drinks he'd bought still waited. *Peter's right*, he thought sickly. *I shouldn't come here anymore*. He drank deeply of his ale, the hand holding the glass trembling slightly. It was time to find some other place to drink—someplace where he was still wanted. "Here's looking at you, kid," he muttered, and drained his glass. Then he tossed back the pink cocktail, made a face at its burning sweetness, and turned to leave.

A cool touch on his hand stopped him. He looked back and down into Treena's blue eyes. "Not going without me, I hope?" she murmured.

He blinked, surprised. "I thought—" he looked over her shoulder. "That tall guy—"

"Not my type," Treena said.

"He bought you a drink."

She shrugged. "I never turn down a free drink. Come on, let's get out of here."

Art laughed, suddenly feeling better. "With pleasure." The cost of the drinks had been automatically deducted from his account the moment he'd ordered them; he left the empty glasses on the bar, took Treena's arm and started toward the door…only to find it blocked by a tall man wearing a disheveled and suspiciously stained suit, his shock of white hair glowing in the light. He'd stumbled to his feet from a booth as they approached, and now stood between them and their escape.

"Yer a ghoul…good…good lad," the man wheezed. "Standing up for selsh…self."

Art took a deep breath, then wished he hadn't as the reek of whiskey and onions filled his nose. He swallowed to keep from gagging and said, "Councilor Woods. You shouldn't be here. Where are your bodyguards?"

Woods drew himself up. "Don't need 'em. People love me. Fav'rite Councilor. Four years running. Puke a pup…I mean, look it up." He poked a finger into Art's chest, and then weaved away toward the bar.

Art sighed, shook his head, and led Treena outside.

They emerged into a narrow roadway with four-story stacks of apartments on either side, light gleaming in hundreds of windows, rising up to the skyplate, itself dark except for the pinpricks of light intended to simulate the stars as seen from Earth. Never having seen Earth—never having set foot on any planet—Art didn't have a clue if the effect was accurate or not. His father and the others of the Originals said it was, and he supposed they would know. Unlike them, though, he never thought of those lights as stars. They were nothing but low-energy/high-output LEDs, and unless he missed his guess, about half of the ones that should have been shining up there were burned out.

Something skittered past them down the pale ceramic pavement, a silvery globe with four jointed spider-legs and four manipulator arms: one of the ubiquitous maintenance robots. Art had once been told that on a ship the size of the *Mayflower II* a part failed every three seconds. A dozen micro-factories utilizing 3D printing technology recycled old parts and churned out new ones, and a thousand robots scurried around the habitats fixing and replacing, and yet…

And yet, the LED constellations overhead had dozens of blank spots, the fish were dying in the tropical rainforest habitat, and every day other stories of breakdowns and failures crossed Art's desk…

Crossed his desk, and fell into the black hole of silence imposed by the Council and Crew on any news of problems with ship maintenance.

Art sighed. He looked up at the skyplate again and tried to imagine what it must be like to walk the surface of a planet with nothing between him and space but a few insubstantial kilometres of gases. He'd watched hundreds of ancient entertainments, "films" and TV shows and holographic soap operas, and though to him the *Mayflower II* had always been home and world combined, sometimes he longed for the wonders of those long-gone days, for mountains and oceans and skyscrapers and a vast blue sky of air —

—for *room*; room enough to escape the constant press of people.

People like Peter. "Bastard," he muttered.

"Was he really a friend of yours?" Treena asked. In the cool darkness she seemed much younger than she had in the overheated bar.

Art put his arm around her and she snuggled close. "He was my best friend, once. But we—drifted apart." He started walking, away from Rick's Place, from Peter, and from memories.

"Because he's a 'make-work jerk' and you're—"

"I shouldn't have said that," Art muttered.

"But that's why, isn't it?"

"Yeah, but I still shouldn't have said it."

"Why not?"

"I pulled rank on him." He shook his head. "That's a Council trick. A *Crew* trick."

"That's all right," Treena said brightly. "You practically *are* Crew."

He almost hit her. Instead he stopped, there on the ceramic street, until he could say, gently, "I'm not. I'm Shipborn. Like him. Like you."

"But—"

"Don't talk." Art roughly pulled her close. "Haven't we got better things to do than talk?"

She nodded and smiled, back on familiar ground. "Where—"

As if there were any choice. He could no more take her to his home in Habitat Three then he could have fixed the matter-antimatter reactor that powered the ship. "Your place," he said, and let her lead him away into the artificial night.

◣ ◢

Night still filled Habitat Three when the insistent beeping of Art's alarm dragged him from the depths of sleep. "Shit," he said. The alarm immediately cut off, responding to one of several swear words he'd programmed the system to recognize as meaning he was awake. Simultaneously the lights came on, stabbing a lance of pain into his fogged brain.

He'd only been in his own bed for a couple of hours, but

it was 0500 and he had to be on the air at 0630. Knowing if he closed his eyes he'd be asleep again in an instant, he swung his legs over the side of the mattress, lurched to his feet and stumbled into the bathroom.

The pulsing water of the shower brought him to some semblance of full wakefulness, but as he stepped out of the stall and grabbed a towel he glanced at his image in the full-length mirror, expecting to see bloodshot, puffy eyes looking back at him.

Instead he saw what he always saw—a 32-year-old man with features some people thought were *too* good-looking, a carefully nurtured tan that covered every inch of his lean, muscular body, straight, chestnut-brown hair now spiky with moisture, and blue eyes that met his quizzically. "You can't go on like this," he told his reflection. "You'll never live to a ripe old age if you don't get your rest."

He snorted and turned toward the smaller shaving mirror over the sink. Old age on the *Mayflower II* would be *very* ripe. Overripe, in fact. Stinking, rotting ripe. "Canned fruits, that's what we are," he muttered as he ran the shaver over his chin. "The universe is a cellar and we're all preserves."

Pleased with his metaphor, he grinned at his clean-shaven face, then went back into the bedroom and dressed in what he thought of as his uniform: a dark-blue jacket, a light-blue shirt, a nondescript red tie, all of a style no one else on the ship wore—anymore than he did, when he wasn't on duty. Then as quietly as possible he slipped out, taking care not to wake his parents.

If he'd lived on his own, of course, he wouldn't have had to worry about it...but his father, the esteemed—by some—Councilor Randall P. Stoddard, had made it clear that any application he might make for housing elsewhere would not be approved. He wanted his son close at hand. And since any housing Art might have been able to get even without his father's interference would most likely have been Habitat Eight or Nine at best, Art had never tried too hard to change the elder Stoddard's mind.

Their house, in Neighbourhood One, was only a short walk

from the nearest intraship transport access station. The stacked, teeming warrens of the higher-numbered Habs weren't for the residents of Habitat Three. Here, trees of uniform height and shape bordered the ubiquitous cream-coloured ceramic pavement; bicycles, identical except for colour, stood on kickstands beside the walk to each square house. Despite white paint and blue, carved shutters and lawn sculptures and variations in landscaping, their basic sameness could not be disguised.

Here and there no disguise had even been attempted, and a house bore the unmistakable stamp of mass manufacture proudly, like a sign of distinction. These were the homes of the Councilors, Earthborn every one of them, appointed by the government on Earth before the ship launched and in power ever since...and Art, son of a Councilor, had lived in one of them his entire life.

He strode down the walk and turned right, breathing in the sweet scents of flowers and other growing things. In Habitat Three, every house had its own manicured plot of oxygenating greenery, potted trees and banks of flowers and even the occasional vegetable crèche. Art's route also took him past the edge of the central park, a manufactured bit of "wilderness" impenetrably dark this early in the morning, when even the "stars" were switched off and the only light came from the widely spaced lightposts, but he didn't spare the shadows a second glance. There was nothing to fear in the dark in the *Mayflower II*'s controlled environment.

Even so, he suppressed a start as a maintenance robot burst out of the darkness and crossed the street not five metres ahead of him, scuttling over the pale ceramic surface like a giant black spider. He snorted at his own foolishness and walked on.

His footsteps echoed back to him from a side street, so that it sounded for a moment as if he were being followed—but he knew he wasn't. Down in the mid-Habs they sometimes followed him, or crowded him—he was as much of a celebrity as the *Mayflower II* had, after all—but no one ever followed him in Habitat Three, which, along with the identical Habitat Four, was home to Councilors and high-level bureaucrats. They knew him for what he was: someone highly visible and completely powerless.

He thought back to the encounter with Pete, Treena's later efforts to make him forget what had happened notwithstanding. Of course Pete was jealous of him. Who could blame him? They'd played together as kids, back when Pete had lived in Habitat Three as well, before his family's fall from grace. It wasn't Pete's fault his dad, senior administrator of the Population Management Authority, had gone crazy and started making wild accusations against the Prime Councilor…not to mention the Captain. But it sure as hell wasn't Art's fault, either. And Pete hadn't been a kid anymore by then. He could have stepped away from his father, kept his own nose clean. No way he'd have stayed in Habitat Three or Four, but he might have hung on in the mid-Habs. Instead he'd defended his father to the bitter end, and after the freak accident involving the maintenance robot had made some pretty wild accusations himself about his father being murdered. *He's lucky he's even doing make-work*, Art thought. *In the early years the Captain might have spaced him.*

Now he saw Art doing all right for himself, and wondered why it couldn't be him. Especially…

Art sighed. Especially since he'd almost screwed up as badly as Pete.

He remembered the night. He could hardly forget it, what with his father reminding him every couple of weeks. He'd been nineteen, Pete a year older. They'd been out drinking in the mid-Habs. Pete had been going on and on about how his father's death hadn't been an accident, how someone had altered the maintenance robot's programming, made it kill him. Everyone knew the robots were incapable of harming anyone. But somehow it had started to make sense, especially after the fifth beer and second—or was it the third?—whiskey. They'd staggered out of the bar in search of a maintenance robot. Even drunk as they were it hadn't been hard: there was always one around, like the one that had just startled Art. They'd cornered it and beaten it to pieces with a chair they'd stolen from the bar. The robot had finally quit twitching just as the Peacekeepers arrived. The 'keeps had hauled them up to Administration, processed them, locked them up in the brig. It had been the last time Art had seen Pete until the night before in Rick's Place, and Art knew he could just as easily have ended up a make-work jerk, too, except…

…except *his* father was a Councilor. Art had only been in the cell for an hour before his father had shown up, tight-lipped and furious, and hauled him out of there. An endless lecture later, Art had been on probation, kept on such a short leash by his father he hadn't even seen the mid-Habs for another five years. By that time his father had landed him his current position as Information Dissemination Specialist.

He tried to shake off his black mood. So who cared what the other Shipborn thought? They were wrong. He was more like them than they knew. He didn't like the way the Council ruled, deciding where people would live, what jobs they would do, what they could hear and see and read, forcing women to have children, forcing those children into whatever roles they saw fit. But what could he do about it? The 'keeps didn't wait for trouble before arresting troublemakers, and what good would getting arrested do anyone?

All he was doing was making the best of things—and sometimes, he had to admit, things were pretty good. After all, however some of the Shipborn felt about him, there were plenty of others to whom his closeness to the Council and Crew didn't seem to matter—including a lot of girls. Like Treena.

A short distance ahead a small red-and-white sign identified the intraship transit station. The pod inside would whisk him up the habitat's "boom" (properly known as the Service and Transit Conduit) to the Core, and from there to Habitat Two, the Administration Hab. Habitat One, of course, was Crew Country: home not only to the crew, but to the ship's bridge, CentComp, and associated control systems, tucked away on a restricted-access deck above the Hab's skyplate.

There were no habitats further "up" the Core: forward of Habitats One to Four there was only the massive sphere of the Forward Service and Propulsion Module, a place where only maintenance robots ventured except in extraordinary circumstances. It housed the projectors for the powerful electromagnetic fields that had kept the *Mayflower II*—at least so far—from a catastrophic encounter with some anonymous bit of space matter while moving at relativistic speed, and itself nestled in behind the huge umbrella-shaped Forward Shield, a solid chunk of reshaped asteroid that was the last defense against such collisions.

Currently the Forward Module also housed the matter-antimatter reactor and the propulsion system, for the *Mayflower II* was decelerating. For the first fifteen years of the ship's journey the reactor and the engines had resided in the Aft Module, accelerating the giant vessel at a constant 0.3 g to almost the speed of light. Now they were just as enthusiastically slowing its journey, though what lay at the end of their long downward slide no one knew…or at least no one was talking about it.

Supposedly there was a good chance of finding a habitable planet in the system at which they had been aimed so many years ago. Art's parents certainly believed it. Art had his doubts.

Art stepped inside the waiting pod, and sat on its worn vinyl seat of faded blue, patched in one spot with a bit of duct-tape—presumably the work of an actual human being, not a spectacularly lazy maintenance robot.

"Please place palm on the scanning panel for biometric evaluation," said a pleasant female voice, and a panel slid aside in the front of the compartment, revealing a glowing blue square. Art placed his hand on the square and it blinked green as CentComp ensured he was indeed Arthur Stoddard and had the necessary clearance to visit the pod's preprogrammed destination, the Administration Hab. For all he knew it sniffed his sweat, too.

"Identity confirmed," said the pod. "Please ensure all hands and feet are inside the pod and say 'Go' when ready to depart."

"Go," said Art. The pod door slid shut and acceleration pressed him back against the seat.

There were no windows; like an elevator, the pod moved people from place to place without ever providing them a glimpse of the rather utilitarian spaces they traversed. He felt the change in momentum as the pod crossed from Habitat Three's boom into the Core. There, subject only to the deceleration forces, his stomach flip-flopped as his weight abruptly dropped to what he'd been told it would have been on Mars, not that he had any way to tell.

Momentum shifted again as the pod moved from the Core along the boom to the Administration Hab, and then he felt the pod slow and stop, the door opened, and he stepped out into the access station, once more at normal weight.

It was never night in Admin Hab, since no one actually lived there; instead the skyplate gave a featureless white light that replicated a day of high overcast on Earth. The buildings were almost as featureless as the sky: white blocks marked with a few mirrored windows and dark blue doors bearing white text identifying each building's purpose. Signs on the corners directed newcomers to "Food Production" or "Population Management"—former workplace of Peter's late father—or any of dozens of other administrative offices, but Art barely glanced at them; although he'd gotten lost in Admin Hab a few times in his early days on the job, now he could have found the studio in his sleep. A couple of times he thought he had.

Three lefts, a right, two blocks and another right, and he stood in front of a dark-blue door like all the others, labeled "Internal Communications." A bar of light flashed over his face again, and the door swung inward. He strode down the carpeted hallway beyond to the studio at its end. His techies, Teresa and Norman, were running a quick system check, huddled together head to head behind the control board. "'Morning," Art said and received brief, distracted nods in return. He withdrew back down the hall to the office, and checked his messages. Nothing new from Crew or Council; that meant the morning 'cast would basically be a repeat of the previous evening's. Art queued and previewed the necessary video files, ran over his script, and still found himself with twenty-five minutes to kill until the scheduled recording time. There was nothing particularly stopping him from recording early—except for his agreement with Teresa and Norman to always leave them with half an hour alone in the studio to "double-check the equipment." He figured he knew *exactly* what equipment they were double-checking, and he wasn't about to interfere.

So he stayed where he was, his thoughts inevitably falling back into the same track as before.

No, it wasn't fair for Peter to blame him for his job. It wasn't as if he had wanted it: he had *wanted* to join the *Mayflower II*'s small professional acting troupe, the Relativistic Pilgrims, but there'd been no chance of that after the escapade with the maintenance robot. The artistic director had privately confided to him once at a party that it was a damn shame, since he had "a fine voice." The director had been hitting on him at the time, though, so he wasn't sure if he should take the compliment seriously; certainly he'd lost interest once Art had made it clear he was straight.

No, Art's job was entirely his father's doing. Randall P. Stoddard was one of the original Councilors, the ones appointed by the bi-partisan Launch Committee before the *Mayflower II* had so hastily set out. In his late thirties then, he was now pushing seventy, and he had never lost his almost fanatical loyalty to the Crew, a loyalty engendered in part by the way the Crew, all career military, had fought off an attack, just a week before launch, by a force from who-knew-where on Earth. Crew had died that day to save the ship and its passengers.

In fact, so far as Art knew, not one of the original Councilors objected to how the Crew ran the ship…well, none except for Jonas Woods, the Councilor he'd stumbled over—literally—at Rick's Place. He'd been appointed as a sop to the Liberty Party, a party so far out of the mainstream of political thought that it was generally seen as a joke—except that it had powerful and wealthy adherents who had made it clear they would withhold their support, both financial and moral, for the building of the ship if he were not included.

Woods had made some fiery speeches in support of individual liberty and responsibility in his early days—Art had covertly watched a couple of them, although he'd only been able to do so because of his relatively unfettered access to the ship's official records; most Passengers would never have been able to get near those recordings.

But despite that—or maybe because of the fact those early attempts at rabble-rousing had gone nowhere—Jonas Woods had long since sunk into drunkenness and debauchery, and as someone who was quite familiar with drunkenness and debauchery, the fact Art even thought of it in those terms was telling.

Jonas Woods was a joke, his long, rambling, pointless speeches having even given rise to a new description, "pulling a woody," applied to anyone who talked a long time without saying anything of note. (That it was also something of a double entendre had probably contributed to its popularity.) The days when he was not a joke now lay more than thirty subjective years in the past—ancient history, as far as Art was concerned. And no one else questioned the Crew.

These days, the Crew kept to itself. Despite his job, the only Crew he had ever met personally were Peacekeepers—and even most of the 'keeps were actually Shipborn, although Crew Shipborn were a different kettle of fish than guys like Pete.

Habitat One was off-limits to everyone but Crew: a modern version of the Forbidden City of ancient China. Even the Prime Councilor did not have access. At its heart, like a spider at the centre of a web, dwelt Captain Harold Nakos, supreme authority of the ship—and a man no one not of the Crew had seen in person since shortly after Launch.

Sometimes Art wondered if the Captain still lived. But he never said that out loud—especially not where his father could hear it.

Norman stuck his head in the door. His face was flushed. "Ready for you now, Art."

"Thanks, Norm. On my way." Art gathered his script and went into the studio.

The rest of the day passed in normal routine; he had interviews with three people and spent an hour getting vid of a dozen maintenance robots, supervised by two harried engineers, scuttling around the river recycler in the Habitat Five, the Forest Hab, which had recently been giving the stream a unique colour and odor definitely not in the original specifications.

Art doubted the vid would ever air. Two stories he'd submitted for approval the day before had both been rejected without explanation. Art frowned at the Crewcomm terminal. One story had been about a mysterious fungal infection that had wiped out a whole tankplot of green peppers, and the other about the loss of half a day's credit transfer records after an unexplained power surge. Both were already the talk of the mid-Habs—but he'd had no choice but to ignore them.

He cleared the screen with an angry swipe. Six months ago he had not only been allowed to report on a similar computer malfunction, he had been ordered to. And agricultural die-offs due to disease or tankplot malfunction were nothing new; every other week, it seemed, some fruit or vegetable crop had to be re-started from the genetics bank, while everyone did without. They'd once gone six months without potatoes, and it had been nearly that long since he'd seen a tomato. Why wasn't he supposed to say anything about it anymore?

He was reduced, in his evening recording session, to reading practically the same script again, except for two frothy human-interest bits, one on the 85th birthday of the oldest Passenger, a man born just after the inaugural meeting of the Caliphate of the Holy and Oppressed and just before the destruction of Ottawa provided the impetus to Unification, and one on an amateur sculptor who made models of the ship out of scrap metal. Art allowed himself the cynical thought that that could quite plausibly be considered a political comment; he was surprised the Council censors, much less the Crew ones, had allowed it.

The only "hard" news was already ancient history: the publication of the latest lists of women required to attempt conception and the men designated as acceptable fathers. Sure, the semi-annual "Sperm-'n'-Eggs" list was big news—and had led to the previous night's energetic and entirely pleasurable, if exhausting, activities with Treena, and since he was on the male side of the list he was more than happy to continue to draw other eligible women's attention to it—but still, three days after its release, it wasn't exactly *new* "news," was it?

Norman gave him the traditional thumbs-up as he finished the recording, then closed down the control board and headed off, hand-in-hand with Teresa. Art watched them go and sighed. Teresa was young and sexy and...completely uninterested in him. Unfortunately, even though she was on the current Egg-'n'-Sperm list, so was Norman, and that suited them both so well Art knew he didn't stand a chance.

Not that it stopped him from fantasizing every once in a while.

He'd just reached the door when his terminal beeped three times, the high-low-high pattern indicating an incoming voice call. For a moment he considered ignoring it, since he was officially off-duty, but then he decided reluctantly it could be important. He went over to his terminal. "Answer," he said. "Internal Communications, Stoddard here."

He expected the screen to light with the image of the caller, but instead it remained stubbornly blank; and the voice that spoke was both distorted and neutered. "Why didn't you report on the cred-transfer breakdown?"

Art frowned at the blank screen. "Who is this?"

The voice laughed, the distortion giving it an eerie, horror-movie sound. "Who knows what evil lurks in the hearts of men? The Shadow knows."

Art blinked in surprise. He'd have bet he was the only person on the ship who would have gotten that particular ancient pop-culture reference. "What?"

"I've got something for you. I know who caused the data loss. Interested?"

Art sighed. Every problem brought the crazies out of the deckplates. "A power surge caused the data loss."

"But who caused *that*?"

"Who? Don't you mean what?"

"No," the distorted voice said. "I mean who. I can tell you. If you want to know."

Crazy, he thought again, and *Call the 'keeps*, another part of him urged.

But it has to be a hoax, he argued with himself. *Do you really want to waste the Peacekeepers' time on a hoax? Time enough to call after you talk to this nut, if you have to. Play it safe.*

"Well?" the voice said impatiently.

"I'm interested," he said cautiously.

"Good. Take the pod as usual. We'll meet you."

"Meet me? Where? There's no place to—"

"As long as we know, you don't need to, do you?" The line went dead.

Art stood still for a moment. He could still call the 'keeps… but then he swore at his own faintheartedness and quickly finished closing up. Five minutes later he stepped out into the ever-bright Hab and made his way to the pod.

Halfway there, the lights went out.

Art stopped dead, shocked. The lights *never* went out in Admin Hab. Never. It was a given. Had something drastic happened? *Have we hit something?*

The lights came back on.

He gulped. *Coincidence*, he thought. It doesn't have anything to do with that mysterious voice.

He was almost able to convince himself.

The pod trip back to Habitat Three was uneventful, though Art held himself tensely the whole time, waiting for something to happen. When he stepped out into the transit station, he took a quick, nervous look around. Again, he saw nothing unusual.

A prank? he thought. *Could be...*

Peter! Peter or one of his friends. That's gotta be it.

Convinced he'd solved the mystery, he set off down the street toward his parents' house.

Well, half-convinced: he couldn't help taking quick looks around as he walked down the dimly lit street, the skyplate shining with "stars" above him but little else in the way of artificial lighting except for the widely spaced glowing lightposts, casting fuzzy patches of silver on the scuffed ceramic street but making the darkness between them even blacker.

As he approached the park, he quickened his pace. Just beyond the park's patch of deeper night he could see the more concentrated glow of Neighbourhood One. The park was two hundred metres wide. He was maybe fifty metres into it when all lightposts along the street went out at once.

He stopped in confusion, heart suddenly racing; an instant later two dark figures leaped out of the shadows.

Chapter Two

One of the figures jerked a bag over his head. The other seized his arm, twisting it behind him and propelling him off the street and onto the grass of the park. "Not a sound," a harsh voice whispered in his ear—a woman's voice.

"Are you—" Art began nevertheless, then gasped and fell silent as his arm was given a painful jerk.

They hurried over the grass; stopped. He heard a scraping sound, then a hiss. His arm was released. It ached, and he rubbed it as the voice said. "There's a ladder. Turn around. On your knees. Find the top rung."

Breathing hard, he did as he was told. He felt the rung, eased himself backward, climbed down. He could tell there was someone below him; someone else came after. The hiss repeated, then the scrape.

A single fluorescent tube flickered to sickly blue life, and Art saw his assailants for the first time. Skin-tight, non-reflective black cloth covered them from head to toe. He'd already known one was a woman; the other was a man…or boy, judging from his slim build. Each wore a sheathed knife on one hip. Cold eyes glittered at Art from behind black masks.

He took all that in an instant: then his vision focused, with laser-like intensity, on the long black barrel of the evil-looking rifle pointed at his stomach. Art went very still, though a voice in the back of his head was shouting. *How did they get a weapon? Only the Crew and 'keeps have weapons! Is this a mutiny?*

And, of course, the central question also kept racing around his panicked brain. *What do they want with me?*

Peripherally he saw bare ceramic walls and a floor of dented, rusty metal panels. He finally tore his gaze away from the rifle's sinister muzzle and looked past it and the boy holding it to the woman. He found his voice, even if it wasn't as steady as he would have liked. "What is this?" he demanded. "You asked me to meet you so you could tell me who was behind the data loss. I met you. Why hold me at gunpoint?"

"Just playing it safe," said the woman, her contralto voice contemptuous. "Just in case you called the 'keeps. That's what Philip said you'd do. He said you belong to the Crew and Council and you'd call the 'keeps as soon as I cut the connection. I said if the 'keeps showed up he could shoot you. So now we're waiting to see if there's a knock." She jerked her head upward, toward the top of the ladder, though the hatch they had descended through was out of sight.

Art swallowed. "I didn't call the 'keeps." *Although I thought about it*, he thought, but he wasn't going to tell them *that*. Art looked at the boy, presumably Philip, but the youth's aim never wavered.

"Philip isn't very trusting," said the woman. "Especially not of a professional liar."

"I don't lie!"

"You don't tell the whole truth. That's a form of lying."

"I suppose the real truth comes from people who dress in black and carry guns?"

"Maybe." The woman circled him. He followed her with his eyes. *She moves like a cat*, he thought. *Closing in for the kill...* "Have you ever heard of the Crawlspacers?" she said abruptly, stopping behind him.

Art laughed. He couldn't help it. "You're not serious!"

Instantly the woman's knife was at his throat. "Very serious," she said softly. "Very, *very* serious."

Art held perfectly still until the tip of the blade moved away from his jugular. "All—" he began, then cleared his throat and tried again. "All right. You're Crawlspacers. What's that got to do with the data loss?"

"Philip is rather good with computer systems," said the woman. She didn't re-sheath the knife.

Art looked at the boy with the rifle. He gazed levelly back. "But *why*? What did you hope to accomplish?"

"Sometimes you have to shake people to wake them up."

"The computer could just as easily have failed on its own."

"Exactly." The woman moved closer again, so close he could feel her breath on his cheek. Her eyes bored into his. "Come on, Stoddard. You're not stupid. Figure it out."

"I don't—"

"You know the truth, even if you don't broadcast it." She banged her booted foot sharply on the rusty metal floor, and Art jumped. "This ship is coming apart—physically and socially. You won't tell the Passengers, so we found our own way to do it."

Art had been thinking the same thing only hours earlier. But he wasn't about to concede anything—not yet. "The *Mayflower II* was carefully designed to maintain an Earth-like environment for as long as is necessary to reach any of a number of systems identified as having potentially habitable planets, and we know we're decelerating." Even if the Crew hasn't seen fit to tell anyone, even the Council, exactly how much longer they had to travel; his father had complained about that often enough. "It will last long enough to—"

"Shut up, parrot!" the boy snapped.

Art shut up.

"There's something you don't know," the woman continued. "Something hardly anyone knows. But something everyone *needs* to know. Something everyone has a *right* to know." She leaned in close behind him, whispered in his ear. "We're almost at our destination. And there's a habitable world there…but the Captain doesn't *want* us to know."

Art stared at her. "But…why *wouldn't* the Captain want us to know that? That's the whole reason for—"

"Because we're not going to stop," the woman said bitterly. "The Captain is just going to grab some raw materials and start accelerating again. Maybe for another thirty years. Maybe longer. Do you really think the *Mayflower II* will hold together that long?

"Even in that sanitized pap you spew every day the signs are everywhere: fish dying in the Forest Hab, the Prairie Hab a desert as dry and cold as Mars. The maintenance robots not only can't keep up, they're starting to break down, too. That computer failure we induced wasn't the first, and it won't be the last—and that's not a threat, because we won't have anything to do with it. The air smells funny, it's getting colder all the time, the water in some Habs is literally sickening—we're even rusting, for God's sake!" She banged the floor again. "The *Mayflower II* is going straight to hell, and taking us with it."

"But...but it makes no sense," Art said. "The Captain knows better than anyone else what shape the ship is really in. Why would he want us to keep sailing along like...like the Flying Dutchman?"

"We don't know why," the woman said. "Only a handful of officers know why. We just know it's the truth."

"Even if it is," *which I doubt*, Art thought, "exactly how are you helping matters by wrecking things? What's next—a few well-placed bombs?"

"We're not killers."

Art pointedly did not look at the weapon pointed at his mid-section.

"We're just trying to wake people up. We have to make them angry. The Crew has control of the ship and all the weapons..."

Except for the ones you *seem to have*, Art thought, but didn't say.

"...but there are only four hundred Crew and more than ten thousand of us. If the Passengers rise up, protest, demand answers, the Crew will have to tell us what's going on."

"What if you find out what's going on and you agree with it?"

"Then we agree with it. The point is we'll have a say! *The people have a right to know.* Isn't that what journalists used to say?"

That was the second time she'd used the phrase "right to know." It was a curiously old-fashioned way to talk. *And who says I'm a journalist? A minute ago I was a parrot.*

Out loud he said, "What if the Crew decides to just seal off the Passenger Habs and let them go to hell? Habitat One is self-sufficient. Everyone knows that."

"They've got the same maintenance problems we do," the woman said. "And the Crew aren't monsters."

That surprised Art. He had her pinned as an anti-Crew fanatic. Especially with the costume and the weapons. But she was almost making sense.

It worried him.

The boy, on the other hand…Art didn't like the icy glitter in his eyes behind the mask. And the rifle had never wavered.

Get out of this in one piece and figure it out later!

"All right, so you think we're almost to a habitable planet but the Captain doesn't intend to let us stop and get off. You're convinced the ship is falling apart and we can't survive another few decades. Is that right?"

"He *can* be taught," Philip said.

"Quiet," the woman snapped. To Art, she said, "That's right."

"So what do you want *me* to do about it?"

"Tell the rest of the Passengers," the woman said. "Rumors are rumors. But if you say it, it becomes official."

Art snorted. "You think people will believe it because I say it? You said it yourself; I'm just a mouthpiece for the Crew and Council. Lots of people—especially Shipborn—probably think I'm lying most of the time. Why would they believe me if I told them *that*?"

"Because it's so obviously not what the Crew and Council would tell you to say," the woman said. "And because of this." From a snap-down pouch on her belt, she drew out something shiny and round, about the size of a thumbnail: an ordinary memory disc. "There's only one file on this. It's been decrypted into a standard video format. And you're going to send it out live over the Shipnet the next time you go to work."

Art stared at the disc as if it might bite him—because, he thought, it almost certainly *would*. "What's on it?"

"The truth."

"That's not very helpful."

"It wasn't meant to be."

"I'll preview it."

"Don't. The Crew is looking for it. Plug it into a computer anywhere on the ship and it will set off an alarm."

"Including the one at the studio."

She shrugged.

"I'll be arrested." *Or worse*, he thought. Officially there was no capital punishment aboard the *Mayflower II*, but unofficially… he thought of the "fluke accident" that had killed Peter's father. "Why should I risk that for you?"

"It's not for me, Mr. Stoddard. It's for all of us. All of the Passengers. Earth- and Shipborn. It's for freedom. For the right of everyone to have a say in their own fate. Supposedly this ship was launched to preserve an island of freedom as the Earth fell into a new Dark Ages. Instead we've brought our own oppression with us. The Council and Officers are a bunch of aging men and women appointed by people who have been dead on Earth for centuries. Why are they still running our lives, especially those of us who are Shipborn? When do *we* get a say in how things are done?"

She's not the one in charge, Art thought suddenly, listening to her. *That has the sound of something she's learned, something she's been taught…by someone else. Freedom? A right to know? That's talk from Earth. Someone else is pulling her strings. And not a Shipborn…but then, who? Someone on Council?*

If they were still in the first year or two after launch, Art thought, then Jonas Woods, the "Liberty Party" representative, would have been the logical candidate…but not after twenty years of heavy drinking. Still, there were others, unhappy with their lack of influence, Councilors his father spoke of in disparaging terms in his rare unguarded moments. They were certainly resentful of the Prime Councilor. Could that resentment have swelled to include the Captain himself?

The woman interrupted his train of thought by leaning in close again. “You watch a lot of old movies, don’t you, Mr. Stoddard? Remember that old slogan….power to the people? *We’re* the people. You’re one of us.” She took his hand, opened the fingers, and laid the disc in his palm. “And with this, you can empower us.”

Art stared at the disc as if it were radioactive—as, in a sense, it was. The woman’s request was ridiculous—play a file from a highly suspect source, without previewing it, knowing it was contraband? The ’keeps would be on him in minutes. And it wasn’t as if it could possibly do any good. The Shipborn could protest, every Passenger Hab could rise up in revolt, the Council could be lynched, and it wouldn’t make any difference. The Captain would do what he damned well pleased, and the Crew would support him. Crew Country wasn’t just an expression, it was a reality; Habitat One was its own separate country, where the Captain was King. Crew women gave birth to Crew kids who were now becoming Crew themselves. No one else could ever join the Crew and no one from the Crew ever joined the Passengers.

The woman was delusional, no matter how much she talked a good game. He shook his head and held out the disc. “No.”

She made no move to take it. “There’s another reason you should play it.”

“What?”

“Are you really that stupid?” Philip said. He prodded Art’s stomach with his gun. “Because we’ll kill you…and take it up with your replacement.”

The woman said nothing, but she caught Art’s eye and nodded slowly.

Art swallowed. “Well, when you put it like that…” He pulled his hand back and dropped the disc into his jacket pocket.

“Very good,” said the woman. “One more thing.” She reached

out, grabbed his wrist, pulled it toward her, and shoved his sleeve up to expose his forearm. "Philip?"

Philip slung his rifle, pulled out something that looked like a short pistol from a pouch at his belt, and before Art really knew what was happening, pressed its barrel against his skin. He squeezed the trigger. Art felt a short, sharp pain, then a numbing spray of cold.

Philip put the "pistol" back in his belt, unslung his rifle, and pointed it at Art's midriff again. The woman released his wrist, and he snatched his arm back, rubbing the place where he'd just been…shot, he guessed.

"What was that?" he demanded.

"Just know that we will always know where you are on this ship, and what you're doing," the woman said. "*Always*."

With that, she bent over and picked up the black bag that had covered his head before.

"Wait!" Art said. "He's Philip—but who are you?"

"Just a Shadow. You can call me that—if we ever meet again. Which we won't. Not where you'll recognize me, anyway. Turn around."

He did as he was told. The bag was jerked over his head. In darkness he felt his way up the ladder. The hatch grated open. He climbed out. The hatch grated closed. Philip—presumably—seized his arm again, frog-marched him across the grass of the park, then spun him in place three times and gave him a hard shove. He fell headlong, raised up, yanked the bag off his head, and stared wildly around.

He was alone, in the middle of the park, the lights of the residential area where he lived gleaming through the trees. Brushing dirt off the knees of his suit, he climbed to his feet and set off. In minutes he was back on the familiar route to home—but now the dark shadows along the way seemed threatening, and the air colder than ever. He hurried out of the park, shivering, and reached the brightly lit streets of Neighbourhood One with relief.

The door to his parents' house slid open as he approached it.

"Good evening, Art," said a warm and cheerful voice as he entered the front hall.

"Cancel welcoming routine," he snapped at the computer.

"Arthur, dear, is something the matter?" asked his mother, coming into the living room from her studio. She wore an artist's smock over a rainbow-hued metallic jumpsuit—the latest Shipborn fashion. She always kept up with the latest trends; she seemed to think it made her and her rather pedestrian paintings of old Earth landscapes avant-garde. For a moment Art wanted to tell her the truth. Once upon a time she had been able to make everything all right. But not anymore. She wouldn't believe him; or if she did, she would call the 'keeps at once, and Art didn't want that. If anyone was going to call them, it would be him.

He shrugged. "Rough day."

"I saw your newscast, dear. I thought you did a very good job." She turned back toward her studio, saying over her shoulder, "Supper's whatever you can find. Your father's in the kitchen now."

"All right." Art started down the hall toward the kitchen, then hesitated and told the house, "Privacy lock." As the shutters whirred over the window glass and bolts snapped home in the door, he went into the kitchen. His father, thickset, gray-haired and scowling, sat at the table studying the glowing screen of a tablet computer, taking periodic bites from a vat-ham sandwich.

He looked up and frowned at Art. "Why the privacy lock?"

Art set about making his own sandwich, taking bread, cheese, vat-ham, an onion, dill pickles and a jar of faux-mustard from the refrigerator. He wished he had a tomato. He wished *anyone* had a tomato. "Overeager fans."

"Must be male," his father grunted. "If they were female you'd be chasing *them*."

Art concentrated on slicing the onion without slicing himself. His eyes watered. For some reason the onions had been getting stronger and stronger recently. A little more and they'd be inedible.

"When did you get in last night?" his father asked.

“Late.” Carefully, Art spread the not-quite-mustard.

“Late? You mean early, don’t you? Who was it this time? Raylene? Jennifer? Suzy? Or have you moved on again?”

Art cut a slice of cheese. “I really don’t think it’s any of your business,” he said without looking around.

“You’re still living in my house,” snapped his father. “That makes it my business.”

“Only if I bring them here. Which I don’t.”

“Hmmph.” For a moment there was silence. Art laid the onions and pickles on the bottom slice of bread and reached for the vat- ham. Just another minute and he would be—

“The Council asked me if you would speak at the Crew Day celebration next week,” his father said abruptly. “I told them you would.”

Art froze with the ham in his hand. “What?”

“They’d like you to talk about what an honour it is for you to keep the ship informed on behalf of the Crew and Council, how important it is for all of us to remain united in the support of the ship’s leadership…the usual sorts of things that get said on Crew Day.”

Very slowly Art laid the slice of ham on his sandwich, then turned to face his father. “No.”

His father stared at him with eyes as blue as his own. “I beg your pardon?”

“I won’t do it. You had no business agreeing on my behalf.”

“I think I did,” said his father in a dangerous tone. “I think it’s about time you took your job a little more seriously. You don’t seem to have any problem accepting the perks that go along with it—like whomever you spent the night with. But there are responsibilities you’ve been shirking. You’re the public face of the Crew and Council. It’s time you used your position to help promote unity, to squelch some of the unrest in the lower Habs. You’re Shipborn. You’re trusted. You have a unique opportunity to do something worthwhile with your life. It’s about time you got started.”

"I said no." Art turned back to his sandwich. His hands shook as he finished assembling it. "The Council will just have to find somebody else." He picked up his plate and started out, but his father shoved his chair back and blocked his way.

"I've put up with this as long as I can," his father said in a low, intense voice, his lined, craggy face only centimetres from Art's. "You're thirty-two years old and so help me, I've waited every one of those years for you to show that you cared about anything important. I stood up for you when you and that drunken friend of yours destroyed the maintenance 'bot. You'd be living in those warrens down in Hab Twenty if I hadn't. I got you this job. It took more wheeling and dealing than you'll ever know, but I even got you re-instated to the Council Succession List as my replacement should anything happen to me. You're *royalty* on this ship. You should be grateful. You should be doing everything you can to prove you deserve it. Instead you seem to think you can just drift along and that's good enough. Well, it's not! This is a spaceship, not a planet. It's a closed system. There's no room for shirkers. And that's what you're becoming—a shirker. You want to do as little as you can to get by, and spend the rest of your time having fun. You're just like the rest of the Shipborn!" His voice rose. "It's no wonder things are falling apart! You just don't care!"

"You're wrong, Dad," Art said. "The Shipborn care. We just know there's nothing we can do about it." He pushed past his father and retreated to his room, passing his mother in the hall. She gave him a puzzled look, then went into the kitchen. Art closed and locked his door, shutting off the sound of his father's angry voice.

He put his plate on his desk, then sat on the bed and took out the disc Shadow had given him. For a long time he just held it. Funny, in a way his father had echoed the argument he'd had with Shadow. They'd both tried to convince him *he* could somehow do something to stop the downhill slide of the *Mayflower II*. Of course, they had vastly different ideas as to *what*.

The giant vidscreen built into the wall to his right,

automatically activated by his entrance, flickered silently with a mid-20th century Technicolor Biblical epic. Waves crashed over an army of Egyptian charioteers. Art sympathized.

Very carefully he set the disc on the bedspread. Shadow expected him to simply play the video it contained into the Shipnet. She couldn't just upload it; everything was pre-screened. But *he* could. Not only that, he could force it to the foreground of every monitor in the Passenger Habs. Nobody would be able to escape it, and there'd be no putting the genie back in the bottle once he'd released whatever was on it into the wild.

If he *didn't* do that, she'd said the Crawlspacers would kill him. He rubbed the spot on his arm where he'd been injected with something…a tracker at least, possibly a listening device.

Possibly a kill switch, he thought suddenly. *What if it contains poison? What if they can trigger it remotely?*

Powerful incentive. But if the file on the disc was really that ship-shaking, what would the Crew do when he played it?

It had to be proof of some kind of what she'd said: that they were decelerating toward a habitable world, but that the Captain did not intend to reveal that fact; that instead he intended to simply take on raw materials and then accelerate again, toward the next system in the catalog of possibilities identified from Earth.

Unless she was lying. What if it were something else? She wanted him to insert it into the Shipnet. What if it contained a virus, something that would attack the shipboard computer systems, maybe CentComp itself? They'd already committed sabotage on a small scale. What if they were duping him to commit it on a far larger scale?

He couldn't imagine why. But that didn't mean it wasn't true. The Crawlspacers were clearly fanatics: revolutionaries, and historically, revolutionaries hadn't always worried about what would happen after the revolution was won, what would replace the oppressive-but-stable society they destroyed. It was always easier to destroy than to rebuild.

No, he thought. *Somebody has a plan. Someone stands behind the Crawlspacers, someone with a clear idea of what he or she wants to accomplish. Someone wanting to seize power for him or herself. And who may not care anymore about the ordinary people than the Crew does. Maybe less.*

He should destroy the disc, call the 'keeps, tell them everything that had happened. They'd protect him.

Wouldn't they?

Could they?

Even from whatever the Crawlspacers had stuck in his arm?

He picked up the disc, stared at it in his palm. He remembered the stories that had been cut from his report that day, and so many days in the past. The Council, and especially the Crew, wanted the Passengers kept in the dark about the true state of the ship—and he was helping them do it.

And the Council and Crew, he thought, *say Crawlspacers are a myth.*

He remembered an earlier fight with his father, when he'd made the mistake of mentioning the legendary group at the dinner table. His father had exploded, "There aren't any Crawlspacers—they're just a made-up group to add glamour to any Shipborn brat who feels like wrecking something. You young people don't know how good you've got it. You should have been on Earth just before Launch, or on the Station when it was attacked. Then you wouldn't be complaining. You'd be glad to be on the *Mayflower II*, glad to be away from it all, honoured to be going to a new planet, the way we were honoured."

"Some honour," Art retorted. "The Shipborn don't have any choice about any of it—where we're going, how the ship is run. That's left to the Earthborn. When do we get a say?"

"You cannot run a ship like a democracy," his father said. "Order and control are vital. Discipline."

"Making women breed to order," Art shot back. "Telling people where to work, where to live. Spying on them every minute of the day. I thought this ship was supposed to preserve freedom among the stars?"

"When we get to Landing—"

"If," Art said.

"*When*," his father insisted, with an angry glare, "controls will be loosened…at least, once the colony is secure. But until then—"

"Until then?" Art said. "And how long until then? Forty years? Fifty? A century? Two?"

"Quiet!" his father thundered. "I will not have the Mission questioned. Not in my house!"

Art had kept his mouth shut after that. He could *almost* understand, he supposed, how his parents felt; they had fled a troubled world, and had created on the ship an island of stability they didn't want disrupted. And of course his father was one of the lucky fifty named to the Council. A promising young member of the party in power—and son of an elder statesman of the type government buildings were named after—he had every reason to support the status quo. He even clung to the—near-delusional, in Art's mind—notion that someday Art would inherit his position on Council, either in flight or in the colony-to-come, and thus carry on his family's long tradition of political clout.

Art knew that the Council saw the decline of the ship's systems as one more reason to even more fervently support the Crew, who, after all, were the only ones who understood the working of the ship. The Passengers, aside from those who had been included for their political or public relations clout, had been chosen for their colonizing skills—not for their ability to run a starship. The Council undoubtedly thought the society they had created within the Habs wasn't bad at all—a bit small-townish, perhaps (Art had heard his mother occasionally reminisce fondly about life in Earth's huge cities), but at least people were getting on with their lives, not just marking time while the ship sailed across the galaxy at relativistic speed.

Yes, he could see their point. But from his perspective, their "not bad" society was pure sham, an elaborate stage play with no plot, one that would taper off to chaos as the set collapsed around the actors and finally the theatre roof caved in. Unless the ship found a habitable planet in the system it was decelerating into even now, the journey would continue for another who-knew-how-many decades, shiptime. What would be left of the decaying ship and the people within it after that many years had passed? If any Passengers were alive at all, they would probably be eating each other, carrying clubs and talking in grunts.

So why shouldn't I play Shadow's video on the Shipnet? he thought. *There's no way it can do any good, but on the other hand, it can't hurt.*

It can hurt you, a more cautious and less-angry part of his mind reminded him. *It can hurt you a great deal. Your life is as good as it gets on the Mayflower II. You've got money, you've got girls, you're famous. "Royalty," as Dad put it. Why rock the boat?*

"Sometimes you have to shake people to wake them up," Shadow had said—but if rocking the boat didn't wake anybody up, and he didn't think it would, it would only get him wet—or drowned.

Yet what if she were right? What if whatever was on that disc *would* make a difference, but he turned it over to the 'keeps? Then he really would have become nothing more than a tool of the Council and Crew.

There was only one way out of his dilemma, he thought, getting to his feet. He had to preview the chip, despite Shadow's warning. And he thought he could do it safely. Their house was shielded, like all the Councilors' houses. There was no way the Crawlspacers knew what he was doing in his own room; no signal could possible get to them from here, or from them to the chip in his arm. And he had an old dumb vidplayer that didn't connect to Shipnet, ancient technology even before it had been brought on board the *Mayflower II* by some kid who'd since grown up. He'd seen it in with a bunch of miscellaneous electronic junk while doing a story on the ship's automated recycling systems. The story had been a puff piece, designed to show how well the ship's systems continue to operate. He hadn't been allowed to show the video he'd shot of two maintenance robots tearing each other apart as each fought to recycle each other. He'd grabbed the old vidplayer on a whim, thinking its on-board memory might have some old movies he hadn't seen before, but it had proved to be blank. Still, it had been sitting on the floor of his closet ever since. If it still worked...and if it were compatible...

It did, and it was. It powered up at his touch and the disc slid easily into the slot in the side. The screen lit up...and Art froze as he recognized the face of Captain Nakos, thinner and craggier than the prime-of-life version that stared grimly at Passengers from the walls of government offices all over the ship.

The Captain began to speak, and for five minutes Art stood there, listening, unmoving. *Shadow is wrong*, he thought. *This wouldn't just shake the ship—it will plunge it into chaos. Maybe even mutiny.*

Which, of course, was just what Shadow wanted.

The disc contained a top-secret announcement from Captain Nakos to the senior officers of the Crew, explaining to them why, although a habitable planet had been detected in the system into which they were decelerating, they would not be ending their long flight.

"The planet," he said, voice grim, "is already inhabited."

Art stared at the screen, feeling as if the old vidplayer had just delivered an electrical shock. *Aliens?* he thought, with a mixture of terror and excitement. *Aliens?*

"We can see large cities and other structures through the ship's eyes. We do not detect any transmissions, which does not mean they don't exist. Our ability to detect any transmissions has been degraded by the extensive damage to hull structures during our journey, and they may be using a technology that is entirely strange to us.

"In any event, it doesn't matter. Our orders are clear," the Captain continued. "Should we find the planet we are approaching inhabited, we are to avoid it entirely and continue to the next system on our list." He took a deep breath. "This ship may contain all that remains of the human race. We dare not risk contact with the inhabitants of the planet.

"But we face a dilemma. The ship's systems are deteriorating and despite our best recycling efforts, we are getting low on necessary volatiles and other raw materials. Our course of action will therefore be as follows: we will decelerate into the system but stay clear of the inner planets. We will assume orbit around one of the gas giants in the outer system, from whose atmosphere and moons our automated harvesters should be able to extract the materials we need. We will linger only for as long as is absolutely necessary, and leave the system as quickly as possible. We will answer no transmissions from the inhabited world, and should ships approach us, we will break orbit immediately and begin accelerating out of the system."

The Captain paused. "I am sure you are aware of how this information would be received by the ship's Passengers," he said. "The Earthborn are loyal, but this might shake that loyalty. The Shipborn…" He shook his head. "The social unrest might well endanger the ship itself. Which is why our official story must be that although we have reached our destination, no habitable planet has been found, and we are simply replenishing supplies before resuming our long journey.

"This is not what we hoped or expected to find at the end of what we must now consider only the first leg of our quest," the Captain concluded. "Many of us, despite our best life-extension efforts, may not survive to the next planetfall, and we will have to think long and hard about that in the days to come, and how to ensure that the ship can continue functioning and fulfill its mission as the original Crew and Council age and die. Our disappointment is great, our future challenges greater. But despite all that, our duty is clear. I am confident each of you understands the importance of carrying it out."

The vid ended.

At the same moment, the privacy shutter over his window drew open of its own accord. Startled, he looked out—and saw, silhouetted against a streetlight outside, the unmistakable, bulbous shape of a 'keeps vehicle.

Six red dots of light suddenly appeared on his chest. "Mr. Stoddard, please stand very still," boomed an amplified voice.

With great care, Art raised his hands.

Chapter Three

The 'keeps were very good at what they did. In short order Art was ushered at gunpoint into the street, where the black, eight-wheeled armored personnel carrier waited, its electric motor humming faintly. His father watched grimly from the doorway, while his mother followed him out in stunned silence, unable to believe that her son could be in any kind of trouble with the 'keeps. "I'm sure it's all just a mistake," she said finally. "Your father will straighten it out in no time—"

"Mary," said Art's father, "Be quiet. I'm the one who called the Peacekeepers."

Art felt as if he'd been clubbed. He blinked stupidly at his father. "What?"

"You heard me." His father glared at him, his face blotched red with fury. "Did you really think you could get away with watching something seditious in my house?"

Art suddenly understood, and his own anger rose, threatening to choke him. "You had the AI monitoring my room!"

"Ever since you smashed that maintenance robot," his father said. "It was part of the probation agreement."

"But my probation ended eight years ago!"

"I never saw any reason to change the programming," his father said. "Looks like I was right."

Art stared into his father's eyes. They stared back at him like blue stones, hard and unyielding. He glanced at his mother. She looked down, twisting her hands together.

So that's the way it is, Art thought. *So much for family.*

He turned his back on his parents and his home, and walked down the sidewalk toward the 'keep vehicle.

Nothing stirred in the street. Every shutter and door was as tightly closed as Art's had been until the 'keeps had overridden the privacy locks. *What about the Crawlspacers?* he wondered. *Are they out there somewhere, watching me?*

His forearm itched. But nothing else happened. No poison flooded his system.

Well, none he was aware of. It could be slow-acting…

Now you're just being paranoid.

An officer waited at the door to the APC. "Mr. Stoddard," said the officer. "Please get in."

Prodded by the 'keep at his back, he climbed into the vehicle's red-lit interior and sat in one of the dozen thinly padded black chairs that lined the windowless metal walls. He kept his eyes on the floor until the door slid shut, shutting off his view of his home and parents. It was almost funny, he thought; his own arrest would be another story the Crew and Council wouldn't let anyone hear. He glanced up at the officer. "I have to have a newscast on Shipnet by 0630, you know," he said. "The whole ship will miss me if I'm not there."

"Somehow I doubt it will spark a revolution," the officer replied dryly, and the APC began to move.

And of course he was right, Art thought. Sure, people would notice he was gone, and those who lived in Habitat Three would even connect his disappearance with the night's strange goings-on. But they wouldn't talk about it. *Don't rock the boat*, he thought—his own creed. *Things are bad enough—don't make them worse.* The Earthborn and most of their go-along-to-get-along Shipborn children would figure the Crew must have had a good reason for taking him in, and the more discontented of the Shipborn, like his old "friend" Peter, would just think, "Serves him right," and order another drink.

Apart from his parents and—maybe—Treena, he could think of no one who would really be concerned about him.

Except Shadow, he thought suddenly. *She'll know what's happened. Maybe she'll try to rescue me—*

He shook his head. Not a chance. He'd lost his usefulness by being captured. She'd just make another copy of that explosive vid and try to find some other way to get it onto Shipnet.

The officer gazed impassively at the wall behind Art. In the red light his face looked hollow, inhuman. Art shifted his weight in the uncomfortable chair and wished they would get wherever they were going. But for several more minutes they rolled smoothly along. When the vehicle finally slowed, then stopped, the officer rose and, as the door opened, led Art out.

They were at the transit station: he'd guessed as much. They boarded a pod with 'keep markings. The officer spoke. "Voice ID."

"Captain Gerrold Keepness," the pod said in a grim male voice, the complete opposite of the pleasant female voice used by the public pods.

"Habitat One," said the officer.

The pod began to move, and Art swallowed, hard.

Habitat One.

Crew Country.

If the 'keeps take you to Habitat One, you never come back, the Shipborn whispered. Art had never really believed that, because no one he knew had ever actually known anyone taken to Habitat One. Certainly he'd never been there. But it looked like that was about to change.

And he had to admit the prospect of him coming back from it was, indeed, slim.

At least from now on, I'll be shielded from anything the Crawlspacers can do, he thought. *Surely they can't track me once I'm in Crew Country.*

It was small comfort.

There were the usual strange sensations as the pod made its journey. "Down" changed position a couple of times. Art's weight grew less, then more; less again, and finally settled back to normal. At last they arrived, the door opened, and Art had his first glimpse of near-mythical Habitat One.

It was underwhelming: just a plain white transit station, indistinguishable from the one they had just left. And much to his disappointment, his guards didn't lead him out of the station into whatever "natural" environment the Crew enjoyed; instead, they took him through long white corridors marked only with cryptic blue and red signs with, to Art, meaningless labels: "COM4," "NAV2," "SDS1" and the like.

Eventually they passed through a pressure door into a new corridor that ended twenty metres to the left in a bright red door labeled "EVA Airlock" in bold white letters. To the right, however, the corridor stretched as far as Art could see, punctuated at intervals by dark blue doors.

They went only a short distance before stopping before one of those doors. "Mr. Stoddard," said the officer, tapping the lockpad, "Until such time as our investigation of your quarters is complete, you will remain here."

The door slid open and lights came on. The officer motioned Art in, and he entered cautiously, expecting a dismal cell; instead he found himself in a small but well-furnished chamber. *Hell*, he thought, *most of the Shipborn crammed into Habitat Twenty would* kill *for a place this nice*. There was a bed, covered with a black bedspread; a white synthiwood chair and table; even a Shipnet terminal and an automated food dispenser. A smaller chamber off the main one contained a shower, bath and toilet.

"Someone will come for you shortly," said the officer, and stepped out. The door slid shut behind him.

Art immediately tried it, just to be sure it was locked. It was. Then he tried the Shipnet terminal. It was deactivated. Finally he tried the food dispenser. At least *it* worked, and, despite its limited menu, proved capable of producing a decent cup of semicaf. Art sat at the white table, stared at the gray walls, sipped the steaming black liquid and thought even blacker thoughts about Crawlspacers, the Council, the Crew, his father and his own stupidity.

Finally his body reminded him that it was the middle of the

night, Passenger time, at least; he didn't know if the Crew kept to a different schedule. Yawning, he stripped off his clothes, took a shower, and tumbled into bed. In spite of, or maybe because of, everything he had been through that evening, he fell asleep almost instantly.

Far too soon he woke to a painful poke in his side. The man standing over him did not wear a Peacekeeper uniform; instead, he wore the crisp whites of the Crew. Art didn't know how to read the insignia, but a nametag on the man's left breast read FIACCO. "Get up," the new man growled. "The Captain's ready for you."

The Captain! Art shaved quickly and pulled on his clothes; then "Fiacco" hauled him out of the room and prodded him at pistol-point down the corridor. His thoughts whirled. Was he really going to meet Captain Nakos, the man no Passenger had seen face to face in almost thirty years?

It appeared he was. They passed several more dark-blue doors, then stopped outside one painted gold. CentComp scanned Fiacco's face, then Art's. The door slid open. They stepped out of the plain white corridor into one richly carpeted in red and paneled with dark wood, decorated at discreet intervals with sculptures and paintings: Van Goghs, Rembrandts, and… *Was that the Mona Lisa?* Art thought, and would have gone back for a second look if not for the incessant prodding of the pistol in his back.

The corridor ended in ornately carved double doors—not the sliding airtight panels of other sections of the Crew Hab, but genuine wooden—or, at least, wood-sheathed—doors, with brass doorknobs. Fiacco stopped Art with a hand on his shoulder, then said, apparently to thin air, "Captain, this is Lieutenant Fiacco. I have Stoddard."

No one replied, but the doors clicked and swung inward. *So why the doorknobs?* Art wondered fleetingly, then Fiacco shoved him forward so hard he stumbled into the presence of the stern-looking man seated behind the massive real-wood desk at the far end. Art quickly gathered his feet and stood with as much dignity as he could muster. Fiacco stepped back into the hallway and the doors closed again, leaving Art alone with the Captain.

Captain Nakos looked much as he had in the illicit video Art had watched that had landed him in the Captain's august presence: high-cheek-boned, dark-skinned face, clean-shaven, black hair streaked with gray and cut in a short military style. The Captain's white uniform was perfectly pressed and every brass button sparkled. His brown eyes regarded Art as though the younger man had escaped from the swamp in Hab Six. "Computer, record," he snapped.

"Acknowledged," said the same female voice the transit tube used.

"For the record, you are Arthur Randall Stoddard?"

Art swallowed. "Yes, sir."

"Your occupation?"

Don't you know? Art thought, but all he said out loud was, "Information Dissemination Specialist: Civilian, sir."

"Very good. Now tell me, Mr. Stoddard, do you recognize this?" The Captain held up a data disc.

"It's a data disc, sir," Art said. Apparently he was going to be forced to state the obvious. Ordinarily he would have found that darkly humourous, but he was having a hard time finding any humour in his current situation. Certainly there was not the slightest trace of amusement in the grim face of Captain Nikos.

The Captain shoved the disc into a slot in the wooden desk that Art couldn't see from his angle. A vidscreen popped up, and the video Art had watched earlier began to play. The Captain stopped it with a touch of his finger to the screen. He looked at Art. "Do you grant that this disc was found in your possession?"

It could be a different one, Art thought, but of course it wasn't, and there was no point in pretending otherwise. "Yes, sir."

"How did you get it?"

Art owed Shadow no loyalty; he hadn't asked to be involved in her mutinous activities. For all he knew she had already been captured and was being questioned next door. Yet still, he hesitated.

"Mr. Stoddard," Captain Nikos said in a voice that somehow contrived to be both perfectly level and full of menace, "we can make you tell us. I would prefer not to have to, and I can assure you, *you* will find that preferable, too."

Art swallowed....and told the story.

The Captain's face betrayed no reaction to the news that there was a secret organization devoted to the overthrow of the established order...*no doubt because it isn't news to him at all*, Art thought. Nor did the Captain ask for more information about the Crawlspacers. Instead, he asked, "Why did you feel you had to view the chip, Mr. Stoddard? Why didn't you simply turn it over to the 'keeps as your duty demanded?"

Because I'm an idiot, Art thought; but out loud, he heard himself say, "Curiosity, sir."

"And tell me, Mr. Stoddard, now that your curiosity is sated and you know what is on that disc, would you go ahead and upload its contents to Shipnet it if you had the opportunity?" Captain Nikos smiled a small cold smile. "Not, of course, that you are going to have that opportunity."

Art opened his mouth to say, "No, of course not," then closed it again. He realized he didn't know the answer. He had never thought, when he'd previewed the vid, that Shadow might be telling the truth about the impact it could have. But she had been. The fact he stood before the Captain proved the vid wasn't a hoax. Playing it really might force change—even revolution.

But there was a big gap between, say, increasing Passenger input into climate control decisions and triggering what could be a bloody civil war. The consequences of playing the vid could be worse than the consequences of not playing it. After all, if the Passengers never knew the truth, at least they'd be no worse off, would they? What they didn't know couldn't hurt them.

Or help them, another part of his mind niggled. *Remember what you told yourself when you decided to preview that vid. Knowing what you do now, if you still had the chip and didn't play it, you'd be declaring yourself on the side of the Crew, deciding, like them, what everyone else should or shouldn't know. Don't the Passengers deserve the truth? Shouldn't they have a say in their own future?*

Neatly balanced on the horns of his internal dilemma, Art said nothing at all.

The Captain snorted. "It doesn't matter. Your mere possession of this chip, Mr. Stoddard, is a serious enough offense for us to do with you whatever we feel necessary."

Art felt cold. *Those who go to Crew Country never return...* "Shadow approached *me*!" he blurted out, then hated how weak it made him sound.

"You kept the disc. You viewed the file it contained. You might have uploaded it."

"The Crawlspacers still have the file. They'll find some other way—"

"There is no other way," said the Captain. "Only a few Crew have the clearance to upload material directly to Shipnet. As of, oh, roughly the time you were arrested, no Passengers have that ability. Shipnet is secure."

"They can still tell people..."

"They can. But who will believe them without proof?"

"They could play the vid on a non-networked player, like the one I used," Art said. "If my father hadn't been spying on me—"

"There are very few places on this ship where you could have played that vid and not been detected," the Captain said. "And even if the Crawlspacers did find a way to play it for five people, or ten, it would still be nothing but rumor...and this ship is awash in rumours." The Captain smiled. "Some of them planted by us... and, in the past, helpfully spread by you. Who believes the rumors? No one, Mr. Stoddard. Especially not one as outlandish as this." The smile faded. "Your friend Shadow—"

"Not my friend!"

"—admittedly found a weak link in our chain of security: you. Humans are always the weak link in security. But you, as it turned out, were also the weak link in her scheme. And she will have no opportunity to try again. We have closed down the Information Dissemination service, Mr. Stoddard. Your job has been terminated, and you will not be replaced."

Art had expected to lose his job. But he hadn't expected it to be abolished. Nor had he expected the news to hurt as much as it did. "But that's a vital service!"

"Information necessary to the smooth functioning of the ship will come directly from the Council and Crew. As it always should have. The office you held was merely a sop to some of the…less hard-headed members of the civilian leadership in the early years after Launch."

"So much for free speech," Art snarled.

The Captain snorted. "Free speech has always been limited by the need to provide security, Mr. Stoddard. Whenever a society faces an existential threat, free speech is the first thing to be curtailed."

Anger swelled in Art. With nothing left to lose, he said bitterly, "You military types have never changed, have you? You see a civilization on a habitable planet and you immediately assume it's a threat."

The Captain shook his head. "It has nothing to do with me, Mr. Stoddard. My orders are clear. I am not to risk the safety of this ship by approaching any inhabitants we might find on the planets we approach. And if *they* approach *us*…my orders cover that, too."

"The people who gave those orders have been dead for centuries!" Art said.

"That does not change my duty."

"Just following orders, huh?" Art said. "Where have I heard that before?"

To his surprise, the Captain's mouth quirked. "Have you ever heard of Godwin's Law, Mr. Stoddard? The first person in an argument to make a Nazi analogy loses?" The smile faded. "We are quite possibly all that remains of the human race, Mr. Stoddard. If we turn our back on our duty, if we fail to keep faith with those who launched us into the abyss, we could be responsible for the destruction of humanity. I will not take that risk." Captain Nikos studied him a moment longer, then nodded sharply. "Mr. Stoddard, thank you for your cooperation. When I have discussed your case with my senior officers, I will decide what is to be done with you." He touched something on his desk and, behind Art, the wood-sheathed doors swung silently open. Fiacco stepped into the room. "Lieutenant, please return Mr. Stoddard to his quarters," Captain Nikos said.

"But—" was all Art managed to get out before Fiacco hustled him out. The doors closed firmly behind them and locked with finality.

His anger carried him straight-backed and jaw-outthrust to his room, but as Lieutenant Fiacco locked him inside, it drained out of him, leaving him more frightened than he wanted to admit. He looked at the clock on the wall above the darkened terminal and saw that it was 0636—just the time he would normally have been making his morning 'cast. Instead he was locked in the bowels of Crew Country, and not only was he not making a newscast—neither was anyone else. Nor would they ever again. And "ever again" could be a very long time, if the Crew stuck to its determination to bypass this planet.

There must be some way to get word to someone in the lower Habs, Art thought. *Maybe they'd let me send a personal message—to my parents—a code—*

The idea fizzled at once. His father had sicced the 'keeps on him. He'd immediately report any attempt at covert communication. And there was literally no one else he could turn to. Peter? Treena? They would no more risk anything for him than—

—than he would have for them.

How did it come to this? he thought. *How did I end up thirty-two years old without a single person I can turn to when I'm in trouble?*

It pained him to admit it, but his father was right. He had been drifting along, only interested in himself, in his own comfort. He knew better than most the troubles besetting the ship, but as long as they didn't afflict him personally his chosen course of action had always—*always*—been…

Don't rock the boat.

It occurred to Art then that even if he had broadcast the chip, it might have made no difference. He thought of the Shipborn drinking themselves into unconsciousness in Rick's Place, down in Habitat Twenty. He was hard-pressed to picture them rising in revolt no matter what the provocation. Revolutions were unpleasant, and messy. Much easier to sink inexorably—but at least comfortably!—into oblivion.

The vid was like everything else, he thought with a kind of grim satisfaction: useless. It wouldn't have accomplished anything. His mistake hadn't been failing to trust Shadow, but believing, even for an instant, that anything he could do would matter in the long run. He had forgotten the reality of life on the *Mayflower II*, and all he had really succeeded in doing was throwing away his own reasonably comfortable position.

He gave up on foolish schemes of escape, lay back on the bed and closed his eyes, secure in the familiar cold peace of being powerless.

Two hours later he jerked awake, certain something was wrong—but with no idea of what it was.

Then he felt a strange vibration, unlike the normal hum that throbbed through the ship all the time, different even from the occasional grinding motion of the pods during deceleration. It seemed to be coming from the floor, but surely that was ridiculous; there was nothing below him but—

The Crawlspacers! he thought in sudden excitement. *The tracker they injected me with must still be working. They're coming to rescue me…*

Or coming to kill me.

He was nothing to them but a tool that had broken in their hands, after all.

Heart pounding, he scrambled to his feet.

The vibration stopped, started again, stopped; then suddenly the cabin shook and rang with a sound like a vast hammer crashing against the hull. The clock on the wall flashed and died.

And then Art heard a noise that terrified him more than the Captain had, more than Shadow had, more than anything in his waking moments ever had—the rising howl of wind, outside in the corridor, whistling past his door.

There was no wind in the Habs, only a gentle breeze from the ventilation systems. What he heard now was no breeze, but a hurricane, and could mean only one thing—a hole in the hull.

He swallowed, hard, and stared at the door. If it should give—

But it held, and after a moment the sound of the wind died away. Was the corridor now a hard vacuum? Art thought so for a moment, until he heard a new sound from outside—gunfire, a rapid crackling of it, a pause, another burst, then a quick, high-pitched buzzing. One more gunshot cracked, and something rang against the cabin door and whined away. Art steadied himself against the wall, chewed on his left thumbnail, and stared at the door as though by mere force of will he could see through it.

Voices approached, muffled and unintelligible. They stopped outside his door. Something snapped and sparks and acrid smoke burst from the inoperative lockpad on his side. A moment later the door slid open.

Air rushed briefly into the corridor and Art's ears popped. But he hardly noticed; he was too busy staring, open-mouthed, at the huge creature in silver armor filling the doorway—and pointing a long black tube right at him.

Chapter Four

The apparition said nothing; just scanned the room quickly, then stepped back into the corridor and let in a small, more lightly armored figure, its face, too, hidden by a mirrored golden visor. It took a white bundle from the pack on its back and flung it at Art, who caught it by reflex and then shook it out in response to an impatient gesture. It proved to be a spacesuit, though far lighter than anything Art had ever seen before, and so thin he found it hard to believe it would protect him from vacuum. Nevertheless, he had little choice but to put it on. It bagged on him as though designed for the massive warrior in the hallway.

From the stranger's pack next came a clear helmet, which snapped firmly over his head, and a white briefcase-like box with hoses and wires protruding from it. This was thrust into Art's hand and swiftly hooked up to the suit. Then the stranger touched a control on the box and the suit stiffened around Art. The air he was breathing took on a metallic tang.

The stranger yanked him out of the room and propelled him down the corridor, the large warrior bringing up the rear and moving backward, watching behind them. Once a bright red beam lanced out from his weapon, ripping the air apart with the ear-rasping buzz Art had heard through the door. He couldn't turn around to see who or what was the target; all he could focus on was the end of the corridor, where the red door labeled "EVA Airlock" was…missing.

Blackened firemarks splayed out from its edges across the white wall and twisted metal littered the floor. Red light flashed a warning in the suitroom beyond, where the bulkier spacesuits with which Art was somewhat familiar stood like mute sentinels.

The reason for the warning was clear: the inner door of the lock itself had likewise been blown apart. The outer hatch, set in the floor of the airlock, had an ominous, bloody cast in the pulsing scarlet light. Art swallowed. They couldn't mean to open the outer door with the inner door blasted away. They couldn't—

His two companions shoved him into the lock and crammed in with him, their hands clamped vise-like on his arms. A moment later the outer door dropped open beneath their feet.

The hurricane of escaping air and the spin of the ship tossed them into space like bullets from a gun, surrounded by a jet of glittering ice crystals. Art screamed as stars and vast walls of metal whirled around him. Everything steadied, and he realized with enormous relief that his captors had some way of maneuvering. Dimly he realized he was still screaming; he stopped.

The impulse to resume was almost overpowering a moment later, however, as he took stock of his situation.

He had never really appreciated before the incredible size of the *Mayflower II*. Habitat One was now a gigantic metal cliff curving away from them, spinning steadily. The ship's name crawled past in letters three times his height, battered and gouged by decades of travel at speeds where even the minute number of microscopic particles that got through the repulsing fields hit like explosive bullets.

As they slowly drew away, the enormous sphere of the Forward Service and Propulsion Module came into sight, overhung by the rust-red Forward Shield, a vast flattened umbrella shape outlined by a brilliant corona: just the fringe of the eye-searing energy pouring out from the main matter-antimatter engine, which had made the move from stern to bow through the Core when deceleration began.

The ship continued to recede. Now he could see the *Mayflower II*'s entire structure: the six layers of boxy Habs, four to a layer, spaced equidistantly around the Core, each large enough to house five hundred people comfortably…*and considerably more uncomfortably*, Art thought. Each was attached to the "trunk" of the Core by a movable "stalk": a Service and Transit Conduit, through most of which Art had travelled aboard the transit pods.

The entire ship rotated to generate the illusion of gravity. The adjustable "stalks" kept the apparent "down" within the Habs at right angles to the floors by angling them as necessary to perfectly match the divergent vectors of acceleration/deceleration and spin. When deceleration had begun, while Art was a teenager, there had been one particularly exciting day when things had gone a bit awry, and the Habs had suddenly all seemed to have steeply sloping floors, much to the detriment of cherished china collections. Still, aside from the minor havoc caused by those and other falling objects and sloshing liquids, there had been no lasting effects: and as the ship's systems finally compensated, "down" had reassuringly returned to its familiar location.

Watching the Habs slowly spinning away from him, Art saw long scars in the metal, blackened places, deep pits. Arrays of instruments and antennae also spun by, reduced in places to twisted wreckage by some cataclysm of the long flight. Neither the electromagnetic nor solid shields had stopped *everything*, it seemed. *Even out here*, Art thought, *you can see the ship's deterioration.* Someday something would fail and couldn't be repaired—and then even if they found a habitable world, they would be blind to it.

A habitable world—as his fear ebbed, Art realized he had been staring at the ship without even thinking about the fact that there actually *was* such a world nearby. He twisted his head around inside the helmet, but could see nothing but stars—including one so close and bright he couldn't look at it.

Close enough, in fact, to be thought of as a sun instead of a star.

He looked from one to the other of his captors. The larger one was as motionless as a deactivated robot, as it very well might be, for all Art knew. The smaller one kept looking at a glowing blue panel on its wrist, peering ahead, then glancing back at the panel again. It looked human, or at least humanoid.

Maybe they are *human*, Art thought. *Maybe they're Crawlspacers. Maybe they stole one of the shuttlecraft. Maybe they gave up on telling all the Passengers in favour of saving themselves. Maybe they're rescuing me.*

Maybe. But it felt a whole lot more like a kidnapping.

The smaller figure pointed. Art peered in the direction indicated, but couldn't see anything at all—including stars, he suddenly realized. Something was blocking them—something small, compared to the *Mayflower II*, but still substantially larger than they were.

That hole in the sky grew, until at last it took on solidity and became a ship, black and non-reflective, a ship Art was quite certain was not in the *Mayflower II*'s inventory. In fact, it looked far more like ships he had seen in old science fiction movies: sleek and bulging with pods from which protruded things with a strong resemblance to the beam-rifle Art had already had too close a look at.

Light flared at one spot on the hull as a hatch slid open. It swelled before them, and with impressive last-minute maneuvering they floated neatly through it. The hatch closed, air hissed, and a moment later the inner door swung aside. At the same time Art felt himself getting heavier and heavier, first touching what had become the floor, then standing on it. Within seconds he had close to ship-normal weight—perhaps a little more. *We can't be spinning*, he thought. *Not with the floor down there, at right angles to the hatch.*

Which meant artificial gravity. Which he'd always thought was impossible.

These were definitely *not* Crawlspacers.

The smaller of whoever—or *whatever*—they were turned off Art's life support. To his rising panic, it next disconnected the hoses and motioned for him to take off his suit. He gulped. Just because these things could breathe whatever gases filled the spaceship didn't mean *he* could.

But he had no choice. He could already feel the air going

thick inside the suit. Heart pounding, he unsealed the helmet and took it off.

For a moment he held his breath, then gave up and let it out with a whoosh, sucking it in again a moment later.

Aside from an odd spicy smell that he couldn't quite place, the air seemed indistinguishable from what he had breathed every day of his life.

The larger figure reached up and touched its mirrored helmet, and the helmet became instantly transparent to Art, as presumably it had been from the inside all along.

Art's imagination had been busily filling the two armored suits with all manner of hideousness, much of it drawn from the same movies in which he had seen ships like this. But to his shock, the entity revealed when the helmet came off was undeniably human: black hair and mustache, dark brown eyes, red, fleshy nose, and a whiff of very human sweat. He said something harsh and unintelligible when he saw Art staring at him.

Art glanced at the other "alien" and put that hypothesis down the recycle chute for good. This time he found himself looking into large green eyes framed by short red hair. Full lips covered white teeth that flashed in a smile at the big man. She said something just as incomprehensible as he had, and the big man shrugged and smiled. The woman laughed, then finished struggling out of the armor, which stood on its own when she was done with it like a trophy in some ancient castle.

The man asked something, and the woman nodded. Beneath her armor she wore a light blue jumpsuit; emblazoned over her left breast was a stylized silver eye. On her sleeve were several other emblems, and Art, glancing back at the man, saw that while his jumpsuit bore the same insignia, it fell well short of her tally of stripes and stars. The woman commanded, then.

But it was the man who hoisted his black weapon and pointed it at Art, and kept it there as the woman led them both down the corridor.

Fifteen metres along, they came to a T-intersection. To the

left, the corridor ended after a couple of metres in a forbidding black door. Red lettering on it confused him further—some of the letters were Roman, but some looked Cyrillic and others more like mathematical symbols. He shook his head in bewilderment. If these people weren't aliens, they had to be from the ship—but they *couldn't* be from the *Mayflower II*. Therefore they were aliens. But aliens would not use Roman letters, even mixed in with gibberish. And aliens who looked like the red-haired woman seemed improbable, to say the least.

Prodded by his armed guard, Art turned right, to see ahead of them another woman, uniformed like his escorts, hurrying away from them, looking at some kind of glowing tablet. She knocked on a door, which slid open to let her in. A bald man looked out, shiny head turned toward Art. Their eyes met for an instant. The man stared with obvious interest, then Art's escort barked a word and the man withdrew in a hurry, the door sliding shut an instant later.

Art and his escorts passed that door and two others before a fourth slid open at their approach and Art was ushered into what was unmistakably a med chamber, the equipment sleek and compact but still recognizable: vital-signs monitors of various kinds, a blood-pressure cuff dangling from a box on a metal stand, a sterilization autoclave.

A third man, wearing white, stood beside the table. The woman pointed Art to it, and, encouraged by a poke from the gun, he lay down, though he didn't exactly relax.

The white-coated man stepped forward and started to strap Art to the table. He struggled, but the big man held him down until the whitecoat finished the job. Then from a tripod by the bed the man in white lifted a silvery metal circlet connected to a flat black box by a red wire. Innumerable horror movies featuring mad scientists sprang immediately to Art's mind, but he could do nothing as the circlet was lowered toward his head except cast pleading eyes at the woman, who gazed at him with avid interest but no sympathy.

Then the circlet touched his skin and everything went black.

◣ ◢

Only an instant later, it seemed, he woke and jerked upright, forgetting about the restraining straps.

But the straps were gone.

So were a great many other things.

He was no longer in the med chamber. Instead, clad only in shorts, he lay between beige sheets in a wide and comfortable bed in a room that might have been in Habitat Three. Bright light streamed through an open window that framed a square of vivid blue.

Blue?

He scrambled out of bed and to the window.

Beneath a turquoise sky, hectares of bright green grass and spiky, blue-green trees stretched farther than any space on the *Mayflower II* permitted. Impossibly far away, that expanse of vegetation finally ended in a high white wall, overgrown with trailing plants abloom with bright red flowers. Beyond the wall rose angular white buildings far taller than could ever be built on the rotating ship; buildings such as he had only seen in movies.

He took a step back. So much space, and no matter how far he looked, no walls enclosed it. He was no longer *in* something but *on* it, and his legs felt shaky at the thought.

"So, you're awake," said a woman's voice behind him, and he spun to see his red-haired captor from the ship standing just inside the door.

"You're talking!" he blurted.

"So are you," she pointed out.

He blinked. "No, I mean I can understand you!"

The woman's left eyebrow lifted. "Listen carefully to yourself."

"What—" Art began, then stopped, astounded. The word he had just spoken was not English. Neither, he realized, had been anything else he had said so far. "How—" he began again, but his voice trailed off as another strange sound emerged.

"We headjacked you," the woman replied. "A direct interface between a computer and your brain. It's a very efficient way to learn, but it has one side effect—it knocks you out. In your case, for just about twenty-four hours."

"Twenty-four—" As that sank in, Art suddenly became aware of other sensations. "I'm hungry."

"Breakfast is ready." She pointed out the door behind her. "Out here."

Art cleared his throat. "One other thing..."

The woman touched a panel by the door. A second door that had been invisible a moment before slid aside, revealing a gleaming white bathroom. "There are towels and soap in the shower, and fresh clothes in the closet—there." She touched another switch on the panel and a third door opened, close by the bed. "I'll wait outside." She walked out.

Art hurried into the bathroom. The fixtures were strangely shaped, but not unrecognizable. The shower took him the longest to figure out, and he almost scalded himself before he learned how to control it, but within twenty minutes he emerged from the bedroom refreshed, clean-shaven, and wearing some of the clothes he had found in the closet, a loose-fitting green shirt with puffed sleeves and tight black pants of some shiny material that tucked into gray, calf-high boots. He felt ridiculous, but presumably this was what the natives were wearing, although the woman was in the same uniform she had worn on the ship.

He walked through a short cream-carpeted corridor into a larger room with a bright red couch, two red chairs and a low glass table at one end and, at the other, on a slightly higher level, a nook with windows on three sides. At a second glass-topped table sat the woman, the sun bringing the planes of her lean face into sharp relief. Steam rose from silvery platters and plates, and with it a smell that made Art's mouth water. He crossed the room in a hurry, passing the closed front door, and the woman gestured at the meal. "Help yourself."

"Thank you," said Art with feeling. He sat down and dug in

to meat, fruit, bread and—were those eggs? Whatever they were, they were delicious—not that taste mattered much, after his long unintentional fast.

The woman ate only a little, and didn't talk, occasionally glancing out the windows as people in uniforms like her own crossed the park at a distance. When Art finally slowed she stood and said, "Let's get started."

"Started?" Art wiped his mouth with a blue napkin and looked at the woman warily. "Started doing what?"

The woman descended from the nook, crossing to one of the red-upholstered chairs and motioning Art toward the other. "Asking questions and answering them, of course. Why do you think you're here? To have lunch?"

Art blinked. "This is an interrogation?"

The woman didn't look up; she was rummaging in a slim black handbag beside the chair. She pulled out a glossy black hemisphere like a paperweight and placed it on the table. "You'd prefer a dark cell with rats running around your chained ankles and the sound of distant screaming? Maybe something involving rubber hoses or electrodes attached to sensitive parts of your anatomy?"

Art blinked again. "Um…no?"

The woman looked at him and smiled briefly. "Sorry. You'd be amazed how many people think that's what my job entails." She touched the "paperweight"; it beeped. "I am now recording our conversation, audio and video," she said. She cleared her throat. "Commander Avara Torrance al Morali, conducting initial interrogation of subject taken from *Mayflower II*, identified in their records as Arthur Randall Stoddard, Information Dissemination Specialist: Civilian."

Art stared at her. "How do you know—?"

"Although your ship's Crew is unable to intercept or decipher *our* communications, *theirs* are an open book. We have been monitoring everything going on aboard the *Mayflower II* for some time. We had already identified you as a person of interest. Your arrest only heightened that interest. And when the Crew was so accommodating as to incarcerate you in a cell easily accessible from the outside of the ship, we decided to *carpe diem*."

"But…who are you?"

"As I just stated," she said impatiently, "I am Commander Avara Torrance al Morali."

"Commander of *what*?"

"I am an officer of the State Security Intelligence Network—SSIN."

Art ran a nervous hand through his hair. Organizations with names like that had never been good news for the heroes in old movies. "Sounds ominous."

"It's supposed to." She leaned forward. "Now, let's start at the beginning. Please confirm your identity."

"Uh—you had it right. I'm Arthur Randall Stoddard."

"And you were the Information Dissemination Specialist: Civilian aboard the Geneva Pact Starship *Mayflower II*?"

"Yes…"

"What did that job entail?" Morali's steady green gaze never left Art's face.

Lying, Art thought, but out loud he said, "I was supposed to keep everyone informed as to what was happening on the ship—subject to Crew and Council approval, of course."

"A propagandist, then."

Art started to protest, then wondered why. He shrugged. "Yeah."

"Why were you arrested?"

"Don't you *know*? If you've been listening in on Crew communications—"

"For the record."

Art hesitated. These people had blasted their way into the *Mayflower II*, and, for all he knew, killed Crew in the process. Add to that the rather threatening name of Commander Morali's organization and the signs didn't exactly point to them being allies.

Not allies of the Crew, *at least*, Art thought. *But the Crew is lying to the people. They arrested me, fired me, and held me prisoner. I don't owe* them *anything.*

"Well?" Commander Morali prompted.

To hell with the Crew, Art thought, and told his story straightforwardly and completely. When he was finished the commander looked thoughtful.

"So only the Crew—and these 'Crawlspacers'—know that the *Mayflower II* is approaching Peregrine. The majority of the ship's population, though it knows the ship is decelerating, is unaware of the presence of a habitable planet in the system it is approaching, much less that that planet is already inhabited. Interesting." Commander Morali touched the black hemisphere. It beeped again. She put it back in the handbag, and stood. "Thank you, Mr. Stoddard. I'll have some more questions later." She turned to go.

Art jumped up and grabbed her arm. "Wait just a—" He found himself instantly on his back, arm tingling. The commander stood over him with one fist drawn back and cold green eyes locked with his. He swallowed and lay very still.

Commander Morali held the threatening pose for a moment, then relaxed. "Sorry," she said, but not as if she meant it. She stepped back and let him scramble to his feet. "Reflexes. What did you want?"

He backed away a little. "Answers to some of *my* questions."

The commander considered. "Fair enough," she said at last. "There are some things I can't tell you, but you deserve to know the basics." She motioned him back to his chair, but remained standing herself. "You were captured because we needed information about what was happening on board the *Mayflower II.*"

"Why not just call them up and ask?"

"The Parliament of Protectors wished to know for certain what it was dealing with before initiating any contact."

"The Parliament of Protectors?"

"The planetary government of Peregrine." She snorted. "Yes,

I know," she said. "The Parliament of Protectors of Peregrine. The PPP. Which can also be pronounced as…" She fluttered her lips in a long raspberry.

Art laughed.

"That's not funny," Morali said, face deadpan. "Laugh again and I will be forced to kill you."

Art's laughter died instantly. Morali stared at him coldly for a long moment, then her mouth twitched. "We all call it that," she said. Her brief smile faded. "But, ridiculous name or not, the Parliament of Protectors is tasked with protecting this planet. And knowing what we know of your ship, we felt it best to attempt to gather intelligence first and contact the Crew later…if ever." She studied Art. "What do you know about your ship's launching?"

Art recited from schoolboy memories: "War seemed imminent. The New Caliphate of the Holy and Oppressed and its allies, the League of Exploited Nations, had launched weapons platforms. The Geneva Pact countries had followed suit. When construction started on the *Mayflower II* in 2088 pundits were calling it the Second Cold War; five years later, the cold war was threatening to turn hot. The starship was one of the main sources of tension—the LEN claimed global resources were being 'wasted' on it while the Caliphate simply issued a fatwa against it and called for its destruction by the faithful. There were several unsuccessful attempts at sabotage, one of which resulted in the destruction of a shuttle carrying 150 passengers. As the rhetoric ratcheted up, the Pact's leaders feared the launch of nuclear weapons against the ship…as a precursor to, or as part of, all-out war. The Pact's leaders hurried completion of the ship and selection of its crew and passengers. Terrorists attacked the Station just before Launch, but failed to stop it."

"Very good. But incomplete. What you don't know is what happened afterward: the Launch, and the Station attack, almost precipitated the very war the ship was fleeing—but not quite. Things remained tense for years, but war never broke out, despite dozens of incidents and crises. The Caliphate fell apart in bloody sectarian strife early in the 22nd Century, and the League of Exploited Nations did not have the willpower or technical know-how to continue to threaten the Geneva Pact, which soon subsumed them into itself, forming, for the first time in human history, a true world government.

"But the world was still a rather nasty place during the decades of what we now call the Troubles: widespread starvation, environmental degradation, rebellions and revolts that had to be firmly squelched by the government. The tide didn't really turn for the better until 2128—the year that a research team at the University of Saskatchewan, led by physicist Heinrich Umstattd, discovered a way to make faster-than-light travel a reality."

"But…FTL is impossible!" Art blurted, then wished he hadn't, since…

Morali cocked an amused eyebrow at him. "Right. Which means, clearly, that you are hallucinating your current surroundings: a house in a city built by humans on a planet some four hundred light years from Earth—a city that has been here for more than three centuries."

Art nodded dumbly.

"The Umstattd drive opened up the galaxy; but first, it opened up the solar system, allowing travel at substantial fractions of the speed of light from planet to planet: Earth to Mars in hours instead of months, for example," Morali continued. "The enormous resources of the outer planets became profitable for exploitation. Earth became wealthy—very, very wealthy, to the point where poverty was all but eradicated. Religious strife certainly wasn't eliminated—there will always be those willing to kill for their god—but prosperity for everyone at least reduced the number of fanatics, and the risk was reduced even further by laws enacted during the Troubles that restricted knowledge of, and access to, any technology the government, in its wisdom, deemed a potential threat to public safety. When only the government has weapons—or even the most advanced communications and transportation systems—then the government, and the people it…

serves...have little to fear from those who would overthrow it."

Art blinked. Morali's tone had changed ever-so-slightly as she said that. Her face remained bland, but she had almost sounded... angry.

"We had suspected since the 21st century that habitable worlds were plentiful in the galaxy, and sure enough, the first wave of exploring starships found several. Colonizing starships soon followed, including those that came to this world, Peregrine. Within a century Earth ruled an interstellar empire, unchallenged as the capital for the simple reason that it continued the policies that had successfully protected its rule of the home planet: strict regulation of technology, government control of research, seizure of anything innovative enough to look threatening, and of course the immediate and ruthless crushing of any significant dissent." Morali looked past him, out the windows of the breakfast nook. "Which, in the end, is why it all fell apart," she said softly. "This colony was founded in 2185, Earth time. And just over a hundred local years later, a scheduled starship failed to arrive from Earth...and no starship has arrived since.

"We've never learned why. The Umstattd drive allows ships to travel faster than light, but not communications. When the ships stopped coming, so did the news from Earth and from the other worlds."

"Why didn't you build your own?" Art said. "Surely you knew how..."

"Haven't you been listening?" Morali snapped. "Earth kept a tight lid on technology, and no lid was kept tighter than the one covering the knowledge of starship construction. Earth was worried about uprisings on colony worlds spreading to other colonies or back to Earth itself. By preventing the colonies from knowing how to build their own ships, Earth could always isolate any rebellion before it could metastasize. But in the end...well, my guess is that the rebellion, when it came, came on Earth itself, and all the government's efforts to control any technology that could be used for mass destruction came to naught in a spectacularly fatal fashion." She sighed. "We can build in-system ships using the sublight version of the Umstattd drive—one of those brought you here. But we do not have the knowledge to build starships. Even knowing it is possible, our scientists have been unable to rediscover the trick of it. And our own government…" She bit off whatever she was about to say, instead looking out the window again, up at the blue sky. "Perhaps other worlds have managed it. But if they have, they haven't come here. For just over two hundred local years, we've been trapped in our own system."

Art's brain whirled. They all knew, on the *Mayflower II*, about the effects of relativity—but he was the first to come face to face with them. His parents, who had been a young couple at the time of the Launch, were ancient history to these people—he and everyone he had ever known were anachronisms, relics out of a long-gone and un-fondly remembered past.

"We detected your ship far outside our system, shedding energy like a small nova as it decelerated," Commander Morali went on, looking back at him. "It was too large to be an Umstattd-Drive starship, and much too slow. For a time we thought it was an alien craft—but then we picked up a few internal communications and realized it had come from Earth…and at sub-light speeds, it couldn't have left there recently. Only one non-FTL starship was ever launched. It had to be the *Mayflower II*."

"But why are you so afraid of us?" Art asked. "Why not just—well, knock on the hull and ask to be let in? Even if the Captain doesn't want to talk to you he can't ignore you."

"If we thought he would just ignore us we wouldn't be concerned. Unfortunately, we think, from his actions so far, that he believes the Pact was overrun and we are descendants of his enemies. He's seen our technology; he knows it's beyond his. He's afraid. And frightened men do rash things."

"What can he do? The *Mayflower II* must seem as primitive as an oxcart to you. It can't hurt you."

"Not everything was included in your shipboard histories, it appears," Commander Morali said. "The *Mayflower II* was launched in a time of war, and the thinking that went into it was war-thinking." She glanced up, as though she could see the distant ship through roof and atmosphere and millions of miles of space. "Oxcarts don't carry planet-busting missiles."

Chapter Five

A surge of anger wiped out Art's first blank shock. "That's ridiculous! Our mission was—*is*—to find a habitable world and establish a colony. We *fled* war!"

"Ridiculous? Tell that to the designers. The old records, top-secret when your parents set out, show that your ship is carrying enough matter-antimatter missiles to destroy all life on this planet…and three or four others, if need be."

In the back of his mind Art heard his father going on and on about the terror he had lived under as a young man in a world constantly on the brink of destruction. "The Passengers wouldn't stand for it—"

"I doubt any Passengers know about it. *You* didn't. But your Crew does. It's a military force. You tell me they've withdrawn from the rest of you. I'd wager one reason is to avoid being assimilated into civilian society—though they probably call it 'maintaining discipline.'" She folded her arms. "So, you can see why we're concerned. Now we wonder what to do about it."

Art's anger faded, replaced by the sense of futility that was never far from him. Was this new world as much a dead end as the ship—*because* of the ship? "You must have defenses against missiles. After all these centuries—"

"*Earth* had defenses. But this is not Earth. Anti-missile defense was a forbidden technology for the colonies. After all, we might have used it to protect ourselves against Earth starships coming to put down a rebellion, had we ever rebelled." For a moment her eyes looked past Art instead of at him, but then she shook her head and her gaze refocused. "We've had our battles among ourselves, and we still maintain a military force for internal security. But the technology restrictions have kept weapons of mass destruction absent from our conflicts."

"In other words, you can't do anything." *Just like the Passengers.*

"I didn't say that." Commander Morali studied him for a moment, as though considering how much to say. "There are two options under debate," she said finally. "I suppose it's only fair you know what they are, since in the next few days all the questions you are asked will be aimed at determining which route we should follow.

"The more liberal faction of the government favours negotiation. They're sure they can get the Captain talking to them, and that once they're talking something can be worked out. They see your Passengers as a valuable resource of minds and talents that could revitalize our world…a world badly in need of revitalization, both technologically and politically." She spread her hands. "But the conservative faction, which at the moment has the edge, would destroy the *Mayflower II* to forestall the attack they consider imminent. They see you as barbarians who have travelled forward in time to pillage our planet the way you did Earth."

Art gaped at her. "*Destroy* the *Mayflower II*? But how? How could you destroy something that big if you can't even stop a missile attack?"

"It's easier to stop a single thing that's large and slow than a thousand things that are small and fast," Morali said. "A few of our ships carry high-energy beam weapons that could carve the *Mayflower II* apart in minutes. Not that anything that drastic—or wasteful—would be necessary. A few holes drilled into each of the Habitats…"

Art could see it in his mind's eye—the atmosphere exploding outward, a sudden hurricane ripping apart houses, plants, animals, people, spewing all of them out into vacuum…he knew the ship was slowly dying. But there was a difference between death from old age and murder. "You couldn't!"

"We could. And we may. But nothing has been decided yet.

The raid to capture you was a compromise. Both sides needed more first-hand information. The negotiation faction hoped you might be able to turn the Captain toward talking. Those favouring attack hoped you could tell them more about the *Mayflower II*'s capabilities."

"Why not just go for the Captain?"

"Capturing the Captain…even if we could have fought through the security, which would not have been easy, despite the relatively primitive nature of your technology…might have resulted in the very attack we are trying to avoid. You seemed like someone both knowledgeable and influential enough to be of use, and someone not important enough for your abduction to automatically trigger war."

"What about *your* people? Where does public opinion stand?"

"The people don't know about it," she said flatly. "They have no need to, in the government's view—at least, not until the government knows what it's going to do. Then it may tell them—or not."

Art snorted. "Your government doesn't sound any better than ours."

"Our government is what this planet needs," Commander Morali said. To Art, it sounded like a phrase she had spoken often, almost by rote. "A representative democracy, on this world, in our situation, would be a disaster…*was* a disaster, in the years after the starships stopped coming. The unrest almost destroyed us. But fortunately we had a model for a government strong enough to deal with unrest, and dedicated civil servants willing to take the actions necessary to assert control and hold it."

Art stared at her. "You *copied* Earth's world government? Even after what you—"

"We needed—and still need—a government of dedicated, competent professionals, knowledgeable in all aspects of governance, and that is what we have." Again, the words sounded to Art like a memorized speech. He'd memorized enough of them; he should know. "To periodically overthrow your professional government on the basis of the quite possibly ill-informed opinions of low-information voters would be insane in our situation. When the time is right, democracy will be restored. But that time is not yet."

Then she surprised Art with a sudden smile. "Of course, the people may find out what's going on anyway," she said. "It seems they often do." Her smile switched off as abruptly as it had appeared. "I've been here too long. I have to file my report. I have no doubt I or someone else will have more questions later. In the meantime, I'm afraid you're confined to this apartment."

"No kidding," Art said drily.

Commander Morali raised an eyebrow and one corner of her mouth quirked a little. "If you get *really* bored—" She opened a hidden panel in the arm of the chair, revealing a numbered touchpad. She tapped it once and a section of the wall rolled back from a huge vidscreen. Two people spoke earnestly to each other about sewage treatment. "You may find our planetary network interesting. It includes many entertainment and informational options… all approved by the PPP, of course."

"Of course," Art said dryly. "I'm sure it will make me feel right at home."

She went to the door and out. Art turned to the controls of the vidscreen. There were indeed a number of options available from the planetary network—Peregrinet, it was called. He wished he'd asked Morali why the planet was named after an Earth bird of prey, but he supposed it didn't really matter. He skimmed from screechy music to all-nude theatre—which held his attention for a few minutes before the novelty wore off—to incomprehensible comedy programs, to one channel that seemed to be devoted entirely to scenery.

What he could not find, presumably because it was denied, was anything that provided him with unfettered access to the wealth of information he would have expected a planetary network to contain. No search functions presented themselves. He seemed to have no options but to stream pre-packaged programming.

In the end he settled on the all-scenery channel. He found the endless shots of seaside cliffs, blazing deserts, dank jungles and ice caps intriguing…and a bit overwhelming. *Planets are so big*, he thought. *And yet our little ship is a threat?*

The camera tracked a flight of enormous white flying creatures as they dipped and soared above a bright-green lake, while his mind idled. He knew he should be mulling over what the commander had said, trying to decide how he could convince the planetary government not to destroy the *Mayflower II*.

But what he was actually mulling over was Commander Morali's low voice, the glint of her eyes, the flash of her smile, the way her lithe body filled her uniform, and even the grace and power with which she had sent him crashing to the floor.

Don't be stupid, he told himself firmly. He replayed their conversation in his mind. She had done absolutely nothing verbally or non-verbally to express any interest in him except as a subject for interrogation.

On the other hand, he had done nothing to indicate interest in numerous girls and women back on the ship, either, and that hadn't stopped them. *Maybe that's why I'm attracted to her*, he thought. *Because I'm not a celebrity to her.*

Or maybe it's the red hair…

The birds on the screen were flying over an enormous waterfall, Peregrine's sun creating rainbows in the rising mist…and then suddenly the image changed.

Art found himself looking at two men and a woman, dressed in outlandish, brightly coloured clothes. They tossed rapid one and two-liners back and forth across a triangular table, along the lines of "How many Cabinet Subformal Undersecretaries does it take to requisition a glow-tube?" "Forty-seven: one to fill out the forms and forty-six to process them."

Art grimaced. The Shipborn told that same joke on the Council. Then he frowned. *This* was approved by the PPP? It certainly wouldn't have been approved by the Council. And the way the image had suddenly appeared…

It's a hack, he thought. He grinned at the screen. "You people," he told the three jokers, "are breaking the law." *Too bad Shadow wasn't able to hack into Shipnet. Then she wouldn't have had to use me.*

Uproarious laughter swelled as a half-dozen actors in exaggerated SSIN uniforms chased the comics off the stage. Then a woman appeared in front of a circular seal showing a bird of prey breaking free of leg-chains. Bold black block letters spelled out PFN on its feathered breast. "This is the Peregrine FreeNet," the woman said, "and this is the news."

Art blinked. There was something odd about the woman's face and voice. *Computer-altered*, he thought. *Or maybe she's not a real woman at all; just a computer construct. To avoid the attentions of Commander Morali's SSIN.*

He leaned forward as the woman began to speak, professionally interested in her delivery (smooth, well-modulated—a bit slow, though) while at the same time wondering if there would be anything in this…what was the old word?…*samizdat* newscast about the *Mayflower II* or his own capture. Surely if the people of Peregrine found out the truth, they would push for the government to negotiate…

…or push for it to blow the ship out of space, that nastier inner voice pointed out. *Public opinion is not always the best opinion. Morali was right about that.*

That sounds like Crew and Council talk, he told himself firmly, and concentrated on what was being said.

However, there wasn't much to hear. Most of the news dealt with government corruption and the small-scale activities of what the newscaster called "Liberty Hawks," underground guerillas of some kind. *Planet-bound Crawlspacers*, Art thought.

But the newscast ended with a very strange item. "And lastly, the First Visionary of the Skywatchers has raised tremendous interest among the cult's adherents by announcing that the arrival of the Conqueror of Time and Space is at hand.

"The Skywatchers, formed in the early tumultuous years

after the starships stopped coming, hold that this Conqueror will turn Peregrine into a paradise for faithful members of the cult. However, this is the first time in their two-century history that a First Visionary has said that the Conqueror's advent is imminent. The First Visionary made the prediction during his weekly address to the faithful, which once again found its way onto Peregrinet despite the government's best efforts—much like this newscast." The woman's voice held the hint of a chuckle as she said that, which made Art inclined to think she was a real woman, not just a construct. "Since the whereabouts of the First Visionary is a closely guarded secret, PFN was unable to ask him why this announcement was made now, but experts speculate it is related to an internal power struggle for control of the cult." The woman smiled. "And that's the news for Gamma 34, 487—the *real* news. Up next: the Banned Song of the Week."

The first few seconds of the ensuing sounds drove Art to turn off the vidscreen. *No wonder it was banned*, he thought. *That's not censorship, it's good taste.*

Rather than return to his previous futile (and frustrating) train of thought, he went to the dining nook and gazed out over the park, trying to overcome his lingering uneasiness with all that open space. He'd have to learn to deal with it if he were going to live on this planet—and it seemed highly unlikely he would be returning to the *Mayflower II*.

He thought of the approaching ship hurling a matter-antimatter missile at the city he saw beyond the flower-draped wall and anger surged inside him again, this time aimed at the blind fools who had put such weapons into the supposed lifeboat of the species. No wonder the Peregrine government was afraid, faced with that kind of warrior idiocy. No wonder the Earth government had tried to restrict access to potentially dangerous technology.

On the other hand, if he were Crew and had seen that sleek black shuttlecraft and knew that an armed party had successfully breached the hull and made off with someone—even an insignificant someone like himself—he wouldn't exactly be sleeping soundly, either. And if he were Captain Nakos, his finger might be hovering over the fire button, too.

The situation was deadly—and, as always, there was nothing he could do about it. He couldn't even be sure that trying to persuade the Peregrine government to negotiate was the best action. Wouldn't it be *better* to destroy the *Mayflower II* and its ten thousand passengers than see millions die on Peregrine and the whole planet possibly rendered uninhabitable?

It wouldn't be better for the people on the Mayflower II, he thought angrily. *And they're* my *people.*

Behind him the door slid open, and he turned to see a stranger in a SSIN uniform, flanked by two others without the silver stars the first man wore on his sleeves but armed with the now-familiar but no-less-threatening black beam rifles.

"Now what?" Art's anger carried over into his tone before he remembered what Commander Morali had said about the possibility of more "formal" questioning. He suddenly wondered what "formal" meant.

He got no answer from the apparent officer. "This way," was all he said.

With the armed guards at his heels, Art followed the officer down a very long corridor, carpeted an unpleasant shade of orange-yellow, its white walls punctuated with unmarked khaki-green doors. So far Art was unimpressed by Peregrine notions of interior design.

At a four-way intersection the officer stopped, held up his hand, and very cautiously peered around the corner. Then he jerked his hand forward and they pressed on.

After another fifty metres or so the corridor ended in a black door labeled AIR TRANSPORT. *At least it's not the torture chamber*, Art thought, but he didn't like the notion he was about to be flown anywhere. Commander Morali had said nothing about it. "Where are you taking me?" he demanded, but his only reply was a painful poke in the back with a gun barrel.

The officer pointed something small and silver at the door and it slid open, revealing a cavernous room containing several sleek winged vehicles, all the same unrelieved black as the Peregrine spaceship had been. At the far side of the room a wide door opened onto a vast stretch of pavement. Here and there mechanics in green coveralls probed the innards of the vehicles, but not one so much as looked up as the guards marched Art across the echoing floor to the smallest machine of all, no more than five metres long, with delta wings and a tall vertical stabilizer. The officer pointed with his little box again and the vehicle's transparent canopy popped open. "Inside," he ordered.

Art looked at the airplane and back at the officer. "But there's only room for one."

"Inside!" One of the guards poked Art in the back again by way of emphasis.

"All right, all right!" He climbed in and saw to his further bewilderment that there weren't even any controls; only a smooth black console with a single rectangular receptacle at its centre and a red light glowing beneath it.

Outside the guards were stripping off their uniforms. Underneath they wore mechanics' coveralls. The officer pointed to another airplane, much larger, not far away. "That's ours," he told the other two. "Fueled and ready. If we're lucky we'll have an hour or more before the alarm is sounded."

"And if we're unlucky?" grunted one of the others.

"Haven't you heard? Martyrs get the prime real estate in paradise." The officer reached into Art's plane and snapped something about twice the size of a data disc into the socket in the console. The red light turned green. "Have a nice flight," said the officer, and pushed down the canopy. As the engine whined to life and the tiny aircraft rolled smoothly out into the morning sunlight, Art saw the "officer" stripping off his black uniform, too.

The airplane rolled faster and faster down the runway. No buildings rose in front of Art—only blue-green, spiky trees, and rolling green fields, and, in the far, far distance, at the very edge of visibility, rugged, snow-capped mountains. The whine of the little plane's engine swelled to a shriek, its needle-sharp nose pointed at those icy peaks, and suddenly it was airborne, carrying Art helplessly into the sky.

He willed his pounding heart to slow. He must be safe—there were far easier ways to kill him, if they wanted to—whoever *they* were. To take his mind off the landscape spreading ever wider around him and bringing back his agoraphobia full-force, along with a new feeling that he was going to crash into the blue vault of the sky, he closed his eyes firmly, breathed deeply and slowly, and set his mind to figuring out what had just happened.

Who had his kidnappers been? The "officer" had said something about "martyrs" and "paradise," and that reminded Art uncomfortably of the Skywatcher cult whose leader had just made the Free Peregrine Net news by announcing the imminent coming of some messiah. Maybe the "soldiers" were members of that cult, or at least in its employ.

Or perhaps the mental quotation marks were unnecessary. Maybe they really were soldiers, but held greater loyalty to their religion than their uniform. That would explain how they had been able to so calmly march him through the hangar and put him on a plane with none of the mechanics paying the slightest bit of attention.

Soon, though, Commander Morali or someone else coming to interrogate him further would surely discover his absence and put two and two together.

No wonder the soldiers had resigned from the SSIN so abruptly.

The aircraft droned on and on, at first over farms and smaller towns, then over increasingly rugged, tree-covered foothills, the uneven surfaces below somehow contributing to increasing turbulence above, forcing Art to swallow hard and hope desperately he didn't throw up. All the while the mountains ahead were slowly swelling in size.

Art had no way to measure time, but he thought he'd been flying for well over an hour when suddenly the plane dropped precipitously, driving his stomach into his throat. He swallowed extra hard, managed to keep his gorge down, and then almost lost it again as he looked ahead and saw that the sudden descent had dropped him well below the level of the icy granite peaks. He glanced at the chip controlling the plane from its tiny receptacle in the console and prayed fervently to whomever or whatever might be listening that the programmer had known what he was doing.

He tried closing his eyes, but the thought of crashing into a mountain without seeing it coming seemed somehow worse than crashing into it with plenty of warning. *Right*, he thought with an edge of hysteria. *If I'm going to die, I should at least have lots of time to panic first.*

Opening his eyes again brought him a fair taste of it. What looked like the largest of the peaks in the chain—though that might have been only because it was the closest—rose dead ahead of the aircraft, whose engine, Art was suddenly sure, was labouring, much like his heart. His mouth had gone dry, he discovered when he tried to swallow, but his palms were wet, and he wiped them uselessly on the non-absorbent material of his skin-tight pants, leaving glistening black streaks.

Slowly, oh-so-slowly, the peak began to dip in front of him. Forest gave way to bare rock and vast snowfields, every detail growing clearer as the huge bulk of the mountain filled Art's vision. His eyes fixed on an up-thrust spire of steel-gray rock, topped with ice. *That's where I'll hit*, he thought numbly.

It swept toward him. An alarm squealed in the cabin—

—and then everything happened at once.

The transparent canopy blew off with a bang, flying up and out of sight. Art had one moment to gasp a shocked breath of ice-cold air, and then with another bang, followed by a roar, the seat into which he was strapped launched itself straight up.

Brutal acceleration crushed him. He couldn't turn his head, could do nothing but stare at the sky. Somewhere below him there was the sound of an enormous explosion, the shock wave kicking the seat up even faster.

Abruptly the acceleration stopped. His stomach lurched and he vomited as the seat stopped rising, and began to fall. The vomit streamed skyward, as did a long white plume of material that snapped open an instant later into a wide wing-shaped parachute. Motors whirred on either side of Art's head, tugging on the cables attaching the parachute to the seat. Art cast a terrified look down and saw an orange inferno and billowing black smoke rising from the side of the peak the plane had just failed to clear.

But the ejected seat that bore him, like the plane before it, was clearly under the control of someone other than himself. The parawing banked and began a spiraling descent. The peaks whirled around Art. Cold wind howled past him…colder than anything he had ever imagined. His thin clothes offered little warmth. Already his nose and cheeks felt numb and his teeth chattered. *I'll freeze before I crash into the ground*, he thought.

But he didn't. Nor did he crash. The seat descended into a deep valley down which a stream poured, white water foaming over rocks. Art saw figures down there, indistinct in the shadows. They grew larger.

The seat touched down, bumped once…and then the chute collapsed and the seat, Art still strapped into it, fell over onto its side. A moment later he was engulfed in the chute's slick material. Disoriented, stunned, he lay still in the darkness for a moment.

Voices sounded, muffled by the chute. "Get him out of there. Clear the chute. We've got six minutes before the next satellite. Move."

The chute material was pulled away. Hands unbuckled Art, pulled him free of the chair, hauled him upright. He had a brief glimpse of men swathed in heavy clothing, faces covered with ice-crusted masks, weapons slung from shoulders. Then someone jammed a hood over his head, cutting of his view of everything. Someone else wrapped a blanket around him. Then he was hurried along over uneven ground, tripping and stumbling, arms gripped by strong hands.

Suddenly the quality of the sound around him changed, and

he knew he had just gone from outdoors to in. A hand pushed his head down, kept him bent almost double for another twenty steps. Only then was he allowed to straighten.

The hood was pulled from his head. He blinked in dim blue light that seemed almost blinding after his enforced darkness.

Three men stood around him in a circular chamber hewn out of black rock. Thin glowing tubes attached to the walls with no visible means of support provided the light, silhouetting the men so he couldn't see their faces, which in any event were shadowed by the parka hoods they still wore.

One by one, they dropped to their knees before him.

Chapter Six

The bizarre tableau lasted only a moment, then the men stood. Before he could speak, the man in the middle produced an adhesive bandage and slapped it over his mouth. The man to the right reached out and pulled the hood back down over his head. It was left to the man on the left to explain. “Our apologies, Farsighted One, but of course you know it would be improper for the Lesser Lights to see you unmasked before the Great Service.”

That meant nothing to Art, but he was in no position to ask questions; what felt like leather thongs were wrapped around his wrists, a voluminous cloak was flung around his shoulders, and he was led off, stumbling, down another corridor, its floor rough between his feet.

“Step down,” a voice said, barely in time to keep Art from falling headlong as the floor suddenly changed from rough to smooth. His footsteps began to echo from walls now appreciably farther away

Turn followed turn in quick succession. Once Art heard a quick snatch of sound off to his left, the roar and clatter of a crowd eating, and smelled roasting meat, but his mouth barely started watering before the odour and noise were behind them.

They stopped, and doors swung open, groaning ponderously. When they walked forward again their footsteps no longer echoed from close by, but rang from distant walls. Here the air was even colder, unpleasantly so; but they crossed the chamber swiftly, and then passed through a door so low Art’s guide made him duck. “Stairs,” the man warned, and down they went, Art’s shoulders brushing rock on either side.

The corridor at the bottom was not much wider. They

followed it for fifty steps and stopped. Art heard a metallic clink and a creak, then someone propelled him forward with a hand between his shoulder blades and a door closed firmly behind him.

As hands released his wrists and then tugged at the hood, he expected to find himself in some dank underground chamber, possibly littered with the bones of previous prisoners…

Instead, he blinked in the bright light of a forest glade.

Emerald green carpeted the floor, from which sprouted furniture that looked more like giant mushrooms and puffballs than tables and chairs. Plants grew around the walls, some reaching almost to the sky-blue ceiling, which glowed with sourceless light. Art stared around in surprise, broken by the sudden ripping of the tape from his mouth. "Ow!" he cried, and lifted a hand to his stinging lips.

Only one man still remained with him, standing to his right, the piece of tape dangling from his gloved hand. Startling blue eyes in a dark-tanned face gazed steadily at him from beneath short-cropped black hair. Black eyebrows that might have been drawn with pencil met above a thin, straight nose. "My apologies, Farsighted One."

The voice was deep and smooth. *He'd make a good broadcaster*, Art thought fleetingly, before demanding, "Who are you, where am I, and what am I doing here?"

"Answers will be forthcoming shortly, I assure you," said the man. "But first, sit down. Make yourself comfortable. Can I fix you a drink?"

Art sat gingerly on a giant puffball. "No, thank you."

"You're sure?" His host opened a cabinet by the door, revealing an array of glasses and decanters filled with fluids of every hue. "I have quite a selection of fine melomels and metheglins." He poured something dark from a white ceramic jug into a beer stein, and Art whiffed a flowery scent that made his nose wrinkle.

"I'm sure," Art said. "I'd rather have answers."

His host made himself comfortable on a circular platform shaded by one of the taller plants, took a long, slow draught from his mug, wiped his mouth, then said, "Patience is one of the prime virtues of the Skywatcher, oh Farsighted One."

"Why does everyone keep calling me that?" Art exploded.

"Because that is who you are…even if you don't realize it yet." The man took another drink, then set down the stein and stood, pulling off his parka and tossing it aside. Underneath he wore a plain white shirt and dark blue pants. He took his seat again. "Still, I admit I can see why you might be puzzled."

"I'm considerably more than puzzled," Art said. He suddenly realized that he ached all over, as if he'd been beaten: the buffeting he'd sustained during the ejection from the plane, the parachute descent, the landing, and then his summary detention and blindfolding was going to have him limping for a week. *Could be worse*, he thought, remembering the flaming debris spread across the side of the mountain.

"Perfectly understandable. You were kidnapped from the *Mayflower II* by the SSIN, kidnapped again by Skywatchers, dumped into an unpiloted plane that almost splattered you against a mountain peak and are now sitting on a giant mushroom deep inside a mountain, talking to a man who won't give you a straight answer and keeps calling you by some ridiculous title…have I covered all the bases?"

Two can play that game, Art thought in irritation. "All right, so you know all about me. Let me see what I can guess about you. This," he gestured at the ridiculous room, "is obviously the secret headquarters of the Skywatcher cult. The planetary government wanted me because of what I could tell them about the *Mayflower II*. Presumably you want me for the same reason…although I confess I'm unsure what concern our arrival could be to a handful of religious fanatics on a planet we didn't know existed."

"Very good," said the man approvingly. "Though I'm surprised you've heard of us. The government does not like to admit we exist."

"The *government* didn't. I caught a little item on the Peregrine FreeNet—something about your leader making crazy prophecies about a messiah who is supposed to appear any day now and establish paradise on Peregrine."

The man smiled slightly. "And did they mention the leader's name?"

"No. They just called him the First Visionary."

"Well," said the man, lifting his mug again, "that's me." He drank.

Art blinked. "What?"

"I said that's me." He raised the stein in a toast. "First Visionary Jem Kalas Arklund."

Art looked around at the bizarre decorations. "I should have known," he muttered. "Only a nut would live like this."

"Tut," said Arklund. "Am I a nut simply because I believe in the possibility of a better world? And in any event, you really should learn to like it down here, because it's going to be your home for the next week, at least. After that, I may transfer you elsewhere—I haven't decided yet. Once you have been presented to the Lesser Lights at the Great Service, your physical presence won't be required again until we launch the jihad."

"Jihad?" Art felt a chill, hearing that word from the war-torn past. How many millions had died in the name of jihad? "Holy war?"

"An ancient word, I know—far more ancient for me than for you, oh Farsighted One—but it has a nice ring to it."

"What do you need *me* for?"

"Allow me to explain to you a little of our philosophy." Arklund smiled. "I'll give you the shortened version. As Commander Morali told you this morning—"

"How do you know what Morali told me?"

"A Skywatcher on the cleaning staff planted a listening device, of course."

"Just how many of you are there?" Art said.

"I can't give you an exact number, Farsighted One. Let's just say there are far more of us than the government thinks. In any event, as Commander Morali told you, the starships stopped coming to Peregrine two hundred years ago. Naturally that caused considerable consternation…not to mention violent unrest that was only put down when the current more, um, *forceful* government took control.

"It also gave rise to a great deal of speculation about what happened. There was talk of civil war or plague or other disaster, but such answers only begged the real question, which wasn't 'what,' but 'why'?

"A farsighted man, the First Visionary (first of my title), Mindos Thel, prayed long and hard and was rewarded with a revelation: God put an end to star travel for humanity's own good. Humankind had somehow taken the wrong road, had slipped onto a fatal path. Humans were not meant to take the easy way, said Mindos Thel; they were meant to struggle, and through that struggle, to improve themselves. Umstattd's stardrive made things too easy; instead of evolving, humanity had begun *de*volving.

"Without stardrive, said the First Visionary, man would have to find other ways to bridge the vast distances of space—he would, in fact, have to turn to God for help. Therefore, said Mindos Thel, when at last someone *did* conquer time and space and once more cross the gulf between the stars, it would be because God's hand was on him and with him; and then those who were ready could join him in the paradise that he would create with God's help."

Art stared at Arklund, who had said all that in a matter-of-fact voice, as if it were self-evidently true. The First Visionary drained the last of the liquor from his cup and went on, "It therefore behooved—I've always loved that word, 'behooved'—it therefore behooved men on Peregrine, Mindos Thel argued, to prepare for the coming of this Conqueror of Time and Space, for only those who were pure and holy could hope to join him in building paradise. Those who were unprepared, who had learned nothing from the first disaster, would have no second chance, but would be swept away.

"So Mindos Thel formed an order that he called Skywatchers,

made up of holy men and women who set their minds on the heavens and keep themselves pure—and who always, whatever job they may hold in the world, are prepared to do whatever must be done to see that Peregrine is ready for the coming of the Conqueror."

"But…but that's ludicrous!" Art blurted.

Arklund raised an eyebrow. "Any more so than any other religion?"

"And you believe this?"

Arklund said nothing for a moment. He looked down into his glass. "Yes," he said. "Yes, I believe it. I believe God has a plan for humanity, that our becoming isolated here on Peregrine is part of that plan. I believe the Skywatchers have been chosen to carry out that plan. Because I *also* believe—" he raised his eyes again, and they bore into Art with disconcerting intensity, "—that the world of Peregrine is crying out for new leaders. We are stagnating, dwindling, ground down by an oppressive government and our own shortsightedness and lack of vision. We on Peregrine may be all that is left of humanity, and if we go on as we are now, we will sink down into a cesspool of self-gratification and mindless debauchery, until the very fabric of society is ripped apart and we quit looking to the heavens at all.

"God spoke to Mindos Thel, and those who follow the path God revealed to him have a fire and commitment to building a better world, a fairer, more equitable world, that exposes our so called Parliament of Protectors as the shams and charlatans they are. A world run as the Skywatchers would run it—as God would have it run—would be a better world for all. *That* is what I believe. And that is what I mean to achieve." The determined set of his face softened a little as a small smile twitched up the corners of his mouth. "And even if I *didn't* believe God had a hand in the creation of the Skywatchers, or believed in God at all, I would still recognize one other great advantage of being a Skywatcher: the First Visionary is presumed to have all the answers, and his followers pledge to serve and follow him to the death. So if you need the power to change the world, but can't—*won't*—seize it through political means, the best alternative is to become First Visionary." He spread his hands. "Like me."

He's a fanatic, Art thought. *Like Shadow. Like the Captain. I'm surrounded by them.* "I still don't understand what you need me for."

Arklund's smile faded. "Ah. Well, you see, before I can ask the Lesser Lights to give their lives for me, with complete assurance they will do so, I need one thing: I need *proof* that I am speaking for the Conqueror of Time and Space. Otherwise I might find some of the oaths sworn by my followers are fragile things on which to depend—the fear of death being a great leveler of high ideals. For years I have struggled with this problem, prayed to God to give me a sign that I could then reveal to my followers.

"And at long last, God answered my prayer. Lesser Lights in the military reported that something strange was approaching our system, decelerating from relativistic speed. I did a little rummaging in the data banks and realized what it must be." His voice lost its sardonic edge, became reverential. "It was the sign from God I had prayed for, and I knew what I had to do. A little pressure in the right places in the government assured that a mission would be launched to the *Mayflower II* to snatch someone for questioning. Once that was done, it was easy to trigger a couple of other Lesser Lights to transfer the captive from the government's control to mine.

"And here you are. A man who was born hundreds of years ago, in deep space, and crossed light years and centuries to come to Peregrine." Arklund sketched a quick bow. "You, Mr. Stoddard, are the Conqueror of Time and Space; and now that I have a Conqueror, I, too will conquer."

Well, Art thought with a slightly forced calmness, *you've always complained about being powerless to change anything. Now someone wants you to help take over a whole planet. Not bad.* He cleared his throat. "Why should I cooperate?"

"Two reasons," said Arklund. "One, of course, is that if you do not, you are no longer of any use to me and I will kill you."

"But I'm the Conqueror of Time and Space!"

"If you do not cooperate with me, then clearly you are no such thing," Arklund said with implacable logic. "Which just means the *true* Conqueror of Time and Space still awaits extraction from the thousands on that primitive starship of yours." He shrugged, as if that were a minor consideration. "The second may carry more or less weight, depending on how noble you think you are. It seems likely that the raptors in the government will win out, and the *Mayflower II* will be destroyed. Should you help me take over the government, I promise you that will not happen."

"You'll let the Passengers land?"

Arklund shook his head. "I didn't say that. I said I wouldn't destroy the *Mayflower II*. But I'm afraid I can't let the Passengers down here. Then I would have ten thousand Conquerors, and I'm only allowed—*God* only allows—one. So far only a handful of highly placed Skywatchers in the government and military know of the ship's existence. When I present you as Conqueror of Time and Space I will also show the Lesser Lights images of your ship, to prove you have indeed come to us from beyond. But of all those aboard the *Mayflower II*, you alone have descended to us, to lead us to a bright new future…and that's the way it must stay. Once I am in power, your starship will be allowed to proceed in peace. It will *not* be allowed to orbit our planet or send down shuttles. I gather this will suit your Captain fine, since he has his own orders not to approach our world." He paused. "Well?"

"It seems I have no choice," Art said. *Again.*

"Not much," Arklund agreed cheerfully. "Now, come with me, and I'll show you your room. Then we'll have a bite of supper and you can get to bed. Tomorrow we'll start preparing you for the Great Service."

Three hours later Art lay between silky sheets in an enormous domed bedchamber, staring up at a depiction of the night sky created with thousands of tiny silvery lights, like the skyplates of the *Mayflower II*'s Habs. He felt the need for sleep, but little hope of obtaining it; his mind was whirling.

Like the Crew and Council, like the Crawlspacers, Arklund wanted to use him for his own ends—but this time, Art wasn't going to allow it. He didn't know how yet, but he was determined that the Conqueror of Time and Space would have a very short reign.

For a moment he considered refusing outright to help Arklund unless the First Visionary promised to let the Passengers land, but quickly rejected that approach as suicidal. Arklund's threat had not been an idle one, he was sure; if Art were killed before he was proclaimed to the Lesser Lights as the Conqueror, the First Visionary would be no worse off, but Art certainly would be—and so would the *Mayflower II*. Art was realizing more and more that if any solution were to be worked out between ship and planet *he* would have to make it happen. There was no doubt that this time he *could* make a difference. A *big* difference.

His eyes, which had begun to sag closed, snapped open. Wait a minute. If he were to die *before* being proclaimed Conqueror, that was one thing, but if something were to happen to him *afterward* the First Visionary would have an awful lot of explaining to do to his followers. Arklund was going to give him power to act, expecting him to use it for the First Visionary's purposes. But what if he took the power—and then used it as a lever *against* the First Visionary?

Once I'm proclaimed Conqueror, he'll have to take me seriously if I threaten to reveal myself as a fraud unless he lets the Passengers land, Art thought. *He'll have to!*

With a plan in mind, however vague, he finally slept.

In the morning he emerged to find a stranger waiting in the bizarre living room, a man wearing a Skywatcher robe who also sported the longest nose Art had ever seen and a bald head that shone under the bright light. "I am Sixth Visionary Urstal Sorvan, Farsighted One," he said. "I will instruct you in the ways of the Great Service."

"Doesn't it bother you that your Conqueror of Time and

Space *needs* instruction?" Art had to ask.

Sorvan didn't even blink. "Of course not, Farsighted One. If you pretend not to know the ways of the Skywatchers, who are we to argue? The Conqueror is not a mortal man and his ways are not ours."

"Then whatever I do in the Great Service is correct," Art argued. "Why should I learn a particular pattern?"

"You need not, if you do not wish to. But whether you learn or not, I have been ordered to teach you. So if you will please be seated, Farsighted One…"

Defeated by such logic, Art sat. In fact he had good reason to learn the proper ceremony; he *wanted* the Lesser Lights to believe he was their Conqueror.

The next few days passed surprisingly quickly, as Art put more effort into learning his script for the Great Service than he had ever spent preparing for a newscast back on the ship. Not that he had ever had such a melodramatic piece of purple prose to memorize before. His lines for the Great Service reminded him of the dialogue in the worst ancient science fiction films. *Maybe they'll sound better with the special effects added*, he thought.

In all that time he only saw Arklund twice, both times late at night. The front door of the apartment was always locked, and whenever it was opened, by Sorvan or Arklund, there was another Skywatcher standing outside, armed and watchful.

Art presumed the waxing and waning of the light in the living room ceiling corresponded to planetary days, and when six had passed Sorvan pronounced himself satisfied. "You have learned well, Farsighted One," said the Skywatcher tutor late that final day. He powered off his data tablet and stood. "You are certainly ready for the Great Service tomorrow."

"Excellent," said Arklund, entering the room. He nodded to Sorvan, who bowed deeply and went out, closing the door behind him. "My spies inform me your ship is still more than a week away from orbiting Merlin," the First Visionary told Art.

Art blinked. "Merlin?"

"Sixth planet of the system…the largest of the three gas giants."

"And what will happen when it does reach orbit?"

Arklund shrugged. "There's been no final decision yet. But I must be ready before that in any event."

"You can't take over the government of a whole planet in a week!"

"Can't I?"

"How?"

Arklund just grinned. "Join me for supper. Then go to bed. Tomorrow is a day of destiny—for both of us." And after that he refused to discuss Skywatchers, the Conqueror, the government or any other of the important topics crowding Art's brain.

Art slept poorly; though he was sure of his role in the Great Service, he was less and less certain of his role in Arklund's plan—and of his whole decision to start trying to change the course of events. Having no control had always meant having no responsibility, either. Now he agonized over the question that had come to him briefly back in the airplane: what if he took the *wrong* action? If he continued with his present plan, would he really be helping the *Mayflower II*—or speeding its destruction? What if the government, under attack from within, decided it had to remove the external threat as quickly as possible?

Maybe he should be trying to escape the Skywatchers, to return to the capital. If he went back voluntarily to the SSIN, told them what had happened, surely he could convince them to try to negotiate with the *Mayflower II* instead of destroying it…

The possibility that the ship would strike first he preferred to not even think about. He might have some influence on Peregrine, but he was as helpless as ever when it came to changing things on the ship. And the Captain, having seen his ship successfully raided once, would have an itchy finger planted firmly on the missile-firing button…*if it really exists*, Art thought. He still had a hard time believing that the ship he'd called home all his life could be armed to the teeth with matter-antimatter missiles.

So he had two choices—stick to his original plan of cooperating with Arklund, in the hope that the First Visionary would succeed in taking over the government and would then spare the *Mayflower II*, or escape back to the capital somehow and try to sway the Parliament of Protectors.

He shook his head in the dark. Escape was impossible. He was imprisoned in an underground fortress deep beneath the mountains. Even if he could evade searchers, where would he go? The wilderness could be days' travel on foot in any direction.

His only possible action was the one on which he had already decided: to allow himself to be proclaimed Conqueror of Time and Space, thereby serving Arklund's purposes, and hope that somehow it would also serve his.

Sorvan awakened him early the next morning to prepare him for the Great Service, a long procedure that involved a ritual bath, a haircut and shave, a light breakfast, and finally the costuming.

First came a short, snow-white tunic and tight-fitting gold pants that glittered when he moved. Over his shoulders he draped a thigh-length black cloak that sparkled with tiny jewels set in the cloth like stars in the night sky. His feet went into mirror-bright silver boots; a mirrored skull cap went over his newly short-cropped hair, and mirrored gloves covered his hands, flashing light around the room. From his neck hung a jeweled pendant in the form of an hourglass, representing time as the star-robe represented space; and finally, to symbolize his title of Conqueror, he was given a naked sword to hold. It, too, was mirrored, and had a golden hilt, but the edge and point, he saw, were very, very dull. Arklund did not intend to trust him with even a primitive weapon. (Well, he supposed he could club someone to death with it, but it would take a *lot* of work.)

The First Visionary came in. He was accompanied by two grim-looking Lesser Lights carrying what looked to Art like sniper rifles. Arklund looked him over once, then nodded. "Take him upstairs," he told Sorvan. "You know when to present him?"

"Of course, First Visionary."

Arklund turned to the armed men. "Take your positions." He glanced at Art. "Be certain you have a clear view of the stage."

The two men left without a word. Arklund glanced at a chronometer half-hidden by a two-metre fern. "Very well then," he said. "Let's be about it." He opened the front door, nodded to the guard stationed outside, and went out. A few seconds later Art heard the murmur of a crowd that fell silent almost at once; and then he heard Arklund's voice, though he couldn't make out the words, drifting back through walls and ceiling.

"Our turn," said Sorvan. "Now, remember everything I told you, Farsighted One, and you'll do fine."

"And if I don't remember everything?"

Sorvan shrugged. "Then it will still be fine, of course. You are the Conqueror; whatever you do, you must have a reason."

I could say anything, then, Art thought with sudden excitement. *I could deliver my own message: tell them to welcome the Mayflower II, tell them to attack Arklund, tell them...*

Hard to tell them anything with my head missing. He hadn't missed the significance of the two snipers with a "clear view of the stage."

Art followed Sorvan into the corridor and up the stairs, the armed guard from the door following close behind.

They emerged into a small chamber whose only other exit was a veiled arch. Through a gap in the silver curtain Art could see a brightly lit platform. He sat down on the stone bench built into one wall and listened to Arklund's speech, awaiting his cue.

"...ultimate proof of prophecy is its fulfillment!" the First Visionary was saying, his deep voice rich and compelling. Again Art was struck by how fine a newscaster—or actor—Arklund would have been—except, of course, merely *reading* the news would never have been enough for him; he wanted to *be* the news.

"We have waited, we have watched—we have been faithful!" Arklund boomed. "Generations of Skywatchers have kept their eyes on the stars, kept their lives pure, awaiting the arrival of the Conqueror and the promise of paradise."

Arklund paused dramatically. "Just a few days ago you heard me prophesy that the Conqueror was at hand; that at last our long wait was nearly over, and the time was almost here when we could reach out for paradise and be assured of grasping it, with the help of God and the Conqueror."

"Get ready," Sorvan murmured, but Art was already on his feet and heading toward the archway, a strange excitement gripping him.

"Brothers of the Holy Watch, the Conqueror is no longer at hand!" Arklund shouted then. "He is *here!*"

Art swept aside the veil and strode out onto the platform in front of the hundreds of gathered Skywatchers, the Conqueror's sword grasped firmly in his silver-gloved hand, bright lights glancing from mirrored helmet and boots to strike slivers of illumination against walls, roof and audience.

And after a long moment of silence, every person in the vast hall rose as one and shook the floor with the roar of their acclamation.

Chapter Seven

As one of the *Mayflower II*'s few celebrities, Art had been applauded before. But the polite patter of two dozen Passengers was nothing compared to the physical shock of that wall of approbative sound. It rushed through him with almost sexual force, thrusting him deep into the role that had been chosen for him. At that moment, he felt he *was* the Conqueror of Time and Space, and these were his followers, whom he would lead to the creation of a new world. The words he had to say no longer seemed shallow and silly, but grave, meaningful, and filled with power. He would not have changed them even if he hadn't known about the snipers somewhere high above. How could he change the words of God?

He strode forward to the very front and centre of the stage and planted the sword point-down on the stone, holding it there with his left hand while his right moved in a slow semi-circle from eye to waist, ending in a clenched fist, as though gathering the cheers of the crowd to himself.

The gesture had been taught to him by Sorvan; it quieted the crowd instantly, and as he ended it all the lights went out except one brilliant spot centred on him. Into the sudden silence and darkness Art said, "Children. Fellow Warriors of Light. Faithful Watchers. Greetings.

"You know who I am. You know that I have crossed light-years and centuries to be here. And you know what my coming portends: the end of this corrupt age and the dawning of a new era of light and peace.

"Yet first…*first*, my children, we must pass through a fiery night, the destruction of the old order so that the new may rise, phoenix-like, from its ashes. My faithful servant Jem Arklund has carried out my wishes perfectly. Obey his commands, and our victory is assured.

"And if ever you doubt it, remember this moment. Remember me, standing before you; and remember what I have done." He thrust out his left hand suddenly, and blood-red light drew a clock on the wall, counting the seconds. "I have conquered time!" he roared, and clenched his fist, and the clock slowed, stopped, and then reversed itself.

He lowered that hand to the sword, then thrust out the right. A glittering star field appeared on the opposite wall. "I have conquered space!" he cried, and clenched his fist, and the stars whirled about themselves and were sucked into nothingness.

Then with both hands he lifted the sword above his head. "I am the Conqueror of Time and Space," he shouted, "and now I Conquer Peregrine!"

The mirrored blade suddenly blazed with light so bright it illuminated the whole hall and the hundreds of white faces staring at him, eyes and mouths dark circles to Art's sight. The spotlight went off him, leaving only the blaze of the sword; then it, too, went out, plunging the hall into darkness. A trap door opened beneath his feet and dropped him three metres to soft padding.

The door clicked shut over his head, then a dim light came on in the little chamber where he had fallen and he heard the crowd thundering above him. Arklund began to speak, his voice dim and unintelligible, and Art felt suddenly drained, tired, the energy he had drawn from the crowd gone and his old doubts and fears back *en masse*.

He pushed himself to the edge of the stacked cloth pads, just as a door to his right snicked open, admitting Sorvan and a Skywatcher guard. "Magnificent!" Sorvan cried. "Oh, Farsighted One, it was magnificent! You are truly the Conqueror!"

Empty rhetoric and cheap theatrical tricks, Art thought wearily. *And a good dose of "Voice of God" boom.* But he straightened his shoulders as he stood. Now that he had been presented as the Conqueror, Arklund couldn't repudiate him—or kill him–without repudiating himself and his plans. Maybe now, at last, he could do something positive and help his fellow Passengers and even—God help him!—the Captain and Crew.

Sorvan and the guard led him back to Arklund's apartment. All the way Sorvan bubbled enthusiastically about Art's performance, till Art was tempted to whack him with the Conqueror's Sword.

Once in Arklund's private jungle, he tried to relax while he awaited the First Visionary's return. He stripped off the Conqueror's finery and put on his own freshly washed clothes, and, when Arklund entered, was sitting drinking something cold and sweet Sorvan had found in the kitchen. "Thank you, Sorvan," the First Visionary said. "You did an excellent job of preparing the Farsighted One. You may go."

Sorvan bowed twice, first to Art, then to Arklund, and went out, closing the door behind him. Art wondered if Arklund had noted the order of those bows; one look at the First Visionary's dour face answered him. *Good*, he thought. *I* do *have something to bargain with.*

"How'd I do?" he asked innocently.

"You were—adequate." Arklund pulled off his ceremonial robe and threw it most unceremoniously into the corner. He opened his drink cabinet and poured himself a tall glass of bubbling green. "Not a moment's variation from the script, and your delivery was excellent—as should be expected of a professional, I suppose."

"What's our next move?"

Arklund cocked an eyebrow at him. "Our?"

"Oh, come on, Arklund, I'm not stupid. You've presented me as the Conqueror of Time and Space. Fine; I'm willing to go along—as long as there's something in it for me. And you know what I want."

"A place for your people on Peregrine."

"Exactly. You can do that—*if* you have me to help you take

over. But without me, you have nothing."

Arklund sipped his drink delicately and set it down on one of the mushroom-like tables, then dipped his finger in the liquid and ran it around the glass's edge. The crystal sang a piercing note that grated on Art's nerves and added a threatening undercurrent to Arklund's words. "I watched you closely out there," the First Visionary mused. "I could see you soaking up that applause. All the time you've been down here I've been able to see your brain spinning, trying to come up with some way to turn all this to your advantage. Then, up there, you accepted the power I have given you. You *enjoyed* it.

"I watched that, and I thought, 'Jem, he's not going to be content to just be your mouthpiece any more, even if that's all he was on his precious ship.'" Art wanted to smash Arklund's glass, still singing its painful note, but he held himself still, eyes narrowed. "He's going to want to have a say in the way things are done, and he's going to threaten to quit cooperating as Conqueror unless he gets it," Arklund went on. For a moment his finger stopped and he gave Art a sardonic look. "Did I guess right?"

"Obviously," said Art. "So now—"

"It doesn't matter." The First Visionary dipped his finger again and once more the glass sang. "It doesn't matter because, having proven I have the Conqueror, and that he supports me, I no longer need him. He has told the Lesser Lights to follow me and has pledged to build paradise, just as the prophecies promise. That's all I need; my long-laid plans of revolution can begin. I need not produce the Conqueror again." He suddenly lifted the glass in a toast, then drank from it.

Art felt cold. "You can't be sure of that. Your followers will question you about me sooner or later—"

Arklund set the glass down again. "Perhaps. Which is fortunate for you, since it means I won't kill you."

"How can you kill your Conqueror of Time and Space?"

"We've been over that," Arklund said. "If you refuse to cooperate with my plans, then clearly you are *not* the Conqueror of Time and Space, and the real one has yet to present him—or herself."

That logic made Art's head hurt. "So are you planning to just keep me locked down here?"

"Not down here, no. I occasionally have to call other people to my apartment and I wouldn't want some of my subordinates to see you at, shall we say, less than your best, O Farsighted One."

"Then where?"

"A safe place, surrounded by desert you cannot cross on foot. That is all you need to know." He went to the door and opened it, revealing a man who wore a Skywatcher uniform but who reminded Art more of the 'keeps than of Sorvan. "This is Eskar Vallini, my personal pilot and sometime bodyguard," said Arklund, returning to his seat. "It is approaching midnight outside. No one will see you leave. The corridors are deserted; I have ordered everyone to their quarters for prayer, fasting and meditation."

"You've thought of everything," Art said bitterly, his hopes of bargaining from strength, of finally *doing* something, crumbling to nothing, while the old voice of his despair whispered, *I told you so. I* told *you so...*

"I'm First Visionary," Arklund said. "It's my job. Vallini, he's all yours."

Vallini pulled a pistol from a holster at his belt and pointed it at Art, then jerked it toward the stairs. The erstwhile Conqueror of Time and Space had no option but to obey. He left with what dignity he could muster, without looking back at the First Visionary.

As they traversed the darkened assembly hall and the corridors beyond it, Art hoped against hope that someone would see him, someone who would wonder why the Conqueror was being escorted at gunpoint out of the Sanctuary, who would perhaps cry out and bring others from their quarters. Art was sure, after the Great Service, that he could turn them against Arklund, if only he could get to them...

But obedient Lesser Lights that they were, they remained

sequestered. None of them saw their supposed messiah herded like a common criminal through rough-hewn corridors into a vast cavern that held half a dozen aircraft of varying sizes. Vallini bundled Art into the copilot's seat of a vehicle so sleek and black it practically screamed speed and stealth…if that made any sense. Moments later the plane trundled out into the open and then shrieked into the dark sky.

In all that time, Vallini didn't speak a word to Art. Now he leaned back in his chair and closed his eyes, trusting the flying to autopilot.

Art fought off that old inner urging to give up, to accept his helplessness, and instead studied the control board almost fiercely, afraid if he simply relaxed he *would* give up. He was not foolish enough to think he could pilot the craft, but he *wa*s able to identify the autopilot computer. Screwed into the board next to it was an engraved metal plate giving the manufacturer's name, the date of installation, the name of the autopilot program—and three emergency program codes, for takeoff, landing and straight-and-level flight.

The autopilot had a numeric keypad and a key labeled TRIGGER. Art stared at it and felt his palms suddenly turn damp. His mind was made up, but he knew very well that if the autopilot was not as simple as it looked, he was about to commit suicide.

Maybe that *would throw a glitch into Arklund's plans*, he thought, letting his hand drop down beside his seat, next to the door, to rest on a heavy metal fire extinguisher mounted with a quick-release shackle. He took a last deep breath, and flipped the shackle open.

It sprang with a horrible clatter that brought Vallini jerking upright, instantly alert, reaching for his gun and already turning toward Art. Frantically Art whipped the extinguisher toward Vallini's head. The pilot threw up one arm to block it but was too late; the metal tube crunched against his skull. Blood spattered the canopy. Vallini stiffened and collapsed forward.

His weight on the wheel overrode the autopilot and sent the

aircraft into a sudden banking dive that threw Art against his door and pressed him there with g-force. Feeling leaden, he shoved Vallini back in his seat, off the wheel, then scrabbled at the autopilot controls. He punched in the landing code and triggered it. Though he couldn't see an altimeter, Art *felt* the ground coming up to destroy him.

The plane lurched, trying to level off. The autopilot faced an impossible task—establishing a glide path with too little altitude, too much speed and too steep a dive. The nose came up, flaps went down, reversing engines howled, air brakes screamed. The plane shuddered. Metal popped and creaked. Then there was a moment of darkness and smoke and tearing metal and shattering glass and one final, crushing impact. Art's world went black.

◣ ◢

The blackness gave way to pain and a different sort of blackness—the blackness of uninhabited wilderness on a moonless world. Art blinked up at stars burning almost as steadily as they did in a Hab skyplate, the stillness of the night absolute after those few seconds of thundering terror that were the last things he remembered. The metallic taste of blood was in his mouth.

The plane had crashed. He hadn't imagined that. But he was alive. Was he imagining *that*?

The pain had seemed to fill him when he first woke, but now he began to localize it, his mind automatically taking stock of his body's condition. Innumerable aches clamored for his attention, but his discomfort centred in the knife-like agony in his side. His right arm echoed that pain—and, he discovered with a gasp, if he attempted to move it, out-shouted his wounded flank.

Ribs, he thought. *Broken ribs and a broken arm*. It could have been worse. The blood in his mouth seemed to come from a badly bitten cheek; he wasn't coughing it. He hoped that meant—though his knowledge of anatomy was slim—that he hadn't punctured a lung. And his legs felt relatively undamaged. He ought to be able to walk.

If, of course, he could get to his feet. He tried to sit up and fire flared in his side, dimming his vision and stealing his breath. He fell back again and concentrated on gulping air for a few moments. *Think*, he told himself. *There has to be a way...your left side seems all right. Try rolling over onto it, first.*

Which he did, earning fresh pain but not enough to overwhelm him. With his left arm as lever, he pushed himself to a sitting position, right arm hanging useless. The night grew darker and roaring filled his ears, but after a moment it subsided and what little light there was returned. He took as deep a breath as he could without driving a dagger of pain into his side, and forced himself to his feet. Again his head swam, but only for a moment. He stayed on his feet, and for the first time looked around.

Their flight before he'd attacked Vallini had taken them out of the mountains and into the desert where Arklund's hideaway was presumably tucked away, though Art could see the dark peaks, snow glinting in the starlight, still looming on the horizon. The plane had skidded and spun on its belly in its doomed attempt to land safely, hurling away pieces of itself as it did so—and he had been one of the pieces. The stench of fuel choked him, and belatedly Art realized his clothing dripped with it. God only knew why it hadn't caught fire.

It still might, a part of his brain warned him, which sent him staggering away from the wreckage, not even checking the largest part, where the cabin had to be, to see if Vallini had survived the crash—or Art's blow to his head.

He had another reason for getting away from the wreckage: Arklund. The First Visionary would know soon that his plane had never reached the desert hideout, if he didn't already—Art had no idea how long he had been unconscious. Arklund might feel confident he need not produce his Conqueror of Time and Space again to ensure the Lesser Lights' loyalty, but he would surely have to make sure Art hadn't escaped. He'd come looking along the flight path, and in the vast, flat desert there was no hope he wouldn't find the wreckage. If Art were still nearby, Arklund could take him prisoner again—or simply finish the job the crash had begun.

Neither option appealed to Art. For the first time in a long time he was free, and he intended to stay that way.

Free to die of shock and exposure? The thought halted him. He looked back at the wreckage, now only a dark streak and spots of black against the starlit desert plain. There had to be food there, blankets—emergency supplies of some kind. A first-aid kit, certainly, with painkillers, a splint, bandages to wrap his ribs. But could he hope to find it in the dark?

As he hesitated, torn between the desire to put as much distance as possible between himself and the wreck and the cold knowledge that he might need what the wreck contained to survive, the decision was made for him. A vast sheet of flame exploded across the horizon, scorching Art's face and sending him stumbling back, left arm over his eyes. All-too-aware of his own fuel-soaked clothing, he turned and ran as best he could, every step sending a red-hot spear through his arm and side but taking him further from the hungry inferno.

And then the ground itself betrayed him. The light of the fire behind showed a shadow ahead, but his pain-fogged brain made no sense of it. He tumbled down the slope of a hidden gully in a blaze of agony as hot as the fire he had fled, agony that finally gave way to blessed unconsciousness.

◣ ◢

The next time Art woke the sky was red, and for a moment he thought the fire had followed him and would lick him up after all; but it was only the dawn.

Dawn, and he lay only a couple of hundred metres from the wreck of Arklund's plane!

The pain remained, but no worse than it had been the night before. He rolled onto his left side and again levered himself up until he sat on the slope, facing down into the gully he had rolled halfway into.

There were plants down there, the first he had seen in the desert; scrubby, prickly, gray-green. Ugly—but *alive. A gully, and plants*, he thought. *Water! Even in the desert it has to rain sometime. The water runs down this gully. Down...*

He looked to his right. *Down to a river*, he thought. *Somewhere. Or a lake. And where there's water, there are animals—food. Maybe even people.* And the gully would give him at least some cover from Arklund's inevitable search.

But first he had to do something about his ribs and his arm, or he wouldn't be able to move at any speed or for any length of time. He needed bandages, something to bind his arm and chest as tightly as he could—and the only materials he had were his clothes.

With his left hand he seized the neck of his green, puffy-sleeved shirt and pulled as hard as he could, ripping the material away from his body, using his teeth to pull off the left sleeve and then easing off the right, even that gentle effort causing him to gasp in pain.

Then he tried to use teeth and left hand together to bind the material around him, holding his right arm immobile against his body—tried, and tried again, and failed. The awkward knot he tied one-handed was uselessly loose, while the pain threatened to knock him senseless again. In the end he let the shirt drop in rags to the ground, staggered to his feet bare-chested and sickly furious at himself, and started down the gully in a stumbling, shuffling walk, while overhead the sky turned from red to pink to high, hot blue, and the shade in which he walked shrank away until the sun crept into sight and he felt its full force, first on his head, then slowly down his chest and arms.

For a few short minutes the warmth felt good, soaking the chill from his bruised and battered frame; but as the sun continued to climb sweat burst out all over his upper body, trickling down from under his arms and stinging his eyes; and then even that ceased as the heat increased still further and the dry air evaporated the moisture almost before it could form.

Dehydration, Art thought dully. *Heatstroke. Sunburn.* In old movies, always that same shot, of the sun burning in the sky like a white-hot coin, and then the close-up on the parched lips and heat-crazed eyes of the unfortunate soul wandering through the wasteland… wandering… wandering…

Art felt something hard and sharp digging into his cheek. A stone. *How'd a stone get way up there?* he thought muzzily. The sun burned his back as though he hadn't escaped the fire that had engulfed the airplane after all. *Maybe I didn't*, he thought. *Maybe this is all one final, tortured hallucination of a mind inside a dying body, burning, baking, crisping...am I well done yet?*

Well done? He hadn't done anything well since he'd attacked the maintenance robot. That was when it all started to go wrong. He should have been an actor. Couldn't act? Who couldn't act? Hadn't he convinced all those Lesser Lights he was the Conqueror of Time and Space?

Some Conqueror, lying under the sun, broiling like a steak, dying and not even fighting it.

That self-inflicted jibe drove him to his feet again. He stumbled on down the gully, though within a few steps he no longer knew if he were actually walking or had fallen again and was just imagining he was walking.

There were voices in his head. *Bad sign*, an inner voice tsk-tsked sadly. *Mind's going. Turning to mush.*

Fried mush, he thought, and giggled.

"Look! Over there!" a voice cried.

"I told you it was an airplane!" shouted a younger voice.

"Gloat later—he's on his last legs—look out, he's falling—"

Who's falling? Art thought indignantly, as the ground came up to meet him in an explosion of pain and heat and finally, at last, cool darkness once more.

Chapter Eight

Art's last impressions before collapsing were of heat and dryness; his first on slowly awakening were of coolness and moisture. He sucked like a baby on a teat from which flowed sweet, pure water, balm not only to his parched throat but to his cracked lips. The white-hot light of the sun, which had been torturing him with seeming vindictiveness, had given way to a gentler glow that lit the inside of his eyelids. Something cool and wet soothed his forehead, and wonder of wonders, his ribs were bound and his arm splinted and in a sling, and the pain in both had subsided to a dull ache.

For a few moments all he was really aware of were those pleasant facts, but gradually he remembered the voices he had heard just before passing out, and finally he opened his eyes.A slender black-haired boy, maybe fourteen or fifteen in ship/Earth years, leaned over him, framed by the sun-drenched wall of a tent, holding the nipple of a water bottle to Art's mouth and a wet cloth to his forehead. He jerked back when Art's eyes opened, then turned and called, "Dad, he's awake."

A shadow moved along the wall of the tent and came through the door, resolving into a tall man, tanned and weather-beaten. Like the boy, he wore a loose white shirt and pants, and he swept off a broad-brimmed white hat, revealing hair black as the boy's, but salted with gray. A long black weapon of some kind, weather-beaten and brutal-looking, hung on his back from the strap across his chest. He crouched and studied Art's face carefully, without touching it; feeling the fire in his sunburned skin, Art was glad he had not.

"My name is Kymbal," the man said finally. "Marc Kymbal.

This is my son, Lorn." He stopped and waited.

Art cleared his throat, but his voice still came out in a croak. "Art Stoddard."

Kymbal nodded gravely. "You're lucky we came along, Mr. Stoddard."

"Believe me, I know," said Art, his voice a little stronger. "Thank you."

"Of course, it wasn't *entirely* luck." Kymbal glanced at his son, his face crinkling into a smile. "We saw the fire last night from our camp in the hills and started down at once. Lorn had heard the engine shortly before that, and was convinced a plane had crashed. I thought we might find nothing more than a patch of brush struck by heat lightning. But instead…we found you."

Art, suddenly remembering why he had been on that plane and who was after him, struggled to sit up. Lorn, who was kneeling on the groundsheet beside him, hurriedly slipped an arm around him to help support him. His head swam. "How long?" he said urgently.

Kymbal raised an eyebrow. "About four hours since we found you. It's almost noon. Why the concern?"

Art shook his head, trying to clear it. "Don't you understand? He'll be looking for me!"

"Who will?"

"Arklund. He—"

Kymbal's eyebrows lifted. "Jem Arklund? The Skywatchers' First Visionary? Why is *he* looking for *you*?"

The dizziness in Art's head had passed, but a dull ache had replaced it. "I can't—there's no time to—we have to leave!"

Kymbal nodded to Lorn, who eased Art back down onto the blankets. Art panted, too weak to try to sit up again. "You're not moving until nightfall," Kymbal said. "You shouldn't go out in the sun again for two or three days, at least. A week would be even better."

"Don't you understand? The First Visionary is looking for me! He'll send another plane…"

"Don't worry, we won't let him have you," Kymbal said. His voice hardened. "I wouldn't turn my worst enemy over to that bloodsucker. But dropping dead in the sun isn't your preferred way of escaping him, is it?"

"But—"

"The tent is camouflaged. We look like a rock. There are no traces of the camp to be seen outside. I've had years of experience not being found." Kymbal stood and stared down at Art. "Anyway, when he sees what's left of that plane, he's bound to think you're dead, at least for a while."

"He'll check for bodies," Art said. "And he'll only find one."

Kymbal gave him a sharp look.

"The pilot."

"So." Kymbal motioned to his son to move back, and the boy obeyed. Kymbal sat cross-legged on the groundsheet, and Lorn immediately followed suit, never taking his eyes from Art. "It's several hours until sunset. Why don't you tell me the whole story?"

Art closed his eyes. "You won't believe it."

"It will still pass the time. Lorn, prop him up."

The boy scrambled forward and helped Art sit up a little bit more, stuffing a backpack behind him so he could stay more-or-less upright. Then Lorn settled down on the groundsheet again and resumed staring at Art.

With some hope that telling the tale would convince Kymbal they had to *move*, Art launched into an account of his last eight days, from the moment he heard from Shadow until the Kymbals found him half-dead in the desert. Lorn's eyes widened as Art told them about the starship, and stayed that way as the story progressed. Marc Kymbal, however, sat impassively, listening carefully but letting no reaction cross his brown face.

When Art finished, Lorn said breathlessly, "You really travelled in a starship? And knew people who were born on Earth in ancient times?"

"Lorn," Kymbal said quietly, and his son subsided, but Art laughed.

"Don't let my parents hear you call their birthdates 'ancient times,'" he said, but his smile faded as he thought about his mother and father and everyone else on board the *Mayflower II*, hurtling closer and closer to possible destruction—and not even aware of it. He wished desperately he knew exactly how long it would take the ship to enter orbit around the gas giant…*What did Arklund call it? Merlin, that's it*…and then was almost glad he did not. There was nothing he could do, and to have known exactly how close they were to the time when either ship or planet—or both!—might embark on mutual destruction only made the waiting worse.

A strange sound edged into his consciousness. *The wind*, Art thought, but Lorn's head jerked around. "Airplane! Twin-engine turbojet."

"Arklund!" Art cried. "I told you—" He bit off his words and held his breath as the sound grew nearer, swelling into a roar that passed right over them, then dwindled again as the plane banked for another run over the site. Three times the airplane thundered overhead, and each time Art's heart skipped a beat; then the sound faded back the way it had come, and he breathed easy again.

"At least that part of your story checks out," Kymbal said calmly. He stood, brushing sand from the seat of his white pants. "I suggest you sleep until dark. Lorn will leave you the water bottle."

The boy turned toward his father sharply and opened his mouth, but closed it again at Kymbal's firm look and somewhat sulkily dropped the bottle onto the groundsheet by Art's head. He followed his father out, with a final glance over his shoulder.

Art shifted uncomfortably on the hard ground; no effort seemed to have been made to remove any stones before pitching the shelter, and the blankets did little to soften their edges. Nor was the tent as cool as it had first seemed when he woke. Sweat ran from his bare chest, leaving muddy streaks. But at least he had water. He took another sip from the bottle, then cradled it in his left arm. Within minutes he was asleep.

He woke in darkness and started up, disoriented. A light moved across the tent roof and to the door, and a moment later Kymbal entered, a flashlight in his hand. “Can you walk?”

“Of course,” Art said, with more assurance than was warranted, considering the way he felt. He *had* to be able to walk, because there was no way he was going to stay there another day, waiting for Arklund to come back to make sure he was dead.

“Then let’s go.” Kymbal backed out of the tent and Art crawled to the door. Slowly, holding onto the tent-pole, he pulled himself upright, then took a trial step. He felt lightheaded and weak, but surprisingly pain-free. Which didn’t make sense, unless—

“You drugged me,” he said accusingly. “The water…”

“Would you rather hurt?”

Art thought about that and shut up.

Lorn touched something on the tent-pole and Art watched, open-mouthed, as the entire tent, more like a cloud than a solid object, was somehow sucked into the pole, which further collapsed until all that was left was a short, thick cylinder about twenty centimetres long. Lorn stuck it into his backpack. The three of them set off down the gully, Kymbal leading, while Lorn hung back with Art and watched him closely as though expecting him to collapse at any moment.

“I’m all right,” he finally said. “Quit hovering!”

“Sorry.” The boy moved off a few steps; but within ten minutes he was back at Art’s side, and Art didn’t have the heart to send him away again.

Art surprised himself on the walk; he was able to keep moving steadily longer than he had expected, and obviously longer than Kymbal had expected, for about midnight the Peregrine native stopped and glanced back. “There’s a cave up ahead in the gully wall where we could spend the night, if you’re not up to—”

“I don’t want to quit,” Art replied stoutly. “Let’s get as far as we can.”

Kymbal grinned, eyes and teeth flashing briefly in the starlight.

"Well, if you can keep it up for three or four more hours, we'll be at the edge of the forest."

"No problem," said Art, and felt he was telling the truth.

But that was before the painkillers began to fade. Within an hour his arm and side were throbbing in counterpoint to his steps, each of which thrust a knife between his ribs. The night grew so cold his half-clad body began to chill. Eventually he took the silvery blanket Lorn offered him, but even its feather-like weight on his burned skin made him gasp.

Still, he kept moving, and was rewarded in the grey pre-dawn light with the sight of a shallow stream, a band of lush grass—and a dark wall of trees. "Next stop, home," said Kymbal; but actually the next stop was a small flat spot, clear of underbrush but still over-arched by trees, which they reached a half-hour later, just as the sun broke the horizon. "We'll stay here through the day," Kymbal announced. "I don't want you in the sun, even with the forest shade."

Art was already sitting on the needle-covered ground. "So who's arguing?" he groaned.

Lorn pulled the tent-pole cylinder out of his pack, placed it on the ground, and touched a control. The pole elongated and vomited out the material of the tent, which erected itself with no further input from the boy, who was already walking away with the water-bottles, clearly knowing exactly where he would find water with which to fill them. Now that he listened, Art could hear the rushing of a stream not far away.

Kymbal handed Art a packet of blankets and ordered him into the tent the moment it had settled. He fell asleep almost instantly, the uneven forest floor feeling as soft as his mattress in the *Mayflower II*.

He woke sore in every joint. His arm and side ached again, and his skin, though no longer quite as angry-looking, still burned. Beside him Lorn slept soundly, curled up like a cat, and Art smiled at the youngster, remembering the boy's excitement when he heard Art's story and thinking how he would have felt at that same age if someone had suddenly appeared on the *Mayflower II* from Outside. Back when he had hoped to be an actor he had even written a play on that theme and submitted it to the theatre. He'd never received a response.

Art wondered how much of his desire to be an actor had been a reaction to the rules and regulations and set-in-titanium traditions of the ship's moribund society. Acting would have been a means of escape, a way to pretend, for a little while, to be someone else and somewhere else.

Now, of course, there was no need to pretend. He really *was* somewhere else, and had even briefly been *someone* else—the Conqueror of Time and Space, no less. His smile faded. Arklund would be looking for him, and they were still too close to the desert…

He tried to creep out of the tent without waking Lorn, but was unable to stifle a groan as his abused muscles protested, and the boy rolled over and sat up at once, eyes wide and hair tousled. For a moment he blinked at Art in bewilderment, as if unable to remember who he was; then he smiled tentatively.

Art smiled back. "Good morning. Or good evening. Whichever."

"How do you feel?" Lorn asked seriously.

"I hurt all over," Art said, then laughed at the boy's worried look. "No, really, I feel much better. Thanks to you and your father. You saved my life."

Lorn looked uncomfortable. "It was just coincidence. I mean, I was sure an airplane had crashed, even though Dad didn't believe it, but I never thought about finding—I guess I just thought everyone would have ejected."

Art started. "Ejected?" He thought back. That red lever at the base of the seat… "I never thought of it." He laughed ruefully. "Which is odd, since I've already done it once, when the first plane crashed into the mountains…but the plane ejected me that time. I didn't do it myself." He thought back to those few terrifying moments that had delivered him to the Skywatchers, and shuddered. "I think I prefer crash-landing."

"Well, maybe." Lorn looked down at the ground and ran a finger over the thin, glistening membrane of the groundsheet. "What's it like in space?"

Art remembered his terror during the transit between the *Mayflower II* and the Peregrine ship, and decided Lorn wouldn't be interested in *that*. "On board our ship, it's not much different than here. Except the sky and the horizon are both illusions. The stars are nothing but tiny lights in the skyplate, and there's no sun…the light comes from everywhere at once…" Lorn looked puzzled, but Art hardly noticed; describing the scene had brought a strange ache to his chest. Homesick? For the *Mayflower II*?

Well, why the hell not? he thought. *I grew up there—and thanks to idiots on both ship and planet, I may never see it again.*

He became aware of Lorn's quizzical look. "Sorry," he said. "I was just—remembering."

Kymbal put his head into the tent. "Good, you're awake. Let's get going. The sun is almost down and I want to be home by midnight."

Art crawled out into the evening chill, Lorn at his heels. A few metres away Kymbal sniffed the air, head up like a wild animal. He turned suddenly. "We'll have rain before morning. A good reason to get going." He paused. "And here's another. I climbed a hill this afternoon and trained my binoculars on the crash site. Another aircraft was there—on the ground. There were people moving around it, sifting through the wreckage."

Art felt a chill. "Then Arklund knows I'm not dead."

Kymbal nodded. "But he doesn't know where you are. And the path we took, we left few tracks. Tonight's rain should obliterate whatever traces there are."

"You shouldn't even have to worry about it," Art said. He hated the thought of putting them in danger, after they'd helped him. "We'll split up. You go on home, and I'll—"

Lorn looked up in alarm, but Kymbal just laughed. "You'll what? Wander in the woods until you starve? What will you eat?

Berries?" He pointed to a nearby bush with a few bright purple berries clinging to the topmost branches.

"If I have to."

"Eat one of those and you'll throw up your guts. Eat five and you'll die in agony. You've got no idea what's safe and what's not."

"I grew up on a spaceship," Art said stiffly. "What do you expect?"

"Nothing, except maybe common sense. Lorn and I didn't save you just to let you wander off and kill yourself now. You're coming home with us, and you'll stay with us until you're recovered, and if Arklund and his Skywatcher goons think they can have you back, they're even crazier than their religion!"

Art blinked at Kymbal's vehemence. "Well, when you put it that way…"

"That's settled, then." Kymbal turned to his grinning son. "What are you smirking at?" he roared. "Strike that tent and let's move!"

"Yes, Dad," said the youth, still grinning. A few minutes later, munching on dry, nutty ration bars, they entered the forest and began to climb.

As they left the clearing Kymbal offered Art more painkiller, but he shook his head despite the growing ache in his arm and chest and the fire in his skin. If they were being pursued he wanted a clear head.

But because of that decision he soon found the going even tougher than the long hike over the desert the night before, made worse by the constant uphill angle and the roots and branches that seemed to deliberately reach out to snare him, stinging his burned skin as he pushed through them. Still, he pressed on, feeling a perverse sort of pleasure in the pain, as though each agonizing step were penance for the mistakes of the past few weeks, or months…

Make that years, he decided finally after stumbling over a root and jarring his arm so hard his head swam. *Or maybe decades. Hell, by the time this is over I will have paid for every mistake I ever made, from drawing on the walls when I was three to previewing the file Shadow gave me.*

After an indeterminate time half-lost in a growing haze of pain and fatigue, Art realized the slope had eased; they began to descend gradually, the change sending a few spasms through his calves and thighs but still a great relief. Ahead Kymbal and Lorn walked faster and faster, drawing away from him, but he plugged on at his steady pace, head down, concentrating on moving one foot after another, not looking up even when distant lightning lit the western horizon and, moments later, thunder grumbled like a Crewman clearing his throat on the public address system.

Then he became aware of a different sort of light, yellow and warm. Wearily he raised his head, which ached in concert with every other part of his body, and saw ahead of him a log cabin that might have been lifted straight from any number of old westerns.

The thunder sounded again, nearer, and as Art approached the cabin, where Kymbal and Lorn and a lovely but puzzled-looking woman awaited him on the porch, the first drop of rain touched his cheek.

Chapter Nine

Rain sleeted against the windows as Art slumped in a chair at Kymbal's kitchen table, wrapped in a blanket which burned against his damaged skin but he snuggled into nonetheless. His host's blonde wife, Melissa, bustled from cabinet to refrigerator to stove, preparing the first real food Art had seen in…how long?

Melissa obviously had dozens of questions, but just as obviously had decided to put them off until she had seen to the needs of her unexpected guest. Art smiled at her when she set stew, bread and cheese before him. "Thank you," he said, and she nodded in return.

Though his mouth watered at the savory odor, he waited until Kymbal and Lorn were also served before taking his first spoonful of the stew—and then it was all he could do to keep from gulping it down. When at last he sat back, feeling more human than he had since leaving the Skywatchers' sanctuary, Melissa's mouth quirked. "Well, Mr. Stoddard, I'll take that as a compliment to my cooking."

He blushed. "I'm sorry. It's just—"

Melissa waved off his protest. "Nothing to apologize for. You obviously needed it." She gave her husband a sharp look with her bright blue eyes. "Now, if someone will tell me exactly what is going on—"

Kymbal nodded to Art. "Go ahead."

He sighed and hitched his chair a little closer to the table, leaning his elbows on it. "Well," he began, "you might say I'm not as young as I look…"

Melissa listened to his tale in astonished silence, while Kymbal gazed into the fire and Lorn listened with a grin that gave way to a yawn as Art again told of his escape/kidnapping from the detention centre in the capital city (which, he learned from Melissa, was called Bagnell, after the captain of the first Umstattd-drive scoutship to land on Peregrine). By the time Art had brought his adventures up to date, the boy slept soundly, head pillowed in his arms.

Melissa's first bundled her protesting son off to bed, where his four-year-old sister Lisa had gone before Art arrived. She returned to the table and poured all three of them a cup of something called "kuf" that might have been an indirect descendent of the semicaf they drank on the *Mayflower II*—itself a synthetic version of true coffee, which, it was generally supposed, only the Captain still had a store of to drink. Art sipped the kuf cautiously and found it tasted slightly better than it smelled—but only slightly.

"So what will you do now?" Melissa said.

Art warmed his hands on the cup. "I don't know."

"You're welcome to stay here as long as you like. You're in no condition to go anywhere right away in any event. Recuperate first, then worry about what comes next."

Art looked at Kymbal, who started to say something, stopped, then shrugged. "She's right."

"Of course I'm right," said Melissa. "And now, Mr. Stoddard, as Marc may or may not have told you, I have had some medical training. Let's have a look at you…" She cleared the kitchen table and had him sit and then lie down on it while she opened a cabinet, revealing a glittering array of equipment, most of which Art couldn't begin to guess the function of. She brought out a scanner that fit neatly into her palm and ran it over his body from head to foot. "The ribs are just cracked," she announced. "And it looks like Marc did a good job setting your arm. You're not in nearly as bad shape as you might have been." She returned the scanner to the cabinet and brought out what looked like a small metal case. She opened it and pulled out two paddle-shaped objects with triggers. "I can't heal you instantly, but I can speed things along," she told him. She set the paddles above and below the splint and bandage on his arm. "Once every twelve hours with these and you'll be back to normal in a few days, instead of six weeks."

She pressed the triggers and Art felt his arm grow warm. After about a minute she moved the paddles to his ribcage and repeated the process. She returned the apparatus to its case. The warmth took a few seconds to fade, and left behind a strange tingling deep inside Art's bones. As Melissa eased his arm back into its sling he asked, "I don't understand. If you're a doctor, why are you living out here in the middle of nowhere?"

Melissa finished fastening the sling, then reached for a jar she had set aside earlier and unscrewed the lid. Finally, as she dipped her fingers into a clear gel and began spreading it over Art's sunburned upper body, she said, "Has Marc told you anything about his life before we came here?"

Art shook his head.

"He was in the SSIN." The gel first stung, then numbed, vanishing almost as quickly as she applied it, taking much of the pain and redness with it. "An officer, in fact. But he was discharged dishonourably."

"Why?" Art said, then hastily added, "I'm sorry, if you'd rather not—"

"For revealing to his superiors the extent of Skywatcher infiltration." Melissa finished his back and came around to his front. "Close your eyes." Art complied and felt her fingers on his face, spreading coolness. He hadn't realized until that moment that even his eyelids were sunburned.

"But why would they discharge him for that?" he asked, eyes still closed.

"They didn't, officially. The *official* charge was dereliction of duty. They put a notation in the duty roster that he had been ordered to stand guard duty one evening, added his acknowledgement—then made sure he never received the order and also made sure there was a disturbance during his watch. He was arrested, court-martialed and discharged with a black mark on his record that would have kept him from ever holding a decent job anywhere on the planet. So we…relocated. To here. People who live out here take pressure off government services in the cities. Not many people are willing to do it. So the government leaves us alone."

She was down to his chest now, her fingers moving surely over his bruised side. Art caught his breath as she touched the skin over the cracked ribs, but she was so gentle he felt nothing. Catching his breath had hurt more.

"I still don't understand." He opened his eyes. "Who were 'they'? Why go to all that trouble?"

"*They* were his superior officers, and *they* were Skywatchers." She finished and stepped back, recapping the gel. "There. Now I'll re-bandage your ribs."

"Then Arklund really is in a position to take over the planet?"

"If his followers believe you're the Conqueror—I'd say he has a pretty good chance." She began wrapping bandage around his torso, maneuvering carefully under his broken arm. "But even the attempt will mean civil war." Her hands faltered. "I'm worried about my parents," she said almost under her breath. "Lorn and Lisa are safe with us out here, but…" Her voice trailed off, and she silently finished the bandage.

◣ ◢

Safe? Art thought the next morning. He sat on a stump in the yard, shaded by the house, having been threatened with dire retribution if he exposed so much as a square centimetre of his body to the sun. *Is anyone safe?* He looked up at the sky, washed pale blue by the night's rain.

Recuperate, Marc and Melissa had told him. *Rest. Don't worry yet about what to do next.* But how could he *not* worry, knowing what was happening in space—and knowing he was the only person who might have had a chance to stop it? If he had broadcast Shadow's file without previewing it…if he had only realized that of course his father would be monitoring everything he did and would turn him over in a heartbeat…if he had fought his kidnappers instead of meekly letting them cart him off to Arklund…if he had made better use of that brief moment of power Arklund had handed him, that moment when he was proclaimed Conqueror and thousands cheered him…would Arklund really have had him shot on the spot if he'd deviated from his script? Would he have dared, with all his followers looking on? *It was a bluff*, Art thought bitterly. *A bluff, and like a coward, I fell for it.*

And that seemed to have been all the power he was *ever* to hold. For a moment he had been a king in this game of chess, but he had squandered it. Now he was a pawn once more, pushed from square to square and momentarily forgotten, or at least misplaced.

Little Lisa's clear laugh rang through the open door of the cabin, and then she tumbled out herself. Blonde hair like her mother's, tied in pigtails, framed wide blue eyes in a heart-shaped face as she stood for a moment on the porch, staring at him just as she had when she first woke that morning and discovered him; she smiled tentatively and, when he smiled back, giggled and ran around the corner of the house.

Art's smile faded as he looked after her. Marc, Melissa, Lorn, Lisa—unless he could get to the edge of the board and transform from pawn into some piece with power, they might be dead within a week.

So might I.

That day and two more went by, and those same bleak thoughts recycled themselves countless times. Lisa began calling him "Arty-art" for some reason only her four-year-old mind could fathom, and surprised him one evening by crawling onto his lap and hugging him. Melissa started to get after her, worrying about Art's ribs and arm, but he stopped her. "Leave her," he said. The warmth of the small body pressed up against his and the arms tight around his neck woke something inside him, a fierce determination that somehow he would stop what was about to happen—stop it, or die trying.

Lisa soon clambered down and shortly thereafter went to

bed, and Lorn was sent reluctantly after her. The three adults remained at the kitchen table, sipping kuf. Art drank it diligently and thought in another year or two he might even grow to appreciate it.

"I've been monitoring the 'Net," Marc said abruptly. "There's been no mention of any starship, or any unrest among the Skywatchers or the armed forces."

"The government wouldn't tell us if there were," Melissa pointed out.

"There hasn't been anything on the Peregrine FreeNet, either."

Art looked up. "You know about that?"

"Everyone knows about it." Marc grinned. "Everyone knows about it, nobody seems to know who's behind it, and so far, at least, the government hasn't been able to stop it. It drives them crazy. Officially, when I was in the SSIN, it drove me crazy, too. But unofficially..." He laughed. "Unofficially, it's the most popular thing on the 'Net."

Something tickled the back of Art's mind. "Does it really do any good?" he asked slowly. "I mean, does the stuff the Peregrine FreeNet puts out change anything?"

"All the time," said Melissa, pouring another cup of kuf. "Practically everyone checks it out—even if no one will admit to it—and, more importantly, believes it; or least believes it more than what comes through official channels. That puts pressure on the government to clean up whatever corruption or mismanagement or abuse of power the PFV has uncovered. And it uncovers a lot. Even on Peregrine public opinion counts for something."

"It's a good thing the Skywatchers haven't infiltrated *it*," Marc said darkly. "Or at least we assume they haven't. If and when the Skywatchers act, that's where I think we'll see the news first. And if those who aren't in thrall to the First Visionary are to stop him, it will be because they got early warning through the PFN."

"But there's been nothing about the starship," Art said.

"No. The government does manage to keep *some* secrets."

Slowly Art grinned. "Maybe it's time to change that."

Marc stared at him, opened his mouth to say something–

—and the lights went out.

"Dad?" Lorn's worried young voice came from his bedroom door. "Someone's outside. I heard him."

Art tensed. Marc moved to the window, a black silhouette against its slightly less black square of the window. "Watch the children," he told Melissa. He disappeared from Art's view. A moment later the door opened and closed as he slipped out.

Melissa went at once to Lorn, hushing his startled questions, and went back into the bedroom with him. For a moment Art sat alone in the dark kitchen, feeling helpless; then, angry with himself for once more remaining passive, he felt his way to the sideboard, where Melissa had earlier been slicing meat. He found the nine-inch blade she'd been using. Holding the knife in his left hand like a short sword—*a* very *short sword*, he couldn't help thinking—he followed Marc outside.

Clouds obscured the stars, and the trees tossed and hissed in the wind that had risen after sunset. Art stood on the porch and peered into the darkness, uneasily aware that ten men could be standing almost close enough to touch and he wouldn't be able to see them, wondering what he hoped to accomplish. *In fact*, he thought suddenly, *this could be a good way to get shot—by Marc*.

But it was because Marc was out there somewhere, risking his life, that Art eased down the porch steps and crept toward the corner of the house. He owed the man more than enough to shoulder some of the risk himself.

He strained eyes and ears to detect anything unusual in the night, but the wind and darkness defeated him. The first he knew of the man behind him was the stiffened hand that chopped down on his wrist, jarring the knife loose. An arm wrapped around his neck and tightened, choking him. Art struggled uselessly, scrabbling at that iron-like limb with his left hand. The sound of the wind gave way to a deeper roaring in his ears, and the night grew even darker—

—and then something made a dull crunching sound and the arm fell away. Art dropped to his knees and clung to the cabin wall, gasping. Marc bent down. “All right?” he whispered, and Art nodded. Marc stood again. “There’s another one out here somewhere—”

A red beam sliced through the night, missing Marc’s head by centimetres. It ripped a flaming chunk of wood from the cabin. Marc whirled and returned fire, yelling at Art to get down, belatedly, since Art was already hugging the ground. Marc’s weapon blazed on full automatic, shattering trunks, scattering needles—and eliciting a brief, horrible scream.

The wind-tossed darkness seemed serene after that blast of flame and thunder. Art raised his head. Marc stood over him like a dark statue. “Who—” Art began, but Marc hissed him to silence.

Long seconds passed before Marc relaxed. “If there were any more, they’re gone,” he said in a normal voice. “I’m going to fix the lights.” He strode around the corner of the cabin and a moment later light flooded the yard from within the house and from the lamps hung high in the trees surrounding it.

Only a metre away lay the man who had first attacked Art, his eyes open but unseeing, the back of his skull caved in. Blood soaked the collar of the black uniform he wore and the ground beneath his head.

Art swallowed. “Government?” he asked as Marc returned.

Marc knelt beside the body and shook his head. “Skywatcher. See the insignia?” He pointed to a small emblem on the dead man’s collar, and Art, leaning closer, saw an eye-within-a-star. “Arklund is mustering his forces.”

He helped Art to his feet, just as the front door opened and Lorn emerged. “Mom’s with Lisa,” he said. “She thinks it’s a thunder storm. What—” His gaze fell on the dead man and he gasped. “You killed him!” His voice held as much admiration as horror.

“He had Art. I had to strike fast.” Marc turned. “As for the other one—" He crossed the yard to the splintered trees. Lorn started to follow, but Art held him back.

"You don't want to see," he said.

Lorn opened his mouth, no doubt to protest that yes he *did*, but just then his mother called. "Lorn. Come sit with your sister."

Lorn turned to the door. "But, Mom—"

"Now!"

There was enough bite in that one word to send Lorn scurrying back inside, after one last glance at the dead man. A few moments later Melissa emerged. She glanced at the body, knelt beside it briefly, checking for a pulse, then closed the man's eyes and picked up the butcher knife from where Art had dropped it. "And just what did you think you were doing?" she demanded as she straightened to face him.

He shook his head, abashed. "I don't know. I just couldn't let your husband risk his life—"

"He wouldn't have *had* to if you weren't here!" Melissa snapped. She took a deep breath. "I'm sorry," she said. "That was unfair."

"No, it's not," Art replied quietly. "It's true. And I know it." He lifted his broken arm in its sling. "How much longer?"

"It can come out tomorrow, though I'd rather give it two or three more days." Melissa studied him in silence for a moment. "You're leaving us, aren't you?" she said finally. "If it's what I just said—"

"It isn't. I knew I was putting you at risk. And now—" He looked down at the dead man. "Look at what I've gotten you into. If these two found me here, so may others."

"I don't think they told anyone," Marc said, coming back across the yard. "They don't have line-of-sight to anyone out here and I doubt Arklund is willing to risk sending messages openly over the airwaves or the satellite links–not yet, anyway. He's dead," he added in answer to Art's questioning glance into the forest.

"But Arklund will find out they're missing and will know

approximately where to look," Art said. "If I'm not here he'll have no reason to bother you."

"We won't be here, either," Marc said.

Melissa shot him a startled look. One hand flew to her mouth. "Oh!" she said in a small voice.

"You're moving?" Art said. He felt sick. What had he done, getting these people involved with his life?

They involved themselves, he thought. *Because they're good people.*

And look what it got them.

Marc shrugged. "This is our second cabin already. Won't hurt us to build another one. Besides, someone moved into the next valley over a month ago. I've been feeling kinda crowded ever since."

"But all your things—" Art said. "It will take forever—"

Marc laughed. "Not planning to carry it all myself," he said. He waved a hand in the direction of the outbuilding. "Packbots in there'll do the heavy shifting."

"Packbots..." Art blinked. "Right."

"Just because we like the frontier lifestyle doesn't mean we don't use modern technology," Marc said. He stared down at the dead man. "Goes against my grain to be run off by the likes of these, I admit." He gave the body a contemptuous shove with the toe of his boot. "They've upended my life once too often. If it were just me, I'd stay and fight any more thugs Arklund cares to send."

"But it's not just you," Melissa said quietly.

"No," Marc said. "It's not." He kissed her on the forehead. "We'll move." He glanced at Art. "You're welcome to come with us."

"No," Art said. "It's time for me to leave."

"What you said before the lights went off?" Melissa said.

Art nodded.

"Well, explain later," Marc put in. "First let's bury the trash." He looked at Art's broken arm and sighed. "Which I guess is *also* up to me."

In the morning, Lorn emerged from his room and started to tell Art about the wild dream he'd had, but Marc stopped him, took him outside and showed him the beam marks on the cabin and the bullet scars in the trees. Art, sitting on the porch, saw the troubled look the youngster gave his father. "Then you really *did* kill the man I saw out here? And another one in the bush?"

Marc nodded calmly. "Yes."

"To save Art?"

"To save Art—and you, and Lisa, and your mother." His gaze slipped from his son to Art, and back again. "They wouldn't have left any of us alive. They *migh*t need Art to keep playing the part of the Conqueror of Time and Space. But they couldn't let *anyone* go who knew the truth." He reached out and fingered the blackened scar on the wall of the cabin. "I'm not proud of what I did, son. But it was necessary. You do what you have to." He sighed. "And here's the other bit of news. We're pulling up stakes. Gotta find somewhere else to live before Arklund sends anyone else our way."

Art looked away. *I should never have come here. It's past time to leave.*

After the noon meal, when Lisa was playing outside with Lorn to watch her, he told Marc and Melissa what he had in mind. "The people on your planet know nothing about the *Mayflower II*. They don't know that your government is planning to destroy it. I'm betting that if they did, they wouldn't like the idea. If your government can't attack in secret, I don't think it will attack at all. So I intend to break their data seal—by getting the truth to the Peregrine FreeNet."

The Kymbals exchanged glances. "It might work," Marc said. "But that won't stop *your* people from attacking *us*."

"I know." Art took a deep breath. "And that means I somehow have to get word to my fellow Passengers at the same time."

"How?" asked Marc.

Art shook his head.

"I see." Marc sat silent for a moment, then said, "Promise me,

Art, that you won't tell our people about the *Mayflower II* unless you can also find a way to tell *your* people about *us*."

"But—"

"Which is better: to save a few thousand lives or a few million?"

"I want to save them all!"

"But you may not be able to," Marc said. "You know it as well as I do. And if you can't—then you *know* it's better to let the PPP act before your ship can." His eyes bore into Art's. "For me…for Melissa…for Lorn…for Lisa. *Promise!*"

Art hesitated. Intellectually, he knew Marc was right. If the planetary government *alone* was stopped from attacking, and Captain Nakos went ahead and fired his missiles, he would indeed be trading thousands for millions. Unless both sides could be stopped, it would be better to let the *Mayflower II* be destroyed than Peregrine.

If you measure lives like potatoes! he cried in inner anguish. *But those lives are people I've known all my life—my parents among them. How can I promise to let* them *die to save* strangers*?*

Strangers? Marc and Melissa? Lorn and Lisa, whose laughter rang outside in the yard? People whose lives were already at risk because of Art, because Marc had brought him home instead of leaving him to die in the desert or fall into Arklund's hands? Marc had saved him yet again the night before…had *killed* to save him. Art owed him many times over.

"I promise," he said finally. "If I can't get the message to both sides, then I won't do anything to stop just *your* government from acting." Determination blazed up in him like a small hot fire. "But I *will* get the message to both sides. What happens after that…" He shook his head. "I don't know. But at least we'll have a hope."

"Sometimes hope is all you can ask for," said Melissa.

Marc's eyes locked on Art's. "Thank you," he said. "I know how hard that promise may be to keep." He smiled briefly. "Now. How do you plan to contact the PFN?"

Art cleared his throat. "I was hoping you might help—"

"He can't, but I can," said Melissa.

Marc glanced at her. "Javik?"

She nodded.

"Javik?" Art repeated.

"A friend of mine. He lives just a few kilometres from here. He can get you into the city, and give you a contact. Beyond that—" She gave Art a hard look. "Beyond that, it's up to you."

Chapter Ten

Two hours later, his arm weak but free of bandage, sling and pain, Art rode with Melissa in an electric truck over a road that was little better than a roughly cleared path in the forest. The truck banged and crashed as though about to disintegrate every time it hit a bump—and the road seemed to have nothing but bumps. "I'd better warn you, Javik's—different," Melissa shouted above the din. "But he'll help you, I'm sure of it."

Art was too busy hanging on to reply, but he wondered, as a hitherto hidden compartment in the control console burst open and dumped assorted nuts, bolts and bits of paper into his lap, what Melissa meant by 'different.'

He found out a few minutes later, when they groaned to a halt in the overgrown, litter-strewn yard of a house that made the Kymbals' plain cabin look like a mansion. Little more than a lean-to, Javik's home was constructed of unpeeled logs and roofed with shaggy branches. Art reached for the door handle, but Melissa stopped him. "We don't get out until he tells us to."

"What if he's not here?"

"He's always here." Her eyes searched the clearing and locked on the shadows where trees overhung a sloppy woodpile. "There."

Art followed her gaze, and after a few seconds of hard looking, thought he could just make out the motionless figure of a man—an *armed* man. With his weapon aimed at them. Art was suddenly very glad he hadn't gotten out of the truck.

They sat there for what seemed like hours, then suddenly the man-shape in the shadows disappeared. "Now, if we're lucky…" said Melissa.

A moment later a man emerged from the door of the shack. Not very tall, stooped-shouldered and graying, wearing well-worn camouflaged military fatigues smudged with sap and mud, he didn't look at all like the menacing figure Art had seen in the bushes—except for the rifle he held in his right hand, the large and nasty-looking handgun holstered on his right hip, and the even nastier-looking knife on the left.

Javik stopped five metres away. "Come out slowly," he ordered. "And keep your hands in the open."

"This guy is going to *help* me?" Art muttered to Melissa.

"Sssh!" she hissed. She opened her door and stepped very carefully into the yard. Art did the same. "Hello, Javik," Melissa said.

He didn't respond; his eyes were locked on Art. "I don't know this man."

"He's a friend."

"Is he?" Javik stepped closer to Art, who didn't need Melissa to tell him to stand very still. "What's your name, *friend*?"

"Arthur Stoddard."

Javik frowned. "A very strange name." For a moment he looked past Art, eyes vague; suddenly they focused. "Ah, I see. A very *old* name. Earth-original. Mutated out of use roughly two hundred years ago. Closest current forms are Artu and Thurr. Why do you wear a dead name, Arthur Stoddard?"

Art opened his mouth to reply; closed it again; looked at Melissa. "Tell him," she said.

So Art told his story again, as briefly as he could. Several times Javik lost focus again, the last time, when Art finished, for ten or fifteen seconds. When he looked at Art again, for the first time his expression held more interest than suspicion. "Thank you."

That wasn't the response Art expected. "What?"

"I have been troubled by anomalies. Your data allowed me to integrate them into the matrix." He glanced at Melissa. "You did right to bring him to me."

Melissa nodded. “He must gain access to the Peregrine FreeNet, and no one is better at gaining access to things than you are, Javik.”

“Well-reasoned.” He turned back to Art. “This afternoon at 1620 an automated tanker carrying sucra will stop at the Kilometre 334 marker of Feeder Road 29 for exactly two minutes. The control cab’s maintenance door will open. Enter the cab.

“The tanker will take you to Bagnell, arriving at approximately 0250 tomorrow. It will stop for another two minutes outside the main gate of the processing plant, where it is to deliver its load. Leave the tanker there. Across the street you will find a communications terminal. Enter the code SPX496. A machine will answer. Leave the following message: ‘Javik sends Iznar his greetings and a gift.’ Then leave the terminal and walk six blocks north. You will find yourself at a citytrans stop on a busy street. Go inside the shelter and wait. Someone will come. Do you understand?”

“I’m not sure—”

“Then listen again.” Javik repeated his instructions. Feeling as if he had fallen into a bad spy movie, Art recited them dutifully. Javik nodded once. “Good luck.” He turned and walked back to the shack without a word of farewell.

Art stared after him, and then glanced at Melissa, who jerked her head at the truck. As they climbed into the cab he asked her, “What was that all about?”

Melissa started the engine and eased the truck out of the yard. She drove back the way they had come, the noise just as horrendous as before. “Tell you later,” she shouted, and Art had to be content with that.

Somewhere along the path they took a different turn, and a few kilometres further finally emerged from the forest onto a smooth four-lane road, the right two lanes separated from the left by broad red stripes. As Melissa turned right something screamed past in one of the far lanes so fast Art hardly had time to flinch before it was gone.

"What the—"

"Courier. Or some government official. Only very important people or very important cargo travel the ziplanes. We stick to the slowlanes. And so will your sucra tanker."

"I'll live." Art began picking up the odds and ends that had fallen from the console compartment. "Now are you going to tell me about Javik?"

Melissa stayed silent for a moment. "Javik was a patient of mine for a while," she said finally. "SSIN brought him to me shot- up, cut, bruised, burned—I've never seen anyone injured that badly recover so completely." She paused. "At least, his *body* recovered."

"His mind?"

"Had been…altered," Melissa said. "He's permanently linked to the 'Net."

"The SSIN did that to him?" Art said, intrigued and horrified at the same time.

"Not exactly." Melissa sighed. "He did it to *himself.* He designed the technology, but the first thing he did once he knew it had worked was to erase his working files—an insurance policy against SSIN deciding it didn't need him anymore. Even knowing it's possible, no one else…well, that I know of," she amended, "has been able to pull it off.

"At one time he could access literally every networked computer on Peregrine, absorb any data that had been stored anywhere accessible from the 'Net…and more than a few computers whose owners thought *weren't* accessible. SSIN used him extensively, as you can imagine. But then someone tried to kidnap him. He summoned help through his link to the 'Net, but there was a fight—a bad one. He was hurt, and they brought him to me."

"So why is he out here?"

"He wasn't the same after his body recovered. He became wildly paranoid. Installing the link had already played havoc with his mind, changing neural connections, doing God knows what to his emotional and mental equilibrium. Marc suspects his kidnappers were SSIN renegades, people he had trusted, and thinks that's what pushed him over the edge. He left the hospital and disappeared. SSIN questioned the entire staff for two weeks, but didn't learn anything. Shortly after that, Marc…we came out here, and—there was Javik. If he hadn't remembered me from the hospital…" She shook her head.

"But if he's hooked into the 'Net, why didn't he already know about the *Mayflower II*?"

"His link has eroded. Technology changes, and security is much tighter—not least because the SSIN knows he's still out there somewhere. Still, clues seep through the cracks."

"Anomalies," said Art thoughtfully.

"Exactly. He could tell something strange was going on, but he wasn't sure what. Now, with your information, he's able to form a more complete picture. That's why he thanked you."

"And why he helped me?" Art dumped the last loose bolt into the console compartment and closed the door.

"He's not doing you a favour," Melissa said. "He *might* be doing me one. More likely, he's just hoping you'll do some damage to the government."

They rode in silence for the next several kilometres, periodically passing stone markers with numbers incised on them, growing gradually smaller—350, 349, 348…and finally, 334. Melissa stopped the truck. "1600," she said, pointing to a chronometer on the control console. "Your ride will be along in twenty minutes."

Art nodded, and opened the door. He paused before stepping down. "Thank you. You've done so much—"

"You needed help. And you're important, Arthur Stoddard. If what you've told us is true, you may be the only one who has a hope of stopping our government and your Crew from killing us all."

"It's true," said Art. "But world-saving isn't really my line of work."

Melissa smiled a little. "To quote the ancient proverb, 'It's a dirty job, but someone has to do it.'"

Art's throat felt tight. "Give my thanks to Marc and Lorn and tell Lisa…tell her Arty-Art loves her."

"I will."

Art hesitated awkwardly a moment longer, then climbed down and closed the door behind him. Melissa backed the truck up sharply, turned it around and drove away; and, feeling very much alone, Art sat down to wait for his ride.

He didn't have to wait long. Precisely on time, the big twenty-four-wheeled tanker rumbled around the curve, its three fat cylinders gleaming white in the high, hot sun. A heart and the company name, Heartlife, blazed red on each cylinder. The tanker wheezed to a halt right beside Art and a hatch popped open in the blank, bulbous cab at its front end, over the humming motor. He scrambled out of the bushes, seized handholds and pulled himself into the dark interior, which lit fluorescently for him, revealing racks of closed metal cabinets, each with two tiny lights in their doors, one dark, the other glowing green.

He glanced back at the open hatch—and yelped and jumped back as someone occluded that light, clambering into the cab in his wake.

The door snapped shut. The lights went out. Art gasped, "Who are you?" into the absolute darkness.

"Don't worry," said a young voice, excited and pleased with itself. "It's me. Lorn."

"Lorn?" Art's heart dropped into his stomach. "Lorn! What the hell—?"

"I hid in the truck before Mom drove away," the boy said. "Jumped out and ran into the woods when we got here. Just made it through the hatch." Art couldn't see him, but he could tell the boy was grinning hugely. "I'm coming with you. I'm coming with you to help!"

"You can't—Lorn, your parents—" Inwardly, Art groaned. "They'll be worried sick, they won't know where you are—"

"I left a note," Lorn said. "Time-release. It'll pop up about the time Mom gets home, tell them where I am."

"But, Lorn—"

"You're trying to save us all," Lorn said, the grin gone from his voice but the determination as strong as ever. "I want to help. I can't hide in the woods when I know what's going on."

"Your parents—" Art began again.

"They've got each other. They've got Lisa. And none of that will matter if the world gets blown up, will it?"

Art shook his head, even though he knew Lorn couldn't see it. "I don't need help, Lorn. You're putting yourself in danger for nothing."

"You don't know what help you need," Lorn said with certainty. "You're afraid I'm too young and I'm just going to be in the way. But I'm not a kid, Art. I can look after myself in the woods…better than you can. I can shoot. I can use a knife. I'm strong. I'm fast." Somehow the grin came back into his voice. "And anyway, I can't get out of here now. Wherever you're going, I'm coming with you."

Art groaned and sank down onto the unpadded metal floor. "Your father will kill me if anything happens to you!"

"He'll kill *me* even if *nothing* happens to me," Lorn said cheerfully. "So it's not worth worrying about."

Art sighed and didn't say anything more.

They rolled along in silence for a while, then Lorn's voice came out of the darkness again. "Smooth ride," he said. "Beats Mom's truck."

Despite everything, Art chuckled at that. But in fact he wished he and Lorn were back in that noisy rattletrap, or in the Kymbals' cabin, or anywhere but where they were, heading to Bagnell, where he planned to do something possibly useless, definitely dangerous, and likely impossible. Taking action, however good it might be for the soul, could be far less healthy for the body. And now he had Lorn to worry about, too. *Stupid kid*, he thought, but in fact his heart wasn't in it; he found it oddly touching that the boy had thrown in his lot with him. *I just have to live up to his expectations*, he thought. *Great. More pressure.*

But staying behind with the Kymbals would have accomplished nothing while still being dangerous…even for Lorn, he had to admit. Should the *Mayflower II* launch its missiles, the remoteness of their homestead would be little protection against radiation and climatic changes, even if they escaped the blast damage. And then, as they struggled to survive in a crippled world, he would have been a drain on their resources—and would have had to live with the knowledge that he had done nothing to prevent the holocaust.

Making sure the truth of the situation got out, if he could, would at least be a gesture—and the right kind of gesture, made at the right moment, could change the course of history. Or in this case, assure that history would continue. And whether he succeeded or failed, at least he would still be trying. It would take a lot of trying to make up for all the times he had just let things happen in his life.

Time passed. He shifted uncomfortably on the bare floor. He heard Lorn breathing heavily and knew the boy had fallen asleep. He wished he could manage it.

The tiny green lights were too small to light the cabin at all, and in the absolute darkness they seemed disconnected from any solid object, simply floating there like stars—or the eyes of small, unblinking reptiles. Art found them disconcerting, and when they showed a tendency to spin around him, he closed his eyes, preferring that familiar inner darkness to the outer one.

And then suddenly he opened his eyes again, and found himself lying on his side on the floor. Cold air, tainted sickly sweet, flowed around him. The cab lights were on, and the door was open. Lorn lay on his side, snoring softly.

Art sat up. What had gone wrong? Why had the truck stopped before reaching the city? Or—

The sky outside was dark, but from somewhere harsh light illuminated pavement and a featureless gray wall. *Bagnell*, he thought. Lorn wasn't the only one who had fallen asleep. They were already in the city!

And how long had the door been open? They only had two minutes! "Lorn!" he said, as loudly as he dared. "Lorn!" He shook the boy. "Wake up!"

Lorn, blinking, sat up. "What…?"

"We have to get out of here—now!"

He scrambled up and out of the cab, Lorn at his heels, glad of his haste a moment later when the door snapped shut and the truck hummed to life again. It rolled away down the street, revealing a mesh fence and, beyond it, an ugly collection of pipes, towers and tubes, topped with tall stacks from which poured heavy blue smoke and the sweetish stench. The truck turned through a gate that swung open automatically for it, and Art read a sign: "Heartlife Sucra Refinery 3. WARNING: Automated Security Systems Active. Trespassers will be targeted."

"Friendly," Lorn commented.

"Let's get out of here," Art said. He led the boy away from the gate. The gray wall continued in both directions, but just a few steps from where the truck had stopped a fluorescent blue triangle glowed over a glass booth—presumably the communications terminal. Art entered it and found nothing but a curved panel of blank black glass. He stared at it. "Now what?"

"You need to call somebody?" Lorn said. "What's the code?"

"SPX496," Art said.

"Personal call," Lorn said, and the curved glass glowed blue.

"Please state code," said a feminine voice. "Or use the alphanumeric keypad." A series of letters and numbers, arranged in a pattern that made no sense at all to Art, appeared beneath the vidscreen.

"SPX496," Lorn said clearly.

"Accepted," said the terminal.

The blue screen suddenly turned dark gray and a man's deep voice replaced the terminal's light female one. "Please state your identity and message. I will return your call later."

Lorn glanced at Art, who cleared his throat and said, "Javik sends Iznar his greetings and a gift." Then he waited.

After a few seconds the screen went black.

"Call terminated," said the computerized voice. "Place another?"

Lorn jerked his head at the door and led Art out. "Now what?" the boy said.

Art took a deep breath of the sucra-perfumed air. So far, so good. "Now we have to locate the citytrans stop…six blocks north…."

He looked around. On all sides rose factories and warehouses—all, as far as Art could tell, devoid of people.

"Um," he said. "Which…uh, which way is north?"

Lorn grinned. He glanced up at the starlit sky, then down again. "That way," he said, pointing off to their right. His grin widened. "Told you I'd come in useful."

"Nobody likes an I-told-you-so," Art grumbled.

Together they walked through streets that echoed only to their footsteps and the clatter and hum of hidden machinery. They passed sign after sign warning of automated security systems, and more than once Art saw cameras and weapons tracking them from gateposts or roofs. He wondered uneasily if their images were even then being cross-referenced with government computers, and if those records might show him to be a missing prisoner of the government—or the Skywatchers' Conqueror of Time and Space. *Iznar*, he thought, *had better have a good hiding place.*

The citytrans stop, when they found it, proved to mark the edge of the industrial section. Across the street from the tent-like structure of grimy steel beams and dingy plastiglass stood a line of bars, with huge, flashing signs that bore no words, only geometric symbols—circles, squares, hexagons, pentagrams. The few people on Art's side of the street stood in couples or trios, conversing in low voices. They gave him brief, searching, suspicious looks, then turned back to their business.

Across the street many more people moved from bar to bar. Women and men alike wore garish, glittering clothing, some of which glowed in the dark. Large patches of exposed skin bore vibrant, painted-on patterns; one or two people seemed to be wearing *nothing* but paint. Art glanced at Lorn, whose eyes were fixed on one particularly statuesque nearly-nude woman, and groaned inwardly. Something *else* he'd have to explain to Marc and Melissa.

"Now we wait," Art said, sitting on the hard plastic bench in the shelter. Lorn sat beside him, and, hidden in shadow, they watched the peculiar parade across the way. Art thought of his mother, always wearing the latest Shipborn fashion, no matter how odd or unattractive. *She'd feel right at home here*, he thought. A bare-breasted woman with glowing blue nipples and what looked like a camera lens in her belly button sashayed by on the arm of another woman. *Or not*, he added silently.

He heard Lorn swallow. "First time in the big city?" he said.

"Yeah…I didn't…I…um…" Lorn glanced at him. "Is the ship like this?"

Art thought about it. "No," he said. "We don't dress…or undress…that oddly." *Mostly,* he thought, remembering Rick's Place, *we just drink.* Judging by the busy foot traffic in and out of the bars, they certainly had *that* in common with the Peregrine folk.

Perhaps twenty minutes later he saw someone new in the crowd, a man at least a head taller than anyone else, who, while not wearing the gaudy trappings or painted skin of most of the people, wasn't exactly dressed in ordinary clothes, either. He wore unrelieved black, including a black mask with a single slit across the eyes and a smaller vertical one over the nose and mouth. He crossed the street and came straight to the shelter. Art scrambled to his feet and still had to look up at that hidden face. "You are Javik's gift?" The man's voice rumbled an octave lower than Art's own baritone.

"Yes. You're Iznar?"

The man ignored him, turning his gaze on Lorn. "Nothing was said of another."

"He's with me," Art said. "Are you Iznar?"

The man stared at Lorn for a long moment, before turning to face Art again. “My name is not important. Follow me.”

He didn’t lead them across the street. Instead they went back a block into the industrial section, and slipped through a door that slid open at the touch of Iznar’s palm to its slick green surface. Stairs beyond led down to a dank tunnel, lined with sweating black pipes and thick blue cables, which doubled back the way they had come. After a hundred metres or so they reached another flight of stairs and climbed it to another green door that likewise slid open when Iznar touched it.

They emerged into an alley between two bars, music in conflicting rhythms pulsating from either side, the only illumination the light that spilled from the busy main street. The light and music alike faded as they moved deeper down that alley and others, each, it seemed, darker, danker, and more garbage-strewn than the previous. Now the only light came from the faint stars shining down into the canyons between the windowless buildings. Something squished beneath Art’s boot and released a nauseating stench of decay; Art swore under his breath. Their guide ignored him, walking steadily ahead, and Art, after trying to scrape his boot clean on the pavement, had to trot to catch up to him and Lorn.

Their path turned several times, until Art had lost all sense of direction. He began to wonder if a knife between the ribs would end this strange journey for both him and Lorn. Javik had sent him here—but how did he know he could trust Javik? A man whose brain interfaced directly with a planetary ’Net—who knew what he might do, and for what reasons? Yet Art had no choice but to keep going. He could never find his way back through the wandering streets. And where would he and Lorn go even if he could?

Finally they turned down a short, dead-end side-alley, lit by a dim blue bulb over a formidable-looking door of red-painted iron. Art’s guide ran his fingers over the door in a complex pattern, and it slid silently aside. The masked man stepped into darkness, then turned and gestured for Art and Lorn to follow. Lorn stepped in without hesitation. Heart in his throat, Art followed.

The door immediately closed behind them, plunging them into complete blackness for an instant before a second door slid opened in front of them, releasing a flood of light. Art blinked at a short corridor that gleamed ice-white under broad glowstrips. At the end of the hallway a red light burned over a blank white door. The man in the mask held up his hand. "Wait," he rumbled.

Art waited. After several minutes that did creditable impressions of hours, the red light went out. Art's guide touched the door; it slid open, and he ducked into the dimly lit room beyond, then stepped aside for Art to follow.

Despite the substantially different technology, Art recognized a vid studio when he saw it. A woman, her face turned away from them, rose from behind a desk Art remembered from his brief look at the PFN, framed by the logo of the hawk breaking its chains. Automated cameras tracked her with faint whirrings as she tugged at her black hair. "Javik's gift has arrived, Iznar," Art's guide announced. "Along with one other."

Art glanced at him in surprise. So it was the *woman* he had been sent to see!

The dark wig came off, revealing short red hair; the woman turned—and Art's startled eyes met the cool green gaze of SSIN Commander Avara Torrance al Morali.

Chapter Eleven

Art opened his mouth, but nothing came out. Commander Morali looked past him at his escort. "You'd better go, Parna." He hesitated. "I'll be fine," she insisted, and finally the big man shrugged and left.

At last Art found his voice. "Iznar, I presume?"

"That's what some people call me. But you can call me Avara." Her eyes flicked to Lorn, and she frowned. "I didn't expect you to be accompanied. Especially not by a child."

"I'm not a child," Lorn said.

Avara grunted, a sound halfway between amusement and disgust. She touched a control beneath the desk, and the room lights came up. For the first time, Art saw another door off to his right. Avara crossed to it. "In here."

Bemused, he trailed her, Lorn at his heels, into a comfortable apartment with almost as many plants in the living room as in Arklund's underground hideaway. The similarity did nothing to put him at ease. Lorn, however, blinked around at the greenery in obvious surprise. "Wow," he said. "It's almost like the forest."

"That's the idea," said Avara. She led them through an archway into a kitchen, where she motioned for them to sit down at a table with a transparent top on chairs with transparent bottoms. "Hungry?"

"Starved," Lorn said. Art, suddenly aware just how long it had been since dinner the day before, just nodded.

Avara took three silvery packets from a cabinet and pulled tabs from them, then set them aside. As they began to swell and steam she pulled a bottle of something golden and glittering from the refrigerator and poured a glass for each of them. Lorn took his and gulped it eagerly. Art tasted his cautiously, then followed suit. Sweet, tart and fizzy, it sparkled in his mouth and quenched the thirst he hadn't even been aware he had.

Avara set the food packets in front of them. Art peeled back the cover of his and discovered a stew of vegetables and meat, savory vapor rising from it.

"Oops, silverware," Avara said, and quickly retrieved spoons for them all.

Despite his hunger, Art ate the stew slowly, trying to make sense of where he was…and who had welcomed them. But he couldn't. He spooned up the last of the thick, spicy gravy, drank the final two swallows of juice, sighed, and finally said, "All right, I give up. What are *you* doing here?"

Lorn paused, his spoon halfway to his mouth, and glanced at Avara, who had only picked at her food. She cocked an eyebrow at Art. "Isn't it obvious?"

"Not to me! Javik said he would put me in contact with the Peregrine FreeNet…"

"This is the central studio of the PFN."

"And you're Iznar."

"I already answered that question." Avara finished her bite of stew and pointed her spoon at him. "Now it's your turn. What are *you* doing here? Do you know that half the SSIN is looking for you? Not to mention, if my sources are correct—and they almost always are—Arklund's Skyguards, his elite army-within-an-army. How did you turn up on Javik's doorstep?" She turned frowning eyes on Lorn. "And who is *he*?"

"I'm Lorn Kymbal," the youth said before Art could say anything at all. "My father and I rescued Art from a crashed plane in the desert. And when the Skywatchers came after him my father killed two of them." He sounded proud. "Art is trying to save the planet and the *Mayflower II*, and I've come along to help him."

Avara had stiffened when Lorn said his name. "Kymbal? Is your father Marc Kymbal? Mother Melissa?"

"Yes."

"No shit." Avara seemed to have forgotten all about Art. "It was wrong what happened to him. That was one reason I decided to start the FPN. Somebody had to try to tell the truth when things like that happened."

"You knew my father?" Lorn said eagerly. "When he was an officer?"

"I knew him," Avara said.

"I was only little," Lorn said. "I don't remember much. Just Mom and Dad…scared. Mom crying. I hated it. Everything was better after we moved into the woods."

"I wish I could have moved to the woods, too. Thought about it. But then I realized I could still do something here." She jerked her head back in the direction of the studio. "And so I have."

"Dad did what he had to do," Lorn said defensively.

"I'm not blaming him," Avara said. "He had you and your Mom to look after. I don't have anyone."

Sounds like me, Art thought.

Avara looked back at him. "So back to my original question. What are you doing here?"

"I thought you knew everything," Art said.

Avara snorted. "I wish. I have extensive contacts inside and outside the government. But there are, as Javik is fond of saying, 'anomalies.' Your presence here is one of them. Why did Javik send you to me?"

Art studied her. "I'll explain why I'm here if you'll tell me something. You obviously run the PFN. You know about the *Mayflower II*, what it might do and what the government might do to it. Why haven't you reported *that*?"

Avara ran one finger up and down the misty outside of her bottle. "A question I've asked myself every day since we brought you back," she said slowly. "I keep getting the same answer—not a very satisfactory one, but all I can come up with. *I don't know what will happen.*"

"What?"

She leaned forward and spoke intensely. "Normally I'd say

tell the truth and let the shit land where it lands. But this is *not* a normal situation. It's not just another story about corruption in the awarding of government sewer contracts or a cabinet minister diddling little boys. I keep running scenarios through my head, and I don't like any of them." She stabbed a finger at him. "Try this one, for instance. I go on the air, tell the truth. The people hear there is a giant spaceship from ancient Earth bearing down on them, carrying matter-antimatter missiles, and that the government is threatening to destroy it. What do the people say? 'Hooray, go to it, save us from the barbarians.'"

"They wouldn't—"

"Wouldn't they? Are you *sure* about that? You were met on Shaymar Boulevard. Do you think *those* people care what happens to your ship? They don't care about anything except their fun. And there are more like them than you might realize."

Like too many of the Shipborn, Art thought.

Avara sat back again. "Or what about *this*? I go public, Arklund hears me, realizes he doesn't have time to look for you any longer, and launches his jihad. The government doesn't want to fight a war on two fronts; it wipes out the *Mayflower II* just so it can concentrate on staying alive."

That one Art *had* thought of.

"And then there's the other charming possibility—telling the story results in such a public outcry the government doesn't dare attack your ship for fear of sparking a massive anti-government uprising…which just means your Captain launches his missiles at a sitting target and we all get to find out what it feels like to be disassociated atoms."

Art winced. He remembered the old phrase that Shadow had quoted to him: *The public has a right to know.* That's what he had told Marc and Melissa, too. But did it? Did it really? What if telling the public the truth could only make things worse—trigger the very tragedy he wanted so desperately to forestall? Again he faced the central dilemma of his fledgling determination to act, to make things happen—what if his actions were *wrong*?

"That's what you had in mind, wasn't it?" Avara said, watching him. "To get to the control centre of the PFN and tell the entire world about the *Mayflower II*, so we wouldn't attack it?"

He nodded mutely.

"Well, forget it. I won't upload that story—not now, with Arklund threatening civil war and the government torn between welcoming your ship and destroying it. Everything is too complicated; a shove like that could bring it all crashing down."

"But that's going to happen anyway!" Art cried, frustrated.

Avara, draining her bottle, stopped with it in her mouth, glaring at him over it, then swallowed and set the bottle carefully on the table. "What?"

Lorn watched wide-eyed, gaze slipping from one to the other as though he were watching a tennis match.

"You know it's true! Broadcasting the story might cause trouble—but *not* broadcasting means disaster for *sure*. Arklund launches his civil war and your government destroys my people. The *Mayflower II* gets its missiles away first and Peregrine is wiped out. Or maybe missiles and beams fly at the same time and nobody survives. Even if revealing the truth has the results you say, we're no worse off."

"But we're no better off, either." Avara was beginning to sound angry. "And those are just maybes. We don't need another variable in the equation." She shook her head. "I won't broadcast the story. In fact, if I'm smart, I'll arrest you and take you back to Security Central."

"In which case I tell them who's behind the PFN," Art snarled. "I'm not going back there. With or without you, I'm going to get this story out."

"How?" Avara said scornfully. "Even if you could get past me—and believe me, you don't want to try that—you couldn't operate my equipment. There are twenty-seven layers of ever-changing encryption and misdirection between the camera in the studio and the backdoor through which the data enters Peregrinet. You don't know anything about any of it. And your technical knowledge—if you even have any—is centuries out of date."

Then why does it seem so familiar? Art suddenly thought. He hadn't really grasped just how ancient he and his shipmates seemed to the people of Peregrine. He wouldn't have expected someone from the 18th century to be able to grasp anything about the *Mayflower II. Technology has changed—the ships and the energy guns show that—but why hasn't it changed more?*

Technological advances must have stagnated somewhere along the line. I wonder why?

But that was a question for another time. "Then I'm leaving," he said. "I'll find some other way." He spun on his heel, took one step, saw movement out of the corner of his eye, and crashed to the kitchen floor. Avara's hand was on the back of his neck, pushing his cheek against the floor, her knee planted in the small of his back. "I could kill you right now," she said softly in his ear.

"Avara, no!" Lorn cried. Avara ignored him.

"And I *will* kill you to protect this planet and my secrets. The PFN is too important to let you bring it crashing down. As far as you're concerned, that door is farther away than the *Mayflower II.*"

The *Mayflower II.* Art's rage drained away as he remembered his promise to Marc Kymbal. "Then *you* tell your people!" he choked out. "Just help me tell the Passengers!"

Avara's hand tensed on his neck, and he gasped. "What?"

"To stop…I have to…"

Suddenly her weight lifted. He gulped air, then rolled over and started to sit up, but Avara's booted foot on his chest held him down. "Say that again."

"Help me tell the Passengers…at the same time as you announce it on the planet! Telling just one side or the other—you're right, that's no good. But if we tell *all* the people, on both sides, maybe, just maybe, they'll stop their leaders from doing something irrevocable." He grasped for the metaphor she'd used earlier. "No new variables—keep the equation balanced." *And keep my promise—a promise I almost forgot. I'm sorry, Marc.*

"Too dangerous," Avara said, but she said it thoughtfully. "It could push both sides into doing something rash, instead of just one. No."

"You admitted it's dangerous to not do anything, either! At least this way there's a chance." He knew what he was about to say could make her very angry and him very dead, but suddenly, he didn't care. "You're scared!" he spat out, aiming the bitter words as much at himself as at her. "You're afraid of failing, so you won't even try! Or maybe you've just been playing, *amusing* yourself with all this Free Peregrine shit, having a good laugh at the people who take it seriously. You don't have the guts to use it for anything that really matters. You're…going…" The boot on his chest pressed down so hard it forced the air out of his lungs and he stared at Avara's white, furious face through a darkening tunnel.

Then suddenly Lorn was on her, pulling at her arms. She threw him off, releasing the pressure on Art's chest in the process. Lorn crashed against the counter and slid to the floor with a grunt, holding his side. Avara took a step toward the youth, hands raised, and then suddenly stopped. "Oh!" she gasped, the sound incongruously soft and vulnerable. "Lorn, I'm so sorry." She knelt beside him. "Are you all right?"

"Um," he said. "Ouch. I think so."

Art lay where he was, happy just to be breathing. Avara turned and slid down the counter until she sat on the floor next to Lorn. She looked at her hands, clenched them into fists, then carefully relaxed them and placed them palm-down on the floor. "My father always told me," she said, in little more than a whisper, "to think twice before acting if someone said something about me that made me really, really angry…because sometimes the things that make us angriest are the things that are true." She met Art's gaze, face pale. "You're right. You're absolutely right. I was ready to kill you for saying it, that's how right you were. I'm sorry." She glanced at Lorn. "To both of you. Thank you for pulling me away from him."

"You're welcome," Lorn said. "Also, ow."

Art finally felt like he had enough air to sit up. "I just told you what I've been telling myself," he said hoarsely. "I think it's starting to work on me. I hoped it would work on you."

She nodded. "Almost too well. So…we'll do it your way. You tell the Passengers, I tell Peregrine." She smiled a little. "Now there's just one thing to figure out."

Art rubbed the back of his neck. "Yeah. How?"

"I've got an idea," Avara said. "You may not like it. But first—" she turned to Lorn. "Take off your shirt. Let's see what I did to you."

Lorn, not without some difficulty, pulled off his shirt. With gentle fingers, Avara examined the growing bruise on his flank where she had thrown him against the counter. Lorn winced a little as she touched the spot. "Well," she said, "I don't think you cracked any ribs or that would have hurt a lot more. Just a bruise. You'll be fine."

"I want to know how to do that," Lorn said as he pulled his shirt back on. "How do you move so fast?"

"Your father could teach you," Avara said. "I'm surprised he hasn't. And if he won't, I will…if we all survive the next few days."

Avara led the way back into the living room, sitting on the couch with Art while Lorn settled, yawning hugely, into the big black armchair in the corner. The myriad blossoming plants scented the air with sweet perfume that unfortunately made Art think of the sucra tanker. "Here's one problem," Avara said. "Just putting it out through the PFN isn't enough. We want more exposure than that."

"But the PFN is the source people trust most…isn't it?"

"Oh, we'll use it to introduce what we have to say…but then I think it's time for the nuclear option."

Art blinked. "What…?"

Avara smiled briefly. "Not literally. That's what your ship is threatening." The smile faded. "I mean figuratively. I think we should flood Peregrinet. Every data channel, everywhere. The soothemusic in the offices. The weathercast. The scenery channel. All blasting the same message: the *Mayflower II* is in our system and the government is planning to attack it."

Art stared at her. "How can you possibly do *that*?"

"I'm an intelligence officer, remember? I've spent years collecting means of access to the government data channels."

"Then why haven't you used it before?"

"Because I can only do it once," Avara said. "There's no way I can do it without revealing who I really am. And revealing all the security weaknesses we've been exploiting. Once done, the PFN is finished—*I'm* finished. So this message you think I should tell the world will be my last." She glanced upward, and Art knew she was thinking of the missiles on the starship. "One way or another."

"Why have you done all this? It can't just be because of what happened to Lorn's father." Art glanced at the boy, who had fallen asleep curled in the chair. He looked terribly young. "Someone in your position, risking so much just to tell stories the government doesn't want told…why?"

In his mind he compared what she had done to what he had *not* done. It was not a comfortable comparison. He kept running into people who had risked their careers or even their lives to do what they felt was right—Shadow, Marc Kymbal, and now Avara—whereas he had always given up, always taken the easy way out, always gone with the flow. Now that he was trying to change that, he wanted to understand what had motivated them.

"It *was* just because of what happened to Lorn's father…and countless others like him," Avara said. "'Someone in my position' sees exactly how the government is abusing its power." She shook her head. "There's no accountability," she said. "Positions in the PPP are filled by appointment. Often as not, they go to the children of retiring members: it's practically medieval. The people in power want to stay in power, and they do everything they can to consolidate that power. The ordinary people get by the best they can, and pray the government takes no notice of them.

A few brave ones move to the frontier, like Kymbal. Government feeds on government. Taxes only go up, they never go down. Nobody innovates…there's no incentive to. You come from four hundred years in my past, and you still recognize the technology. You know why?"

Art shook his head.

"Because the one thing our government learned from Earth was that if you control technology, you control society. Only government-approved technology may be used: technology that, in the eyes of the government, cannot in any way threaten government control. And the process for getting government approval for any new technology is so convoluted, so rife with corruption, that nobody bothers coming up with anything new." She stabbed a finger at the door to the studio. "Half the stuff in there is unlicensed tech from the black market. But a black market is no substitute for a free market. And on Peregrine, nothing is free. The Parliament of Protectors giveth and the Parliament of Protectors taketh away…then giveth to themselves and their cronies. Blessed be the name of the Parliament of Protectors. And the result? A society that's stagnating. A society that's shrinking. A society that's dying…and a lot of people are dying with it. Troublemakers arrested on trumped-up charges—and on our world, everyone is guilty of something if you dig long enough through decades of corruption-encrusted laws—some of them never seen again. Black prisons that don't officially exist but everyone *knows* exist. And then the people like you saw out on Shaymar Avenue, partying their lives away until they end up dead in some alley, raped, robbed or rotted out from within by the latest concoction of the street chemists…no lack of innovation *there*." The rush of words ended. Avara shook her head. "That… all of that, and so much more…is why I started the PFN. Trying to wake people up. Trying to get people to push back against the government. And you know what?"

"It hasn't worked?" Art said softly, thinking as he did so that the Crew-and-Council-controlled world of the *Mayflower II* and the Parliament of Protectors-controlled world of Peregrine sounded depressingly similar. *The operative world is control*, he thought. *Governments are all about control. Unless you have some way to change the people in power periodically, they're going to do everything they can to exert more and more control to ensure they never lose power.*

And if you can't take power away from them peacefully, then...

"Damn right it hasn't worked," Avara snarled, derailing his train of thought. "The PFN is just another entertainment option. The people are so stifled by the thick wet blanket of government control over every aspect of their lives that they don't even *think* of pushing back."

"Except for the Skywatchers," Art pointed out. "Arklund seems to be all about pushing back."

Avara snorted. "Except for the Skywatchers. Whose idea of the perfect world will be one where the government has even *more* control, only this time with more focus on controlling public and personal morality and *way* more executions. *Public* ones for our moral instruction."

"Maybe the arrival of the *Mayflower II* will be the catalyst the planet needs for real change," Art said.

"I've pretty much given up on real change," Avara said. "I'll settle for keeping millions of people from being turned into expanding clouds of plasma." She shook her head. "So. We know what I'm going to do. What are *you* going to do aboard *Mayflower II*?"

"First I have to get there. A ship, like before—"

"A ship will never manage that rendezvous again. Last time they weren't expecting us. Now they will be. And they have other, smaller missiles besides the planet-busters—pretty short-range, but just fine for blowing away a juicy target like a nearby spaceship with a matching trajectory and velocity. And there are only a couple of those deep-space ships like we brought you back on. The majority of the fleet is limited to the inner reaches of the system. Merlin is right on the extreme end of their range."

"Can you commandeer one of those deep-space ships?|"

"No, I can't," Avara said flatly. "They require a specialized crew. I can't fly one myself and I can't assemble a crew without giving myself away."

"Then how—"

"I *can* commandeer one of the shorter-range ships. A scout-ship. And fly it myself. But we can't approach the *Mayflower II* until it's in orbit around Merlin. And even then we can't get in close."

Art didn't like where the conversation was going. "How close *could* we get?"

"Maybe a hundred kilometres. They might not even know we're there, with our stealth technology. Even if they detect us, it's too far for a successful missile attack. We'd just outrun it."

Art remembered the stark terror of crossing just a few hundred metres of space when Avara first kidnapped him, and swallowed before he said, "Then I'll have to cross it on my own—in a suit. I'll be too small and slow-moving for the ship to notice."

Avara gave him a hard look. "You've never maneuvered in space. And if you miss you won't get a second chance."

"I'm relying on whoever takes me up there to do the maneuvering," said Art steadily. "With a perfect velocity match—all I'll have to do is float."

Avara grinned suddenly, surprisingly. "I'll be your pilot," she said. "The velocities will match. And I can program a maneuvering unit to make any small corrections that might be needed." The grin faded. "So. You're on board the ship. Then what?"

"I have to contact the Crawlspacers."

"And how do you plan to do that?"

Art held up his right arm. "They injected me with a tracker of some kind. As far as I know, it's still working. If we could somehow use it to shout out to them that I'm back on board…"

Avara's eyes narrowed. "A tracker, huh? Hold on a second."

She went into the studio, returned a moment later with a small flat rectangular device, glossy black, with a small, glowing screen on one side. "SSIN issue, this," she said. "I use it all the time to scan for listening devices. It should tell me…" She passed it over his arm, glanced at the readout. "It's off," she said. "Probably a power-saving feature. Once it was out of range, it went to sleep." She studied the readout. "Primitive by SSIN standards," she said briefly. "Tracking technology is something the government heartily approves of. We can do better."

She disappeared back into the studio. Lorn mumbled something in his sleep. Art glanced at him as Avara came back in. She carried something that looked a little bit like the device Philip had used to inject him with the tracker back in Hab Three, only smaller and blacker. "Arm," she said. He held it out. There was a spray of numbing cold, then a feeling like he'd been pinched. He drew back his arm and stared at a small red spot.

"That," said Avara, putting aside the injector, "will send out a signal at exactly the same frequency as their tracker, but with *way* more power. If they're listening, it'll knock them back on their heels. Just like the one they put into you, it will let them hear you. Unlike theirs, it will also let *you* hear *them*."

Art blinked. "What? How?"

"Nanobots," Avara said. "They're setting up shop in your ear canal right about now. If they transmit back to you on the same frequency as they're listening, you'll hear them inside your head."

Art thought about tiny robots building a receiver inside his head, and then decided he wouldn't think about it ever again if he could help it.

"So," said Avara. "Then what happens?"

"Well, here's how I see it," Art said. "First…"

An hour later they had the rough details of their joint plans worked out. Sitting side by side on the couch, heads almost touching as they bent over the low table, Lorn snoring softly in the corner, they drafted the messages Avara would broadcast to the Peregrine people and Art to the Passengers. "I don't like that phrase there…" Avara murmured, pointing. "Maybe if we softened it…"

Art yawned. "You could be right."

Avara looked up at him, then past him at a chronometer on the wall. "0440," she said ruefully. "I have to be on duty in two hours." She glanced at Lorn. "I'm glad one of us is getting some sleep." Her eyes turned back to Art. "You look as exhausted as I feel."

"I'm all right. I slept in the sucra truck." He yawned again and laughed. "Okay, maybe I'm a *little* tired," he admitted.

Avara looked down at the pad of paper on which they'd been working. "Maybe it will work the way it is."

Art leaned his head in his hands and blinked at the two messages. "Right now I don't have any critical faculties left. Let's leave them. I'll give them a fresh look after I've had some sleep." He rubbed his eyes and tossed his pen at the table.

It bounced off the edge of the pad and fell on the floor. He and Avara both reached for it at once. Their hands touched. They looked up at each other at the same moment, and Art suddenly found his lips only inches from Avara's.

Without even thinking about it, he kissed her, and after a moment's hesitation she returned the kiss, lighting a fire in Art's head that raced through his body. Slowly the kiss faded and they pulled apart, and Art blinked, licking his lips, which tasted sweet. "Unnnh," he said. "I'm sorry, I didn't—"

"Don't be sorry," Avara said softly, touching his lips with her finger. She leaned forward and kissed him again, and his hands came up of their own volition and pulled her to him.

But after another timeless instant, she pushed away. "I'm the one who's sorry," she said huskily. "I have to go, or I'll be late for duty." She glanced into the corner again. "And besides…"

Art swallowed, hard. "Right," he said, but somehow couldn't bring himself to let her go until she freed herself and stood. "The bedroom is through there," she said, pointing to another door. "Make yourself comfortable. I'll be back in about ten hours and tell you exactly where the *Mayflower II* is, and how much time we have." She hesitated, said, "Good-bye," rather abruptly, and left.

Art sat very still on the couch for a long time, his mind feeling a bit like warm mush. Sleep suddenly seemed much further away than it had a few minutes ago. How had *that* happened? Two hours ago she had been ready to kill him. Now…

And it had been…different. Different than he had felt with Treena or other girls. *Danger adding spice?* he wondered. *Or have I always secretly wanted a woman who could break my arm?*

Finally he shook his head, got up and went to Lorn. "Lorn," he said.

The boy stirred. "Dad…?" he murmured, then opened sleepy eyes and blinked at Art. "Oh," he said.

"You should go to bed properly," Art said. "I'll take the couch if you want the bed."

"Couch is fine with me," Lorn mumbled. He got up from the chair, wincing a little, and stumbled over to the couch. Stretching out on it, he fell asleep again at once, lying on his stomach, one hand dangling down onto the floor. Smiling a little, Art found a blanket in a closet in the hall between the living room and the bedroom and spread it over the boy, then returned to the bedroom, furnished in the same stark black-and-white, silver-and-crystal fashion of the rest of the apartment. He stripped and went into the bathroom, where a hot shower brought back his drowsiness. Sleep claimed him quickly once he slid between the smooth black sheets.

He slept until he felt someone shaking his arm, and muzzily rolled over. "What—?"

Avara stood over him, her green eyes narrowed, tension in every line of her body. "Wake up! We're out of time."

Art sat up groggily. "Were you gone ten hours?"

"Just four. I checked the *Mayflower II's* status first thing. It's going into orbit around Merlin *now*. I've already reserved a scoutship. We take off in less than an hour. Now will you *get up*!"

Beginning to feel some of her haste, he threw aside the covers and reached for his clothes. Her eyes barely flicked over his nude body as he stood. He felt absurdly disappointed about that. "But we haven't had time to finalize the messages—"

"They'll have to do. I've already got bots cracking the security to pull vid of the *Mayflower II*. I can record the voice-over on the ship on my way back to Peregrine. When I get the signal you've reached the ship and are going in, I play my story. It's up to you to get yours out to your ship as soon as you can. Can't you dress faster?"

Art pulled on his second boot and stood. "Done."

"About time. Let's *go*!"

Art followed her out. Lorn was waiting by the front door of the apartment. Art pulled up short. "He's not coming!"

"Yes, I am."

"Yes, he is."

The two spoke together. Lorn laughed.

"He can't stay here," Avara said. "It's entirely possible I'm not as smart as I think I am and alarms are going to start going off all over the place as my bots sink their tendrils into the 'Net. If that happens, the SSIN will be breaking through the door ten minutes later. Even if they don't shoot Lorn on sight, they'll ID him and haul his parents in. The only safe place for him is with us."

"On a spaceship flying toward another spaceship that might just blow us out of space?" Art said. "You call that safe?"

"Nowhere is safe," Avara said. "But that's as safe as any. Now come *on*." She slapped the door; it slid open, and the three of them stepped out into bright morning sunshine. Nothing moved on the street except for an old man sleeping in the doorway of a boarded-up brick building across the way.

"Nice neighbourhood," Art said.

"Nice neighbourhoods have lots of guards, prying eyes, and cameras," Avara said tersely. Her eyes were on the corner to their right; a six-wheeled vehicle, a windowless box on wheels painted a non-descript gray, rolled around the corner, swept silently up to them, and whooshed to a stop. A door slid open.

They climbed into an interior plushly upholstered and

carpeted in blue. To empty air, Avara said, "Spaceport," and the car accelerated smoothly.

"How long?" Art said.

"Ten minutes. This car has SSIN clearance, so other vehicles are making way for us. Another five to the hangar, five to taxi to launch position, ten for preflight checkout, and we're off."

Half an hour, Art thought, his chest constricting. "And then how long until we rendezvous?"

"The way I plan to drive the engines, about four hours."

"Four hours?" Art stared at her. "To a gas giant how many million kilometres away?"

"We may not be able to build a star-drive," Avara said, "but we still know a *few* things about getting around in space in a hurry."

Art looked at her. Her fingers drummed on the armrest between the seats and she was chewing on one corner of her bottom lip. "There's more wrong than just the *Mayflower II* coming into orbit around Merlin, isn't there?"

She nodded reluctantly. "Your friend Arklund knows it's there, too. He's starting his jihad. We're getting reports of mass desertions at military bases, missing equipment, computer systems going off-line. No attacks yet, but it's building. The government knows what's coming." She looked down. "They've decided they can't fight revolution here with that floating missile base in the system," she said without meeting his eyes. "They've ordered the attack fleet prepped and the pilots alerted. It can't be done instantly, but it won't take all that long, either. Once they launch, they're only four or five hours from *Mayflower II*...and then, if nothing has changed, your starship dies."

Art felt cold. "And if the *Mayflower II* realizes what's happening..."

"Then *Peregrine* dies."

Chapter Twelve

"Approaching destination," the car said.

"Windows," Avara said, and portions of the blank gray walls suddenly turned transparent. Looking out, Art saw they were racing toward a gate in a tall wire-mesh fence surrounding the spaceport. It swung aside at the last possible instant. Low, windowless buildings bristling with antennae swept by, giving way to the vast landing field. The car decelerated sharply and stopped beside a sleek, black delta-winged ship, miniscule compared to the one that had brought him to Peregrine. The air around it trembled to a low rumble. "Wow," Lorn said, staring out at it. "We're going on that?"

"We are," Avara said. "Unless someone has figured out what I'm up to and puts a stop to it."

Art didn't like the sound of that.

The car doors slid open. "Wait random," Avara told the vehicle, then climbed down, Art and Lorn behind her. As soon as they were out the doors closed and the car turned and sped back toward the gate. "It will drive randomly around the city until I signal it to pick me up when I land," Avara explained. "Or until someone stops it."

Then she turned toward the ship and placed her palm on the hull. A hatch opened and a spindly ladder extruded. "I can't believe I'm really going into space," Lorn said. He hurried forward, started up the ladder. "I—"

There was a flash and smoke puffed from Lorn's back. He fell backward without a sound, Art barely fast enough to catch him. A sharp smell of scorched cloth and burnt meat assaulted his nostrils.

"Shit!" Avara swore. "Down!"

She pushed Art and Lorn flat to the ground. Another flash of light, and an angry red spot appeared on the flank of the spacecraft. Avara was already rolling over onto her back, sidearm drawn, her eyes on a small square display on its top. It flashed green. "Got you," she snarled, and pulled the trigger. The weapon made a deep coughing noise and something small and silver shrieked away so fast Art barely registered it. A second later an explosion shook the landing field, black smoke and red flame bursting from the other side of a stack of crates a hundred metres away.

"Now! Inside!" Avara cried. "Go! I'll bring Lorn!"

Heart pounding, Art scrambled up the ladder and almost threw himself through the hatch. Avara followed, Lorn slung in a dead-man's carry—maybe literally, Art thought sickly. As he watched her put one determined foot after another on the rungs with the boy dangling from her shoulders, he revised his estimate of her strength upward and was doubly glad she'd decided not to break his neck the night before.

No more shots were fired in their direction and Art helped her bundle Lorn's body into the scoutship. She rolled over and slapped a panel beside the hatch, which locked and sealed with an audible hiss. Art sat on the floor of the short corridor into which they'd emerged, breathing harder than Avara even though she'd been the one carrying Lorn. She was already leaning over the boy, pulling off his shirt. "Is he dead?" Art gasped. He swallowed as he saw the round, black hole in the boy's skin, just to the left of his spine in the small of his back.

"No," Avara said shortly. She scrambled to her feet, slapped a panel to open a compartment in the wall of the corridor, pulled out what looked more like a hot-water bottle to Art than anything else, and placed the "bottle" on the wound. "Automedic," she said. "Now help me get him into a seat. We've got to get spaceborn."

Together they hauled the unconscious boy upright, one arm

over each of their shoulders, and dragged him along the corridor to another hatch which opened at their approach. As he helped Avara pull Lorn into the compartment beyond Art glanced down at the other end of the corridor. Big red letters on the closed hatch there proclaimed ENGINE COMPARTMENT. TRAINED PERSONNEL ONLY. RADIATION HAZARD.

The rumbling vibration, pronounced now, gave Art a funny feeling in the pit of his stomach. He wiped his palms on the front of his shirt.

"Help me!" Avara snapped, and Art turned his attention back to the task at hand, helping her settle the half-naked boy into the left-rearmost of the six seats in the passenger compartment and strap him in, the automedic still clinging to the small of his back. "We'll get him a blanket later," she said. "Now strap in yourself."

Avara sat in the pilot's seat, and Art clambered into the co-pilot's position, surrounded by glowing controls in a riot of colour he was very careful not to touch. "As soon as we're up I'll check you out on the spacesuit," Avara said. "But for now, just hang on." She put a tiny silver plug in one ear and touched a switch. "Control, this is SSIN Scoutcraft XRCI2, exercising emergency clearance authority. Acknowledge."

She paused, waiting, drumming her fingers on the arm of her seat, her eyes flicking out the cockpit window at the spaceport.

"That explosion is the reason I need to get off the ground immediately," she snarled suddenly. "This is an emergency. Why the hell do you think I'm demanding immediate clearance?"

Her eyes returned to the window. Lights flashed in the distance. More black smoke rose. An instant later, the spacecraft shook. Avara suddenly snatched the silver plug from her ear, wincing, and even from where he sat Art could hear the high-pitched squeal emanating from it. "I don't think they're in a position to issue clearance anymore," she said.

"Skywatchers?" Art said.

"Count on it," Avara replied. "So screw clearance. We're going."

"What if there's another aircraft in our—"

"Then this will be a very short flight." She swept her hands across the console. "To hell with slow and easy," she said, as the black screen lit with a bewildering series of coloured shapes that meant nothing to Art. "Hold on." She touched a bright blue diamond. The ship reared back on its haunches, further and further, until they were pointing straight up and all he could see through the cockpit windscreen was fluffy white clouds drifting across a bright blue sky. And then…

"Launching," Avara said, and touched a big green circle.

For a horrifying instant Art was convinced the ship had exploded. The rumble of the engines turned to a deafening, heart-stopping howl. At the same instant he was slammed deep into his seat so hard the air rushed out of his lungs. The fluffy white clouds swelled, engulfed them in an instant of fog, and then vanished. Art fought against the crushing force to draw breath, but despite his best efforts, his vision began to gray around the edges. He watched, as though through a tunnel, the high blue sky deepening to cerulean, to indigo, and finally, almost abruptly, to black, but the acceleration continued, minute after minute, while Avara watched numbers flickering across a trio of vidscreens in front of her, and he drew painful, too-small breath after painful, too-small breath.

Then the acceleration halved, quartered, ended. Straps and buckles creaked as Art and Avara's bodies floated off the seats. Art swallowed, and his voice sounded strange in his noise-numbed ears as he said, "Quite a ride."

"You ain't seen nothing yet," Avara said, and Art blinked at the ancient turn of phrase. "Getting off the planet still takes brute force. But out here we can do better…good thing or we'd never get to the *Mayflower II* in time." She shook her head. "And we may not even so." She leaned forward. "Next challenge. If anyone has guessed what I'm up to, they may have severed my contact with the space navigation satellites…" A star on the console turned from red to yellow, then to green, and Avara grinned in obvious relief. "Not yet!" She rummaged in the breast pocket of her uniform and pulled out a small gold cube. She slipped it into a receptacle on the console, touched a red square. It turned to yellow with a green dot at its centre. "Course laid in and accepted," she said. "We're in business." She paused. "Well, assuming the engines don't blow up," she added thoughtfully. "Since I'm about to overdrive them something fierce…"

Art groaned. "Have you ever heard the expression 'too much information'?"

Avara gave him a toothy grin. "But you and I are all about sharing information, sweetie," she said. "The public has a right to know!" And then she touched a yellow square. It turned green.

Art suddenly sank back into his seat again, but only at what felt like something close to his usual weight. He remembered the artificial gravity on the larger ship that had kidnapped him from the *Mayflower II*. *Must be a side benefit of this "Umstattd Drive" technology I keep hearing about*, he thought. *If you can get around your solar system in a few hours, why* shouldn't *you be able to do something about inertia?* Then he frowned. The ship…hummed, at a frequency that settled into his bones and made them itch in a way he couldn't scratch. He wriggled his shoulders. "What the hell?"

"Side effect of overdriving the engines," Avara said. "I hear it can do nasty things to your insides if it goes on too long. But it shouldn't cause any lasting damage in the time we have to put up with it."

"Shouldn't?" Art sighed. Then his frown deepened. "But what will it do to Lorn…?"

"Let's find out," Avara said. She reached over to her left and pulled a secondary display screen on a jointed arm in front of her. She touched it, and it lit with what even Art could tell were vital signs. "He's stable for the moment," she said. "No vital organs hit. But he's bleeding internally and in shock. He won't stay stable forever. And you're right, the overdrive vibration isn't helping." Her face turned grave. "The automedic can keep him going for a few hours. But not indefinitely. He needs proper medical care."

Art felt cold. "Why is he bleeding? Wouldn't the beam have cauterized—"

"It did, partially," Avara said. "But not completely." She stared at the screen, then shoved it away almost angrily. "Dammit," she snarled. "And I thought he'd be *safer* with us."

"You can take him back to Peregrine, get him into a hospital—"

"*And* get arrested, *and* not get the message out," Avara said. "That's assuming I can even get this ship down and get off of it alive."

"But…" Art's voice trailed off. He glanced back at the boy, whose skin was pale and beaded with sweat. "We can't just let him die."

Avara looked out the cockpit at the deep black of space and the distant, uncaring stars. There was no sign of Peregrine, presumably dwindling away behind them, and Merlin still lay hours ahead. "I can only think of one way to save him," she said slowly. She turned back to Art. "He's going to have to go with you. To *Mayflower II*."

"What?" Art stared at her. "How does that help? Even if I get on board, I'll be on the run. I can't get him to a hospital—"

"Your Crawlspacer friends must have medical facilities."

"I don't know—"

"It's his only chance," Avara snarled, eyes suddenly blazing. "Do you want him to die? Will you tell Marc and Melissa and Lisa if he does?"

Art opened his mouth; closed it again. "No," he said. "No, I don't want him to die." *It's my fault he's even here*, he thought sickly. *I should never have stayed so long with the Kymbals. Should have guessed what Lorn was thinking…it's not* that *long since I was a teenager.* He thought of a smashed maintenance robot and how that one rash action had in some ways brought him directly to this moment. *I survived my foolishness. Lorn deserves to survive his.*

"All right," he said at last. "But…how?"

Avara reached for her seatbelt buckles. "Let's go take a look at the spacesuits."

First, though, she retrieved a lightweight silver blanket from the same compartment from which she had extracted the automedic, and spread it over the boy. He moaned a little at the touch, then relaxed again. "Automedic has him sedated," Avara said. "He's not suffering, at least."

She led Art back down the corridor to a side compartment just short of the humming engine room. It was little more than a closet, hung with eight spacesuits, one for each potential crew member. Art had expected something lightweight and simple, like the suit into which he'd been stuffed during his abduction. But that, Avara told him scornfully, had been a "dummy suit." *These* suits were designed for much longer periods in space. They included food and water and tubes that Avara explained in straightforward fashion while Art tried unsuccessfully not to blush. He had to discard his own clothes and don a special undergarment, then struggle into the suit. Finally he had everything in place and zipped up. "Now what?" he said. "I'm stewing in my own sweat."

"Now take it off," Avara said. She glanced at a chronometer. "We're still more than three hours from where you'll be getting out. Take it off and put it back on again until you could do it in your sleep…and can do it for someone else, too."

Art nodded, understanding. *Lorn*.

He practiced under Avara's watchful eye until she finally said, "Enough."

Panting, covered with sweat, he leaned against the wall. "Now what?"

Avara handed him a bottle of water and a silvery food pack. He gulped the cold liquid and then tore open the pack. The contents, pink as salmon but tasting like…actually, he wasn't sure *what* they tasted like and decided maybe that was a good thing… took the edge off his hunger even if they didn't exactly rise to the level of *haute cuisine*. "We're half an hour from engine cut-off," Avara said as she watched him eat. "There'll be some reaction-drive maneuvering for about twenty minutes to match velocities. You'll be going out the hatch within an hour." She turned her gaze back to him. "Which means I'd better show you one other thing."

He followed her across the corridor to another closet-like compartment. It slid open to reveal a bulky white backpack bristling with nozzles pointing in all directions. Two armrest-like control bars protruded from the sides. A vertical handle protruded from each. "Extravehicular Maneuvering Unit," she said. "Or EMU if you prefer."

"Isn't that a flightless bird from Earth?"

Avara didn't so much as crack a smile. "I wouldn't know."

Tough crowd, Art thought.

Avara pointed at the controls. "Pull both handles back, you go forward. Push them ahead, you slow down. Push one, pull the other, you revolve. For rotation, pull them in toward the centre, then pull back. That spins you head forward, feet back. Pull them in, push them forward, you get feet forward, head back. Got it?"

"Um..."

"Pay attention." Avara demonstrated the controls again. "Now?"

Art nodded.

"Good. Now that you know what they do—don't touch them. Not until you and Lorn have reached the *Mayflower II*." She pulled a gold cube from her breast pocket and plugged it into a socket in the right armrest. "That will get you to the *Mayflower*; it's being constantly reprogrammed by the ship's computer. It will point you in the right direction and use just enough burn from your EMU to get the two of you going. Once you get there, the final adjustments will be up to you. But be prepared: you're going to be out there a long time."

"I know," Art said quietly. "Will Lorn make it?"

Avara was silent for a moment. "I don't know," she said. "It's going to be touch and go. Bu to have any chance at all..."

Art nodded.

For a moment there was silence. Avara was staring at the EMU. Art gazed at her profile. Her expression softened; he could almost see her come to a blank space in her relentless mental checklist of what must be done. For a moment she looked much younger and much more vulnerable. On impulse he leaned forward and kissed her cheek.

She turned her mouth hungrily to him, and for a moment she responded as she had the night before—but suddenly she stiffened and pushed him away. "No."

He gaped at her, breathing a little hard. "Why not? Last night—"

"Last night was—different. I thought we would have a little more time. But now there's no time at all. We could both be dead tomorrow."

"All the more reason—"

"No!" Avara's denial was harsh. "I don't deny I'm attracted to you. You're obviously attracted to me. But I don't know *why*. I don't do anything without a reason—and we don't have time to explore what our reasons are—not now."

"Why does there have to be a reason? What about impulse? If I listened to reason I'd be reading the news on the *Mayflower II* right now."

"And wouldn't you rather be *there* than *here*?"

"A few days ago I would have. But not anymore." It was the truth, Art realized with surprise. "I've got a chance to do something worthwhile for the first time in my life—and I got it by acting on impulse, by doing what felt right at each moment. So what's wrong with this impulse?"

"Do you realize," Avara said, with a hint of a smile, "that you just used reason to argue the merits of acting on impulse?"

Art blinked, then grinned. "Did I convince you?"

"It really doesn't matter, because—" Something beeped down the hall in the cockpit, piercing, insistent. "There's no more time."

After that, things seemed to happen in alarmingly rapid

succession. They returned to the cockpit as the strange engine hum/vibration fell away to nothing, and Art was shocked by the sight of Merlin, a vast yellow sphere surrounded by bright white rings, looming above them. Maneuvering engines fired, several times. Then they were unstrapping themselves, unstrapping Lorn, bundling the unconscious boy into a suit. "I'm going to turn off the internal gravity now," Avara said. "Be ready."

How? Art wondered, but said nothing.

Avara touched a control by the airlock. Suddenly Art's stomach lurched and his feet lifted from the deckplates. Lorn, too, floated up from the deck like an untethered balloon. Avara maneuvered him in front of Art, attaching him to Art with some of the plethora of straps and buckles on the outside of both suits. The boy bobbed there like an exceptionally large baby in a chest carrier, his head just below Art's direct line of sight. *At least I'll be able to see where I'm going.*

Next Avara strapped him into the EMU. When it was all done, he felt huge and awkward, and floated in the corridor, helpless: Avara would have to maneuver him the rest of the way into position.

Avara went forward to do her final checks. Left alone, Art licked dry lips inside his still-open helmet. Within minutes he would launch himself and Lorn across empty space as slow-motion human missiles, trusting to the programming of his EMU to guide them across a hundred kilometres of nothing. And once there he would still have to find a way in and locate his one possible on-ship ally, Shadow—and get Lorn the medical help he so desperately needed.

He wished he had a chip that could take care of that, too.

Avara returned. "Everything's green. Perfect velocity match."

"I never doubted it."

"Don't interrupt," Avara said. "Your Captain may or may not know we're here. Even if he does, we're too far away for him to do anything about it except worry. At worst he might throw a missile my way, but this far out I can dodge it or shoot it.

"Once you're out I'm going to accelerate past his bow—too fast for him to hit," she added in response to Art's look of consternation. "I want all his attention on me to be sure he doesn't spot you. After that you'll be so slow-moving and such a soft radar echo I doubt even one of our ships would be able to detect you." She gave him a penetrating look. "You ready?"

"Yes," Art said, and if the word came out not quite as firm and determined as he had intended, he thought it wasn't bad, considering the sandpaper in his throat.

"Come on, then." Avara drifted back down the corridor. The hatch through which they had entered the ship on the ground bore a bright red warning: SINGLE DOOR. WILL NOT OPERATE IF PRESSURES ARE NOT EQUAL. Avara punched a control on the wall beside that closed hatch and a metal panel slid aside in what had been the deck, groundside. Beneath it was another hatch, labelled "PERSONNEL AIRLOCK," with its own panel of controls. Avara tapped one, and the door hissed open. Lights came up in the space beneath, revealing a small chamber with a yellow-painted door on the far side.

Art, his breath coming in short gasps, closed and sealed his helmet without a word, while Avara took care of Lorn's helmet and life support. Cool air flooded around him, stiffening the suit and drying the sweat from his body. Cool water, too, began circulating through the network of tubes in the special undergarment. Art borrowed a sip of it from the tube that thrust up from under the suit collar as Avara maneuvered him and Lorn into the lock. "Closing inner door," she said, her voice tinny through the helmet. "Hang on for communications check."

With shocking abruptness, the inner door slid shut, leaving him and Lorn hanging in the brightly lit, barely-large enough airlock.

A moment later her voice returned, this time clear and strong in his headphones. "How do I sound?"

"Clear. What about me?"

"Clear. But remember, keep radio silence until you're ready

to enter the ship. Then call me, but keep it brief. I'll back on Peregrine by then, but I'll still hear you…well, some forty-five minutes later, with the speed-of-light delay. Your Crew shouldn't be able to decipher what you're saying through the encryption, but they may detect the signal, and you don't want to give them time to home in on you, or they'll be waiting for you inside."

"I know."

There was a moment's silence. "Good luck," Avara said finally. "To both of you."

"You, too."

"All right." Avara's voice regained its cold, professional tone. "Here we go. Evacuating lock."

There was a hissing sound that attenuated to deep silence.

"Opening outer door."

The outer door moved noiselessly aside, revealing blackness and stars. "Ready to launch?" Avara said.

No, Art thought. "Yes," he said.

"Activating EMU program," said Avara; and something shoved Art in the back and plunged him into space.

Merlin hung above him, its vast yellow sphere marked with the roiling filigree of enormous currents of wind and gas, its rings white and sharp as blades of ice. Beneath his feet he could see only the infinite dark of space and a million un-twinkling stars. But dead ahead…

Dead ahead glinted the long, lumpy shape of the *Mayflower II*, capped front and back by the half-domes of the Forward and Aft Shields, studded along its length by the huge metal boxes of the Habs, like the seeds on some gigantic stalk of wheat. Even a hundred kilometres could not diminish that enormous mass to invisibility.

The sun burned behind him, so that the suit's control lights glowed bright and clear in his own shadow. His eyes went first to the most important, a little green bar on the chest pack, just tinged with red at one end—life support. By his right hand a similar bar recorded the level of maneuvering gas. The faint thrust of the pack continued, accelerating him to a speed of just under four metres per second, while the fuel supply, never intended to be used in such a prolonged burst, dwindled rapidly. When the thrust ended, half the green bar had turned red.

Until that moment Art had managed to ignore the endless space around him, concentrating fiercely on the controls and the slight feeling of acceleration. But when the EMU cut off, all sense of movement ceased, and suddenly he was adrift, helpless, a tiny spark of life engulfed in an enormous and uncaring universe.

Art had lived all his life in space, but had never seen it until that terrifying leap from starship to attack craft. Then there had been no planet twirling away below him, no tiny starship hanging like a model ahead of him, no real sense of the immense emptiness surrounding him—yet it had been quite enough to almost frighten him senseless.

Now there was no doubting his own insignificance. His heart pounded in his ears—yet the unreasoning panic of his first exposure to the wider universe outside the starship did not return. He could still function, and he hadn't screamed—or if he had he did not remember it, and Avara had not reacted.

Even as he thought of the SSIN officer the sleek winged shape of the scoutship flashed past to his right and below him, riding a white torch. In seconds, reduced to a mere spark of light, it zipped past the *Mayflower II* and vanished into the eternal night.

And then he and Lorn were truly alone, a hundred kilometres and eight hours from the ship that had been his home. He hoped desperately he wouldn't arrive there with nothing but a cooling corpse in the suit in front of him.

His heartbeat slowed gradually, and he began modulating his breathing, taking slow, even breaths. His fear faded, became almost incomprehensible to him, like his fear of darkness when he was a child. He had food and water and air; what was there to be afraid of? He was not, after all, the same Art Stoddard who had been carted helplessly, like a piece of luggage, from ship to ship two weeks ago. Considering all that had happened to him since, how could he be? He had lost whatever lingering inbred respect he had still had for the Crew and Council when he had found they had lied to the Passengers. He had lost his passivity when Arklund tried to use him to start a civil war on Peregrine. He had lost his detachment when the Kymbals had saved his life at the risk of their own; and when he had lost all that, his fear had lost the power to paralyze him, the way it had all his life, even though the stakes were higher than they had ever been on the starship.

Last night he had convinced Avara to help him by accusing her of the very fear he knew he was most guilty of; but he knew, now that it was too late to tell her, that it was her *courage* that attracted him to her so strongly. She had never let fear stop *her*. She had acted, setting up the Peregrine FreeNet, almost single-handedly stealing information from the government and giving it to the people. She had done what he might have been able to do aboard the *Mayflower II*, if he'd only had the courage to try it. Maybe he could have found a way to use his access to upload data without being detected, tell some of the stories the Crew kept censoring. But he had been afraid to try, and his excuse had been that it wouldn't do any good anyway.

Maybe it wouldn't have, he thought now, *but I should have tried anyway. Dad was right—I had opportunities, but I wasted them.* He grinned a little at the thought of his father, wondering what the old man would be thinking if he could see him now, sneaking up on the *Mayflower II* in a stolen spacesuit. *Well, here's one opportunity I've seized...though it's probably not exactly the kind of thing Dad was thinking of!*

It might well be his last opportunity to do *anything* that mattered. If Avara were correct, he had less than a day until the attack fleet launched. The Crew had to have already readied its weapons, the Captain just waiting for a reason to launch them. And back on Peregrine, Arklund was playing his own power games.

Art stared at the distant starship and futilely urged his rate of drift to increase.

Time passed. He tried to avoid looking at the chronometer on his chest pack: its digits changed with painful slowness. Instead he gazed up at Merlin, watching in silent fascination as its ever-changing, swirling surface passed over his head. When at last he couldn't stand it any longer, he glance down again, and groaned.

Still five hours to go.

◣ ◢

Sunset took him by surprise. Darkness spread over the planet from behind him, and he passed into night through a band of deep orange light, followed by dark blue shading to black. Merlin became a vast, black circle, visible only by the absence of stars in the void it created, and, here and there, the flash of vast bolts of lightning.

He tried closing his eyes, and dozed, waking frequently but nodding off again. Finally he slept hard, waking to find the chronometer had at last jumped ahead—and the *Mayflower II* had swollen to enormity. The short orbital night had ended, and the sun rising over the limb of the planet lit the ship from behind, giving it the look of an ebony carving gilded with silver.

Art licked his lips. With his target in sight, his velocity of drift seemed even slower than before. The Mayflower grew larger moment by moment, not quite fast enough to see, yet fast enough that whenever he looked away for a few seconds and looked back he was surprised by how much closer it was.

The sun continued to rise, flooding the planet with light. The starship's own terminator crawled around its circumference toward Art, and as the sun moved higher than the *Mayflower II* his helmet darkened automatically.

Finally the ship filled his vision. The EMU's programming was perfect, he realized, even as the forward nozzles vented gas to slow his approach, dropping the fuel level to the point where a yellow warning light began to blink.

By then his drift was no more than a half-metre per second, and the *Mayflower II* looked as big as the planet below. Again he could see the pits and scars on the once-smooth skin of the Habs. In places antennae were bent or fused into useless junk. Warning signs reduced to pale smudges of paint rolled endlessly past as the ship rotated.

He risked another puff of gas to bring himself to a complete stop, and hung motionless relative to the ship, studying the hull. Now came the tricky part, especially with so little maneuvering gas to spare…and Lorn still unconscious—and hopefully still alive—and buckled to his chest. He had to enter through the Core. Even though there were access hatches in the rotating hubs, he hadn't a hope of matching his velocity to theirs.

Originally he had thought to use one of the locks in either the Forward or Aft Service and Propulsion Module. But either would be very difficult, maybe impossible, for the Crawlspacers to get to. And if he didn't make contact with the Crawlspacers in time, all of this would be for naught.

So the Core it was. He knew there were plenty of locks there, of all sizes. But part of the Core's very purpose was to allow quick access to all parts of the ship. If his entry were detected—and it surely would be; security must be high after one successful break-and-enter already—the 'keeps would be on him in moments.

His only advantage, if he had one, was that he knew the ship better than they would expect from an intruder. He hoped that would allow him to evade the 'keeps long enough to meet up with the Crawlspacers.

Taking a deep breath, he gripped the controls and started forward.

The Habs swept by to either side. With deceleration complete, they were no longer angled; they stuck out perpendicular to the Core on their respective booms. It made the approach to the Core far easier than it would otherwise have been.

The Core grew nearer with agonizing slowness, but Art dared not use more thrust. The yellow warning light on his fuel gauge burned bright, the green of the readout the thinnest of thin lines on the end of a long strip of red. If he sped up his approach he might not have enough fuel to slow down, and splatting against the side of the Core like a thrown tomato would be an ignominious end to their journey indeed. The chronometer counted the minutes one by one, until he wished he could shut it off.

Finally the Core loomed in front of him, a vast curved wall of metal. He used another burst to come to a halt relative to it, and hung there, watching it crawl past, the skin moving past him at a brisk walking pace. A series of handholds ran around the entire massive circumference. Art moved in closer. Here goes, he thought, and reached out with his left hand, thinking he'd simply take one of the handholds and let it pull him along.

But he'd forgotten one salient fact about floating in space: gravity might not be a factor, but mass remained unchanged—and his total mass, of man, boy, two suits and EMU combined, was considerable. Pain shot through his wrenched arm and he let go of the rung by reflex. Grabbing the ship had started him spinning slowly. The EMU brought up against the hull and he bounced away. Frantic with the knowledge he might not have enough fuel to maneuver back again, he fumbled one-handed at the EMU's straps, managed to undo them, and started to shove the thing down and away from him by the control arms—then at the last second realized he was turned in such a way that that would cause him to drift away from the ship, and he'd have no way to get back.

Gasping, he held on until his head was angled toward instead of away from the *Mayflower II*, and in the direction of spin: only then did he give the EMU a hard push. It sent him and Lorn back toward the hull, two metres behind him. His previous contact and the new impetus reduced the relative speed of the spin considerably. The handholds grew closer. He reached for one…

…and Lorn, who hadn't moved for hours, suddenly stirred, startling like a frightened animal. His arm flew out and knocked Art's arm aside. He missed the handhold. Worse, they were starting to spin again.

They turned head-down toward the ship, Lorn feebly struggling. The handholds were drifting off to their left. Art stretched out frantically. If he missed again, they'd bounce off the hull and away, drifting off into space, helpless until their life support ran out…

His reaching fingers closed on the handhold. Though his arm took another painful jerk, he held on, literally for dear life.

Almost immediately the sense that they were spinning vanished entirely. Everything suddenly seemed completely stationary except for the EMU, tumbling away, flashing white over and over again in the sun as it receded from his sight around the limb of the central Core.

Now it seemed the Habs, impossibly enormous, hung over him like mushrooms on the end of ridiculously thin jointed silver stalks. Merlin, vast and yellow, swept slowly over his head.

Art took a quick sip of water and waited for his breathing and pulse to slow, the pounding of pain in his arm continuing in time to his heartbeat. Lorn still stirred feebly, clearly not awake, but not as unconscious as he had been. *The sedatives*, Art thought. *The sedatives the automedic were giving him. They must be wearing off. He's in pain. It's going to get worse. I have to get him inside. I have to get us* both *inside.*

Taking a deep breath, he began awkwardly following the line of handholds toward the sun, just able to reach each one in turn over the no-longer-entirely quiescent bulk of Lorn.

He didn't have far to go. As he had known they would, the handholds led within forty or fifty metres to a personnel lock, providing access to the outside of the Core for repair crews and maintenance bots. Art glanced to his right as he passed a lump of fused metal that might once have been an antenna array. *Not that repairs seem to have been exactly expedited recently.*

Holding on to one of the stanchions on either side of the lock, Art studied the simple control panel. It required no access code; all he had to do was hit a green button marked CYCLE and moments later he would be back in the *Mayflower II.*

He didn't think of it as coming home.

He took a deep breath. "Activate voice communications," he said to the suit's computer. A soft beep acknowledged the command. “Avara, Art,” he said tersely. “I’ve reached the ship. I’m going in.” It would be forty-five minutes before she heard him. Then she would tell the people of Peregrine the truth.

It was up to him to do the same on Peregrine…the sooner, the better.

Art punched the green button.

Chapter Thirteen

The outer door stayed closed while the lock cycled—but it stayed closed so long Art began to fear it had malfunctioned. In his mind he could hear alarms ringing in the control room, and see a 'keeps platoon hurrying into pods and zipping through the Core toward him. But just when he was about to give up and try to get to another lock, the door slid aside, a puff of un-reclaimed air forming sparkling ice crystals around him. *More poor maintenance*, he thought. He pulled himself and Lorn into the chamber beyond—they barely fit—and hit the red button next to the inner door. The outer door slid shut and air filled the chamber, bringing with it the sound of pumps.

It seemed to take forever for the lock to cycle. Art didn't waste the time. "Crawlspacers!" he said. "If you're listening, respond on this frequency. This is Art Stoddard. I'm back on board. Crawlspacers! Shadow! Is anyone there? Respond!"

There was no answer. The red button turned green and Art punched it again. The inner door opened, and he pushed forward, then stopped, startled. He'd expected to find himself in a smallish compartment containing spacesuits and racks of tools. Instead he was in a very large chamber, dominated at its centre by a gigantic spherical machine, locked into place atop a steel pedestal and bristling with manipulator arms, antennae, and other things Art didn't recognize. On the far side of the room was a single enormous hatch, obviously providing access to the Core, and suddenly he realized what the thing must be: a maintenance robot, the biggest he'd ever seen, presumably designed to work inside the open spaces of the Core among the transit tubes, the engine track and the massive conduits that kept energy, data, water and oxygen—the lifeblood of the ship—flowing from stem to stern.

He yelped as his perception shifted and it seemed that giant ball of steel was hanging directly overhead. It took him a second to realize what had happened. Even though this close to the Core there was very little spin effect, that didn't mean there was none at all: he and Lorn had already drifted back down to the now-closed airlock through which they'd just emerged. The force had been enough for his body to register it and his brain to decide that the hull was "down" and the giant robot was "up."

Stupid brain, Art thought, as his pulse raced.

He snapped out of his momentary freeze. "Crawlspacers! Shadow! Respond! This is Art Stoddard! Respond, please!" he called, and kept on calling as he unbuckled the feebly squirming Lorn, both of them bouncing gently against the floor of the chamber like almost-exhausted helium balloons. He opened the boy's faceplate. Sweat beaded Lorn's white face. His eyes flickered, and then opened.

"Dad?" he said weakly, the word a knife to Art's chest, then his eyes focused. "Art? Where…what…where are we?"

"*Mayflower II*," Art said. "You were shot. I'm going to get you help." *I hope.*

"Hurts," Lorn mumbled. "Hard to…hard to breathe…"

"Just lie quiet." Art stared up at the robot and the hatch before it. There had to be other ways into the room, but for the moment he couldn't see them. "Crawlspacers! Respond, please!"

And then, just like that, there was a voice inside his head, a female voice that he recognized immediately: Shadow.

"Stoddard! We're getting your signal. We're on the way."

"I've got an injured boy with me," Art said. "Bring medical help."

"We'll be lucky to get there ahead of the 'keeps," Shadow said grimly. "They're on the way, too. Ten minutes."

It was the longest ten minutes of Art's life. He used the time to get out of the suit, but left Lorn in his, afraid of hurting the boy further if he tried to move him. Lorn was becoming more and more alert, though his face remained pale and sweat-slicked. "How did we end up *here*?"

"Avara didn't think she could get you medical help back on Peregrine," he said. "Here…maybe." He touched the boy's forehead. "You're going to be all right."

"Yeah," Lorn said. "Sure."

Two more minutes slid by. Then Art jerked and swore as, from shockingly nearby, he heard the unmistakable sound of gunfire. Something struck the other side of the giant hatch a ringing blow. Suddenly, Shadow's voice was in his head again.

"'Keeps got here first," she said. "They'll be in there with you in a minute. We're trying to keep them occupied—" More gunfire; the sounds inside his head, coming through the link to Shadow. "You've got to hide. They may be under orders to shoot on sight, especially if they think you're an invader—"

"Hide?" Art looked frantically around at the room. "Where—?"

"Dammit!" More shooting. "They got by. Left two behind. We can take them out, but not quickly, and the rest will at the hatch in a minute. Six of them."

"The big hatch?"

"Small one! Forward!"

Art turned his head toward the bow, and spotted the hatch she meant, half-hidden by a rack of green-painted steel bottles.

"Hide!"

Hide where? Art thought. Even if he could hide, Lorn couldn't—

He swore silently. He didn't like the idea he'd just had, but it was the only way he could think of to give them both a chance.

He moved over to the airlock, poked the controls. The inner door slid open, revealing the brightly lit interior they'd come through just minutes before. He turned and tugged at Lorn, who groaned. "What's happening?"

"'Keeps—soldiers—coming this way," Art panted. "I can run, maybe hide. You can't. I'm going to hide you in the lock. No reason for them to look. They'll see my empty suit and assume there was only one of us. You'll be safe. I'll send help as soon as I can."

"They'll catch you," Lorn gasped out. "Just leave me. They don't know who I am—"

"They'll still see my suit. They'll still come after me. And they may have orders to shoot on sight." He pushed Lorn down into the airlock. "Just don't touch the outside controls," he said. "You don't want to launch yourself into space. Keep quiet and you'll be all right." *That sounds like a lie even to me*, he thought. "I'll send help," he said again.

"All right," Lorn said. He closed his eyes and swallowed. "All right. Good luck."

I'll need it, Art thought. He closed the inner door.

"They're almost on top of you," Shadow said in his head.

Art looked around. "Is there any other way out of here?"

"No," Shadow said. "You've got to hide."

"It's not *that* big. They'll find me—"

"If you somehow slip past them—"

"Right," said Art. "Piece of cake." His eyes fell on the suit he had taken off, and he had an idea.

He had to act fast; he barely had time to get into position before the hatch slid open. He heard it but didn't see it: he was curled up on the far side of the maintenance robot, the spacesuit clasped to his chest.

Voices rang in the hall. "Spread out. He has to be in here. There's nowhere to hide."

Almost nowhere, Art thought. Taking another deep breath, he pulled his knees up behind the empty spacesuit, and then straightened his legs as hard as he could.

In the two minutes of grace he'd had before the 'keeps entered the compartment, he'd sealed the spacesuit again and activated its flagging life support. Stiffened by internal air pressure, and with the mirrored visor down, it looked exactly like it must have with him in it…and, as it soared across the compartment toward the controls of the large hatch, looked exactly like someone attempting to escape.

"Halt!" someone shouted.

Well, that's a stupid thing to say to someone in mid-flight, Art thought, even as he edged around the maintenance 'bot. Then again, it had clearly been just to observe the formalities; the shots rang out before the spacesuit had even reached the bulkhead. One arm and one leg of the suit jerked spasmodically as the bullets hit home, the motion only adding to the illusion it contained a living person—*though not one who might be living much longer*, Art thought, as six black-clad 'keeps, faces hidden beneath black helmets with reflective faceplates, soared across the compartment in pursuit. He didn't waste any time watching them: he was already launching himself the other way, toward the still-open hatch through which the 'keeps had come.

He almost made it…but not quite. "It's empty!" someone shouted, and "There he is!" shouted someone else, almost at the same instant.

He reached the hatch. He turned to close it. The controls had been locked open. A bullet slammed into the bulkhead just by his head and he jerked back. He looked frantically up the long straight corridor into which he'd emerged. Shadow was down there somewhere…but so were at least two more 'keeps.

He was trapped. He turned, raising his hands, hoping desperately they weren't really under orders to shoot on sight, knowing it was a vain hope since they already had—

To his shock, the airlock hatch behind which he had stashed Lorn slid open.

A moment later, all hell broke loose.

"Another one!" shouted someone.

Guns blazed.

"No!" Art screamed. He started toward the hatch, though there was nothing he could do to save Lorn…

…but Lorn, it seemed, had already made up his own mind what to do. There was a bang, and then an enormous, howling wind. Art's ears popped. And inside the compartment, the 'keeps, screaming, were suddenly all tumbling toward the open airlock, the airlock whose outer hatch Lorn had just somehow opened.

An instant later, the hatch in front of Art, safety overriding whatever security protocols the 'keeps had used to keep it open, snapped shut. Big red letters blazed on the control panel. PRESSURE LOSS. COMPARTMENT SEALED.

Art gasped. "No…Lorn…"

Guns rang out from somewhere behind him, down the corridor, Art spun. "Got them," Shadow snarled. "Art, you alive?"

Art let the spin push him against the "floor" of the corridor and lay there. "I am," he said dully. "But I'm the only one."

A minute later seven young people in skin-tight black clothing and featureless masks reached him, pulling themselves along the handholds that ran down the middle of the "floor." In the lead was Shadow, who pulled off her mask as she reached him. "Shit's hit the fan now," she said savagely. "It's a shooting war."

"They killed Forbes," said one of the others, voice choked with grief. "They killed him!"

"Yeah, well, we killed two of them back there and…" Shadow's eyes slid to the closed door. "Shit," she said. "Six of them here." She gave Art a look. "How'd you manage that?"

"I didn't," Art said. "It was Lorn."

"Lorn?"

"A…" Art's voice shut down. He had to swallow hard to keep speaking. "A boy. From Peregrine. The inhabited planet."

"A boy?" Shadow said. "There are *humans* down there?"

"Yeah." Art's vision blurred and he blinked away tears. "Yeah, they're human."

"So we got him," said one of others. Art recognized the voice. Philip, who had been with Shadow at their first meeting. Who had seemed way too willing to kill him even then. "Better be worth it. Why didn't we just let the 'keeps have him?"

"Orders," said Shadow.

Art stared at her. *Orders*. He'd been certain these kids couldn't be acting alone. *Although Lorn did*, he thought, and swallowed hard again. “Orders from *whom*?”

“Higher up. Someone who knows what’s going on. Same someone who told us how you were stupid enough to get yourself captured in the first place…and that you’d been kidnapped from the ship by the aliens.”

“They’re not aliens—”

“Yeah, well, we didn’t know that then. Soon as I heard your signal, I checked in. Rescue you, he said. Take you to…well, never mind. You’ll find out soon enough.” Shadow glanced down the corridor. “More ’keeps here any minute. Time to make ourselves scarce. Philip?”

The boy pulled a data tablet from his belt and glanced at it. “Twelve metres this way,” he said, and led them down the corridor; stopped. “There,” he said, pointing. “Wall panel, second from floor.”

Shadow drew a short, stubby black tube from her belt, and pointed it at each corner of the panel. With a pop of equalizing pressure, it came free. Beyond lay a vague space, dimly lit in blue. “Everyone through,” she said. Art squeezed inside with the others. As Shadow turned and resealed the wall plate, he looked around.

They were in some kind of old service corridor, or maybe it had served no other purpose than to allow construction crews access to this part of the ship. The light came from small blue hemispheres that Art knew well: they were an emergency form of lighting that could last for decades—as clearly these had.

Phillip consulted his data reader. “This parallels the main corridor until the junction of the next Hab boom. Ends there, but there’s a shaft Coreward. Should take us to the transit tubes.”

Shadow nodded. “Sir, did you hear?” she said, apparently to thin air. She paused for a long moment, gazing blankly at one of the pale blue lights. “Understood,” she said at last. She looked around at the others. “Pod will meet us in the tube. Let’s go.”

They began pulling themselves along the corridor. “Is there

anything your mysterious patron doesn't know about what happens on the ship?" Art demanded of Shadow as they crawled.

"Very little," she said.

"Did he tell you the *Mayflower II* carries matter-antimatter missiles?"

Shadow didn't react. The others stopped dead. "*What*?" Philip said.

Art didn't look at him, keeping his eyes on Shadow, who halted a few metres farther on. She looked back. "We've got to keep moving," she said.

But the others were looking at Art, not her. "It's true," he said. "The people on Peregrine have the original records from the time of the ship's construction—more than four centuries ago, from their point of view."

"I don't believe you!" Philip said, and the others chorused their agreement.

All except Shadow.

She knew, Art thought. *Even if they don't.*

He turned toward Phillip. "If you don't trust me now you'd better start soon. Otherwise, we're all going to be dead real soon now."

"It's not up to us to trust you or not trust you," Shadow said. "We have our orders. I said *keep moving*!" she snapped to the others, and resumed pulling herself along the corridor.

Art's arms and shoulders ached when at last they reached the place where the corridor/crawlspace abruptly ended in a junction box and some thick cables. To the left…up, at least vaguely…a shaft disappeared into darkness. More handholds punctuated its smooth interior at regular intervals. Shadows started up it. Art followed, watching her heels and thinly-covered legs and buttocks. Ordinarily he would have admired the view. At the moment he was more concerned about whether or not they were all going to be blown out of space by the Peregrine forces.

The climb took roughly forever, and at some point even the slight force of the spin they'd experienced at the edge of the

Core disappeared. Art had another of those weird perspective shifts, and instead of climbing straight up, suddenly found himself, without changing a thing, pulling himself lightly along an endless horizontal tunnel.

The tunnel ended in a hatch. Shadow held up her hand. "Locked," she said. "Philip?"

Again Philip stepped forward. Again he pulled something from his belt. But this time it was a small box with a red light on the back. He stuck the box to the door and pressed the red light. "Clear back," he said.

Art pushed himself back along…or possibly down…the tube. There was a sudden "whump!" and a feeling like he'd been lightly punched in the stomach, and the door swung open. "Transit tube," Philip said. "Back of maintenance access station 201 four metres further on. Should open on approach."

"Then we don't approach it," Shadow said. "Until the pod is here." She gazed off into space again. "Maintenance access station 201," she said. Then, "Yes, sir." She glanced back at the others. "It's coming."

They waited in silence. Art tried to imagine who their mysterious patron/commander might be. *Someone with power*, he thought. *Council, or even Crew…my father?* He snorted at the very idea. His father would hand out the weapons to the firing squad if the Captain ordered his execution.

Even if I save the ship by rebelling? he thought. *Even then?*

He had no answer to that. He didn't know whether that was comforting or alarming.

Three or four minutes crawled by, and suddenly one of the Crawlspacers at the back of the column stiffened and stared back "down" the shaft. "I hear something," she whispered. "Scuttling…"

"Scuttling?" someone else said, but "Sh!" hissed Shadows, and they all listened.

And there it was. A clicking, clacking sound. For a moment Art was puzzled; and then, along with everyone else, he realized what it had to be.

"Maintenance 'bots," Philip said. "More than one..."

"Harmless," said one of the other boys, but Art's eyes widened, remembering Peter's father...

"No!" he cried. "They've reprogrammed them to kill. They're like...antibodies, and we're the infection."

"What?" Shadow stared at him.

"They've done it before! Don't let them close with us!"

The others were already unshipping their weapons, driven by the urgency in his voice, but before they could fire there was a blink of light and the girl at the back screamed and clutched her smoking shoulder, dropping her weapon. Art leaped forward and grabbed it as it floated in mid-air, twisted and fired down the shaft. An instant later the others followed suit. Bullets screamed off of walls, followed by the dull whump of another explosion. Black smoke billowed toward them. Art stared into the darkness. Last time he'd destroyed a maintenance robot he'd felt bad about it. Not this time.

If we got it, he thought.

It appeared they had: no more lasers speared through the smoke and fog.

And then there was a beep behind them. "Pod's here!" Shadow cried, and they bundled through the open hatch into the space beyond. Another hatch, a normal one, slid open, revealing the familiar interior of a transit pod. Soft music wafted out of the interior, along with a puff of expertly freshened air. "Please place palm on the scanning panel for biometric evaluation," said the familiar female voice. Shadow slapped her hand down on the blue square the instant it appeared and it turned green. "Identity confirmed," said the pod. "Please ensure all hands and feet are inside the pod and say 'Go' when ready to depart."

"Go," yelled Shadow. "Go, go, go!"

"Repetition is unnecessary unless requested," the pod reproached her pleasantly. "Please enjoy the journey."

"Where—" Art began.

"No talking," Shadow snapped. "Emily, let me see that shoulder. Take off your top."

The injured girl struggled out of her skin-hugging upper garment. She wore a sleek black bra, revealing a well-muscled torso…and an angry red and blistered patch on her shoulder. She looked no more than sixteen.

Art looked away as Shadow began smearing the burn with a blue paste from a first-aid kit she'd produced from another of her belt pouches. "Skinshield took most of it," she said. "Just a first-degree burn. No lasting damage."

"Hurts," Emily said.

"Yeah," Shadow said. "I know. Keep your top off for now."

Emily nodded and settled back into one of the seats.

After that they rode in silence until the pod abruptly changed direction and orientation. Suddenly Art felt properly heavy for the first time in hours. And then the pod said probably the most shocking thing he could have heard at that point: "Habitat Three."

Art stiffened. "*What?*"

"No talking," Shadow repeated. The pod stopped. The door opened—but again, it opened into darkness, not into a transit station—certainly not into the Hab Three transit station Art had travelled into and out of almost every day of his working life. With proper weight again, they hurried single-file along a dark corridor lit at wide intervals by more of the blue emergency lights.

Art tried to figure out where they were going. Assuming they'd been sliding into the transit station as usual, even if they'd never actually gotten there, then they had to be moving toward… he thought hard.

The park.

The room where he'd seen Shadow and Phillip the first time?

He was right. Five minutes later they were in that room. But they weren't alone.

Standing in the dim light was a tall figure, face hidden by shadow. As they entered, he stepped forward…

…and Art found himself face to face with Councilor Jonas

Woods.

He gaped. "You? *You're* their secret mastermind?" He glanced at Shadow. "He's a drunk!"

"So are you, based on the ship's alcohol-dispensing records," Woods said pleasantly. "But, here you are."

Art shook his head. He couldn't believe it. And yet…

…yet, it made sense. What better way to hide your subversive tendencies than speak about them openly—but convince everyone they were the ravings of a drunk. Woods had been hiding in plain sight.

He remembered all the times his father had told jokes about Woods's latest embarrassing speech in Council chambers or at the opening of a repaired transit station or food hall. (Never the opening of a new one: the closest the ship ever got to anything new was when something broken for years was finally repaired.)

He snorted then. "Can't wait until my father finds out."

"I hope his heart isn't weak," Woods said.

Art stared at him; and even though the joke wasn't very funny it was so unexpected he couldn't help but chuckle suddenly.

"So, Arthur Stoddard," said Woods. "You return from kidnapping, break into the ship, and demand our help. You have plunged us into civil war. I do hope you have a good reason." There was no trace of slurred speech or rambling in Woods's delivery.

"I think I do."

"Then perhaps you had better tell me—tell us," his gesture took in the Crawlspacers clustered behind Art, "what it is."

"Do you still have a copy of the file you wanted me to play?" Art said.

Shadow responded, not Woods. "Of course. But we have no way to get it into Shipnet. Even he," she indicated Woods, "can't do it. No Passenger has that kind of access anymore."

"Previewing it was a mistake," Art said.

Shadow snorted. "Y'think?"

"But I think I can make up for it."

"Can you also make up for the casualties suffered this day?"

Woods said. "By both ourselves and the Crew? Can you make up for the arrests and 'disappearances' still to come, as the Crew begins an all-out attempt to uncover the truth of who just helped you break into the ship? An attempt, I might add, that despite all my precautions may very well lead them to me. Can you make up for the destruction of the only revolutionary force this ship has ever seen—or likely ever will?"

"There will be a lot more casualties than just the handful we've suffered today," Art said harshly. "If we do not act—if what I have in mind fails—then this ship, and the inhabited planet in this system, are both on the brink of destruction."

"They're aliens," Woods said. "Why should I care what happens to them?"

"They're not aliens—they're humans," Art snarled. Again he thought of Lorn, sudden pain twisting in his chest. "Humanity developed faster-than-light star travel after we left. They spread out to multiple planets, including this one. But Earth didn't trust its own people. It kept details of the technology secret. And something happened. The starships stopped coming. Peregrine couldn't build its own. And so for two hundred planetary years, Peregrine has been on its own: no contact with other humans…until we showed up. There may not be any other humans left, anywhere else. For all we know, the humans on this ship and on Peregrine are all that remain of the race."

Thick silence filled the enclosed space after his pronouncement. Finally Wood spoke again. "Well, you haven't lost the knack for commanding attention in a crowd," he said. "Tell us everything you can."

As quickly as he could, Art laid out the situation: revolution below, ships launching, Captain Nikos prepared to destroy the planet if it meant saving his ship, the likelihood that both might destroy the other. "So the fact you've exposed your hand up here and begun a shooting revolution doesn't matter," Art said. "It's all or nothing, right here, right now. There won't be another chance. Down on the planet Avara—Commander Morali—is throwing away her career, maybe her life, to get the message out. She's telling everyone on her planet of our presence in the system, and *her* government's plans to destroy us. But if the *Mayflower II* keeps hanging up here silently, threateningly, that could be worse than useless. If we still look dangerous, the truth may only ignite public support for our destruction—especially with Arklund's Skywatchers attempting a coup.

"There are two things we have to do. We have to tell the Passengers the truth, just like you wanted me to. Tell them there's a habitable planet. Tell them it's *already inhabited*—by humans. I hope that will make them turn on the Crew, force the Captain to negotiate. But in case it doesn't, we have to be in a position to keep our missiles in their tubes...and break communication silence. We have to contact the government of Peregrine—and, thanks to Morali, the *people* of Peregrine—and assure them no attack is being launched, that those of us on the *Mayflower II* want peace. With that message going into every home on the planet, the government won't dare attack us. They won't want any more civic unrest than Arklund is already giving them."

"Without the access to Shipnet you threw away," Shadow said softly, "the only way to get that message out to everyone on *Mayflower II* is to take over the control room."

A murmur ran through the youngsters. Art glanced at Shadow. *Odd*, he thought. *Woods is the adult mastermind...but half the time Shadow does the talking. And he seems fine with that. Who* is *she?* "Yes," he said. "Can you do it? You lot claim you want to change things on the ship. The only way to do that is to take control of the ship. If you don't, there won't be a ship left to change!"

Shadow's eyes narrowed. "You're also asking us to trust you. I did that once before. I trusted you not to be stupid enough to preview that file. It was a mistake. I never make the same mistake twice."

"Not trusting me would be the mistake this time," Art said quietly. "Listen to me, Shadow, Woods..." He glanced around the room. "All of you. Somewhere on this ship you must have parents, brothers, sisters. If you don't help me, you're sentencing them all to death. Along with yourselves and possibly millions more on Peregrine."

Woods looked from Art to Shadow. "If this is to succeed," he said to her, "it will be *your* doing. You know that. And you and I know what that will mean. Unless *you* support this, we disband the Crawlspacers now."

Shadow ran a finger over the barrel of her rifle. "You could order me," she said. "I've always obeyed your orders."

Woods snorted. "And how exactly would I enforce those orders? No, Shadow. You must decide. But for what it's worth…" Woods's gaze slid back to Art. "I believe him. It matches what I know to be true, and what I know of how our Captain and Crew think. And also…" He cocked his head to one side. "This young man is different than when I saw him two weeks ago. Something has…hardened in him. Changed. For the better."

Art's mouth quirked as he looked at the face that, the last time he'd seen it, had been red-nosed and bleary-eyed. "Could say the same about you," he said.

Woods's own mouth twitched. "Touché."

Shadow's moving finger stopped for a long moment; then suddenly her hand moved to the stock and gripped it, and she straightened. "All right," she said. "We'll do it." She turned to the Crawlspacers. "Ponce, Michael, summon all the Crawlspacers to the Hall. One hour. Top priority, top security, no excuses. Leigh-Anne, you and Andrew meet the new arrivals, kit them up: full assault gear, everyone. Philip, you'll brief them when they get there. Blue Delta. You know the drill."

Philip grinned. "Know it? I helped you write it."

"Janet, you're last out of here. Wait until we're all on our way, then activate the alarms and booby-traps. Then high-tail it to the Hall to join the others."

One of the other girls nodded.

Then Shadow turned to Woods. "Councilor? What will you do?"

“Too old to fight,” Woods said. “Too unsteady on my feet.” He winked at Art. “But don’t worry, I’ll make myself useful somehow.” His gaze on Art turned thoughtful, but he didn’t say anything more.

“Thank you for your help, sir,” Shadow said quietly. “The pod…?”

“Programmed a long time ago,” Woods said. “Awaiting your signal from the transit station of your choice.”

Shadow nodded. “Then let’s go. Councilor, you’re first.”

Woods nodded and went to the ladder leading to the surface. He paused just before his head disappeared from sight. “Good luck,” he said, and resumed climbing.

The rest of them went back the way they had come, except for Janet, who remained behind, already opening lockers in the wall and taking out ominous black boxes. At the door Art knew opened into the back of the transit station, Shadow paused. “Good luck,” she said to Philip and the others. “Remember: Blue Delta. Execution at,” she glanced at her watch, “0545. One hour.”

0545. It hadn’t occurred to Art until then to wonder what time it was on the ship. Still early morning.

As the other Crawlspacers disappeared down the corridor, Shadow pulled him into the short corridor that ended in the “back door” of the transit station. She took something from her pocket, touched it, put it back. They waited through two minutes of silence until a light above the door turned green and it slid open.

A pod waited on the other side. They climbed in. The door closed. Unlike every other pod Art had ever been in, this one said nothing. Nor did it ask for biometric identification. They simply began moving.

“Where are we going?”

“You’ll see,” Shadow said. She pulled off her mask. For the first time he saw her uncovered face: dark skin, full lips, high cheekbones. She stared at him with eyes so brown they looked almost black: piercing, intense. She was older than the others: early 20s, he guessed. “In less than an hour Blue Delta will kick in,” she said, quietly but with fierce intensity. "All the Crawlspacers… at least the ones who answer the call…will be asked to commit themselves to taking the ship. You saw the ones with me a few minutes ago, Stoddard. The rest are no older. They're not children, but they're very, very young. They're bored and angry and like to think of themselves as hardened revolutionaries. They're going to take this as a magnificent adventure. It won't even occur to most to them that they may be killed—until it happens. What I want to know is, has it occurred to you?"

Lorn. Again grief seized his heart, squeezed it hard. "Of course I know," he said angrily. "I've already lost a friend…a young friend…on this 'magnificent adventure.' But he'll have died for nothing—and they'll *all* be dead anyway—if nothing is done. They're all we've got. If I could do it alone, I would." I *would,* he repeated fiercely to himself. "But I can't."

Shadow searched his face, then slowly nodded. "I believe you." She sighed. "Councilor Woods and I have talked about this. We both knew we were building up to a mutiny. But the kids…I wanted to wait until they were older. I thought it might not even be necessary, that as the Crew and Earthborn aged the Shipborn would come to power peacefully. Even with successors being hand-picked, things would change. But this planet…this inhabited planet…"

"Peregrine," Art put in.

"Peregrine," Shadow said, as though the hated the name, "has forced my hand." She sighed and closed her eyes.

For a few minutes they sat in almost-companionable silence. The pod swung through an orientation change, out of the Hab and into the Core. "So where are we going?" Art asked finally.

Shadow didn't answer. The pod did.

"Habitat One: Control Level," it said cheerfully. But it didn't stop. It kept moving.

Art shot upright and stared at Shadow. "Habitat One *Control Level?*"

"Where the bridge is located," Shadow said. "Where an assault force of Crawlspacers will show up in," she glanced at her wristwatch, "about forty-five minutes."

Right around 0630, Art realized. *Right about the time I used to do the morning newscast.* He shook his head. *There's poetic justice for you.*

"Shadow," said a male voice inside Art's head, Ponce's voice, and he started, before belatedly realizing that the communications system that had been inserted into him was still working.

"The Crawlspacers are arriving," Ponce said with barely controlled excitement. "Leigh-Anne and Andrew are handing out the assault kits as they come in. Philip is briefing them. Everything's ready."

"What about Janet?"

Ponce hesitated. "She hasn't shown up yet. Should we send out—"

"Negative." Shadow's unemotional voice belied the pain on her face. "If she's not with you yet, she's not coming. The 'keeps have her."

Silence. "But, Shadow—"

"Focus on Delta Blue. That's an order."

More silence. "Yes, Shadow."

Shadow glanced at Art. "First casualty," she said harshly, and pulled the mask over her head; but though it hid her face, it couldn't conceal the hurt in her eyes.

Not the first, Art thought, thinking of Lorn. *Not the first at all.*

He wondered what *his* eyes revealed.

Chapter Fourteen

The journey to the Control Level ended sooner than Art expected. The door opened, and they stepped out into darkness, again apparently in a back-of-the-transit-station crawlspace. "Why are we here alone?" Art said. "Why didn't we come with the Crawlspacers?"

"Because I'm the only one who can get on the bridge," Shadow said. "And because I want you as close to the bridge as possible before the final assault."

Art stared at her back, a metre in front of him. "How can *you* get onto the bridge?"

Shadow snorted. "Let it be a surprise," she said. "Don't you love surprises?"

"Not in this case."

"You'll understand when I do it," Shadow said. "I don't want you to know until then. In case something goes wrong and you're captured."

Art glanced behind him at the empty corridor. "Pretty sure nobody knows we're here."

Shadow just grunted. A few minutes later she stopped. "Control Level is a maze of corridors and compartments taking up a not-very-large portion of the top part of Habitat One, above the skyplate," she said. "The bridge is at its centre.

"You can't just walk into Control Level, of course. Its main entrance, which is just the other side of that bulkhead," she pointed right, "is quite secure, and also guarded at all times, even when there hasn't been an open revolt somewhere on the ship.

"But like the rest of the ship, Control Level has its hidden world beneath the floors and behind the walls. There were two other ways into it we've identified by examining construction reports for the ship, obtained for us by Councilor Wood, using his almost-Crew-level security clearance. One is a forgotten—we hope—maintenance hatch in a fire-suppression equipment room. The other is a ventilation shaft that apparently got left off the final schematics.

"This is the plan," Shadow continued. "Red, Yellow and Green Cells will take the direct approach, using access codes we've stolen to ride pods to the same transit station we just vacated. But unlike us, they'll emerge right into the station. They'll launch a frontal assault on the main entrance.

"Five minutes later, Orange and Purple will come through the fire-suppression room and spread out through the level, ostensibly attempting to open the main doors from the inside. But both attacks will be mainly diversionary. While everyone's attention is on the hallways, Blue Cell—my cell, the one that rescued you—will attack the bridge itself."

"And how do they get in?"

"You'll see." Gazing off into space, Shadow said, "Philip. All set?"

"All set," said Philip's voice.

"One thing I forgot to say. This mission, nobody wears a mask."

Silence for a moment. "Sir?"

"You heard me," Shadow said. "This is our final action as Crawlspacers. One way or another, this ends it! What difference if they know who we are now? And it will keep them off-balance. Even 'keeps will hesitate to shoot teenagers."

Another moment of silence. "Roger, wilco, sir."

"Execute at the time agreed," Shadow said. "Out."

Art wondered how the gathered Crawlspacers in the Hall, wherever that was, would react to the news. How many of them had joined the shadowy organization as a game, a way to break the boredom? How many of them would turn and run when they actually faced the Crew gun-to-gun? How many would simply go home now, to sit and eat breakfast with their parents while their friends fought and maybe died?

He found himself hoping a great many of them would do just that.

But Blue Cell won't, he thought, remembering the tough youngsters who had already fought the 'keeps in the corridor near the airlock. Even the wounded Emily was back in the fight. And as Shadow had said, whatever force the others could muster was really only for show, to keep the Crew occupied while Blue made the killing thrust into the bridge, the ship's brain and heart combined…

…however it was they were supposed to get in there.

Once they *were* in, Blue would have to hold the bridge against the concerted efforts of Captain and Crew to get it back, hold it until the time came for Art and Avara to let their respective people know the truth, and keep holding it until things were resolved, one way or another. Until peace had been made between ship and planet, they dared not let the Crew regain control of the missiles.

Shadow checked her chronometer again. "Time to get into position," she said tensely and tersely. Art followed her down more corridors, twisting and turning until he was thoroughly lost. Finally she stopped beside a sealed hatch. "Our way into the bridge is on the other side of the corridor outside this hall," she said. "Blue will show up on schedule—they're entering control deck through the forgotten ventilation shaft. As soon as they're in position, and the firefights start down by the main doors, I'm going to open *this* door and walk across to another door that in turn opens onto the bridge."

"Just like that?"

"More or less," Shadow said. "This is the back door; main doors are on the other side. Once it's open, Blue rushes in. You bring up the rear. Don't get yourself shot."

"I'll do my best," Art said fervently.

Ten minutes later, right on time, the rest of Blue showed up. Without a word, Philip shoved a rifle into Art's hands. He took it. It felt heavy and menacing in his hands, which were slick with sweat. He wiped them, one after the other, on his pants.

Shadow checked her watch. "Five minutes," she said. "Once I get the door open, Ponce and Maria go first. Get the main doors closed and sealed. Fire only if fired upon—if we're lucky, no one in the control room will be armed. Philip, you're next; secure CentComp. Make sure they can't take over from an auxiliary board somewhere. Andrew, Leigh-Anne, secure the personnel. We'll herd them out into the corridor out the back door. I want the control room empty of everyone except Crawlspacers two minutes after we enter, and the back door sealed as tight as the main. And while all that's going on, Art and I will secure communications."

"And weapons control," Art put in.

"If we can find it." Shadow glanced at her chronometer. "We've got two minutes until the Hub diversion starts; seven until Orange and Yellow hit the hallways; ten until our turn. Hang tough."

They hung tough. Not that Art was feeling very tough. In fact, he was feeling very un-tough, his heart in his mouth. How could Shadow just…just walk across the hall and let them in? It made no sense.

She's going to get us all killed, he thought, but it wasn't like he saw any better options. He bit his tongue and said nothing. As though she'd heard him, Shadow glanced back at him, but she said nothing, either. To Art if felt as if events had acquired their own momentum, and now they were just along for the ride.

The minutes passed, more slowly than Art would have believed possible. Elsewhere on the control deck the other Cells were already fighting, maybe dying. Some of them could even be children of Crew, fighting their own fathers, mothers, brothers and sisters, all so that he could get to the communications console. Second thoughts fluttered through his mind like vultures, seeking the carrion of doubt, but the time for thought was past: it was time for action.

Or it would be, when two more infinite minutes had passed. He wiped his hands again.

Finally Shadow nodded. “Luck,” she said, opened the door, and darted across the brightly lit hall outside.

The moment she appeared, sirens sounded and red lights flashed, but she ignored them. She touched a control panel beside the back door. “My name is Cynthia,” she whispered, as though it hurt her to speak. “Open the door, please.”

And just like that, the back door to the bridge slid silently open.

Shadow stepped to one side as the rest of Blue charged into the bridge. Art heard shots, and his stomach clenched. So much for a bloodless coup. The bridge Crew hadn’t been unarmed after all.

Shadow waited another eternal minute before motioning him forward. Together, bent almost double, they darted through the door, which slammed behind them. More shots rang out, louder now. Shadow twisted left, fired a burst, and threw herself behind a tall bank of electronic equipment. Art, breathing hard, crawled over to crouch beside her. After a moment, unable to bear it any longer, he eased his head around the corner. Nobody shot it off, and as an added reward, he got his first good look at the nerve centre of the *Mayflower II.*

Four concentric circular levels bearing row upon row of glowing screens and touchpads surrounded a holographic display showing the ship’s approach to Merlin, its projected orbit looping around the dirty-yellow sphere from pole to pole. Heavy gray smoke covered the floor like water, settling in a dingy pool around the base of the hologram projector. The shooting seemed to have stopped. Despite a hissed warning from Shadow, Art raised up on his knees to take a better look.

Ponce’s fingers tapped the control pad alongside the double doors on the far side of the room. Beside him, Maria leaned against the wall, clutching her arm, blood welling through her fingers. He could see Philip at one of the consoles close to the hologram projector, fingers flying over a touchpad. At the far side of the bridge a half-dozen Crewmen huddled together, white-faced, while Andrew held a gun on them. A woman in the uniform of a 'keeps officer lay at their feet, clutching her stomach and moaning.

Of Leigh-Anne there was no sign—until Art saw a scarlet thread running from level to level and followed it back up to the girl's crumpled body, lying against the outer wall, which was splattered as red as though someone had flung whole buckets of paint against it. Not far from her a second 'keeps officer sprawled unmoving. Both were missing parts of their heads.

Art swallowed, bile burning his throat, and dropped his unfired weapon.

"Ponce, is that door secure?" Shadow shouted.

"One second—yes!"

"Then help Andrew with the Crew. Maria, how bad are you hurt?"

"Just a nick," the girl said. She had already ripped away the sleeve of her black uniform and was rummaging in her first aid kit.

"Watch the door. Andrew, get those Crew out of here."

"You heard her!" Andrew shouted, voice tight with grief and rage. "Move! And take her with you!"

The five white-faced Crew gathered up the wounded 'keeps woman and, under the guns of Andrew and Ponce, stumbled across to the back. It opened, and Andrew roughly prodded the Crew out it into the corridor outside. The door slid shut again, and Ponce busied himself with the control pad.

Shadow crossed to the bodies of Leigh-Anne and the Peacekeeper officer, knelt briefly beside each, then left them and went to Philip. Art envied her apparent detachment; his stomach churned and he thought he might be sick, not only from the blood that had splattered the once-immaculate control room, but from the horror of the Crew and children gunning each other down.

But it would all be for nothing if he didn't do his part. Shadow understood that; she kept her mind on the task at hand. *Avara would, too,* he thought. *There'll be time later for emotions.*

Maybe.

He joined Shadow at Philip's console. The computer expert's eyes remained locked on the glowing screens before him. "I've reserved all CentComp functions to this unit. Every other terminal in the ship is dead."

"Where's the communications console?" Art asked.

"I already know that," Shadow told him. "I'm more concerned with the weapons control."

"It's not labeled," Philip replied, "but that's it." He pointed to a console set a little apart, in the ring closest to the hologram.

Shadow followed his gesture. "That's a scientific station—hull sensors."

"Disguise. Construction files don't lie."

"Where's the communications console?" Art asked again. "You may know where it is, but I don't."

"There." Shadow pointed to a console near the weapons control board.

Ponce and Andrew returned. "The door is sealed," Ponce reported. "But I don't know how long it can withstand a concerted assault."

"We only need a few minutes," Art said.

Gunfire crackled outside the main doors.

"I hope we have them." Ponce went to join Maria.

Andrew, after one long, blank look at Leigh-Ann's body, choked out, "I'll watch the back door," and hurried away.

Art picked his way through the banks of equipment to the communications console. Shadow moved to the weapons controls. "Give me a schematic of this on Screen 32," she called to Philip, while Art ran his fingers over the touchpad, setting frequencies and ensuring nothing would stop the flow of data into Shipnet. He touched an icon labeled SHIP-WIDE PUBLIC ADDRESS, wishing for a moment he could be in every Hab to hear his voice echo from the skyplates. *Every newscaster's dream,* he thought.

A screen *he* hadn't activated flicked to life, and he jerked out of camera range as Captain Nakos's dark face filled the frame. "Surrender!" the Captain barked, his voice crackling from every speaker in the control room. "Your co-conspirators are all captured or dead." Art chilled; removing their masks had not protected all of the Crawlspacers. "The Peacekeepers are moving into position for an assault. You cannot hold the control room."

Shadow came over to the communications console, likewise staying out of camera view. "I suggest you move your 'keeps back again, Captain," she said, in a voice rougher and deeper than normal. "In two minutes I'm going to open all the airlocks on the Control Level to space."

Nakos's face darkened further. "You'll kill dozens of—"

"Only if you don't tell them *right now* to retreat."

The Captain's lips thinned. He turned and barked a command, then faced them again. "Done. But I warn you, two can play that game. You evacuate the corridors, and all I have to do is send one space-suited Crewman in with a demolition charge to blow the control room doors. You'll find yourself breathing vacuum."

"You won't do that, Captain," said Shadow.

"Won't I?" he growled.

"No. In the first place, explosive decompression would make a real mess out of your control room. And in the second place…" She stepped into the Captain's view. "I don't think you're ready to kill your own daughter."

Chapter Fifteen

Captain Nakos's dark face turned gray. "Cynthia?"

"*Shadow*, Father. Leader of the Crawlspacers. And I have your ship."

The Captain's face went from gray to purple in an instant. "Cynthia, I demand you surrender the control room at once!" He turned and shouted to someone, "Get those men back in the corridor! I want those kids out of there!"

"In thirty seconds that corridor is going to be hard vacuum," Shadow said coldly.

The Captain faced her. "You won't do it. Not with unprotected Crew out there. You've known those men and women all your life. You were a cadet with some of them. They're your friends!"

Shadow tapped her controls. "Check your screen, Father. One of my people is already dead in here, and one of yours. And how many others have died out in the corridors? We aren't 'kids.' We're revolutionaries. We're overthrowing your tidy little tightly controlled world…we've *already* overthrown it." Her voice took on a mocking tone. "You wanted me to be Captain after you, Father. I just didn't feel like waiting. How's that whole nepotism thing working out for you so far?" She glanced at the chronometer. "Fifteen seconds."

The Captain swore, then shouted, "Get back and close that door!"

Shadow moved to another panel. The corridor outside the control room howled with a hurricane wind, a wind that quickly died away to uncanny silence.

Shadow returned to the communications console. "Now, Father, even if you decide you *are* willing to kill your own daughter to regain control, you can't do it in time to stop us."

"Stop you from doing what? *What do you want?*"

"What do I want?" Shadow laughed bitterly. "I want a life that's worth something, Father. That's what all of us want—the kind of life none of us could ever have on this sealed-up tin can. My whole generation has grown up with no purpose, nothing to do, nothing to work for, nothing to look forward to except the rotting away of the ship from the inside."

"But you would have been Captain!" her father exploded. "Why are you throwing that away?"

"Doesn't matter if you're at the top of a heap of garbage or at the bottom, it still stinks," Shadow said. "But the real reason I'm doing this, Father? Because now that you've finally found the habitable planet we've supposedly been searching for, you've not only tried to keep it a secret, you have plans to blast it into rubble…just so you can keep control." Her father stared at her, shocked. "We know all about the *Mayflower II*'s matter-antimatter missiles, father. You really don't have any secrets at all….not anymore."

"You don't understand!" her father exploded. "The planet isn't just habitable—it's already inhabited…by aliens. *They've already attacked us*. They'll destroy us if they get the chance!"

"Aliens?" Shadow's voice lost its sardonic edge; for the first time, Art heard real fury in it. "*Aliens?* You and I both know that's not true, Father. Just another of your lies. The inhabitants of the planet are as human as you and me. *And you still plan to destroy them*."

"What—what are you talking about?" the Captain spluttered. "Humans? Don't be a fool, Cynthia. We were the first starship launched. How could they be humans? Where did you get such an idiotic notion?"

That sounds like a cue, Art thought, and moved into camera range. "I told them," he said.

The Captain's face turned gray again. "Stoddard? But you're—we thought you were dead!"

"It would have suited you better, wouldn't it?" Art said. "But I'm alive, Captain. And I've been on Peregrine, that inhabited planet. The Peregrine government knows all about your matter-antimatter weapons…and since you won't talk to them, they're convinced you're planning to use them. They're preparing an attack fleet. They plan to destroy the *Mayflower II* and everyone aboard her."

Captain Nikos's eyes flicked back to his daughter. "*Now* will you listen, Cynthia? Pressurize the corridor, let us back in. We've got to be ready—"

"We haven't been attacked," Shadow said firmly. "And we won't fire the first shot."

"But *they* might! The people on that planet are our enemy." The Captain really did sound frantic. "Cynthia, you know how vulnerable we are. Think what it would mean if a Hab were seriously holed. Hundreds could die—"

"I'm not an idiot, Father," Shadow snapped. "We won't attack first. But if it looks like attack is imminent, I'll do what must be done. I promise you that much." And then she cut the connection.

Art shot her a worried look. "Shadow—"

She glanced at him, her face cold and set. "I mean it. I'll defend this ship if necessary. It's up to you to make sure it's not necessary."

Art swallowed. He drew from his pocket the wrinkled, sweat-stained blue paper on which he had written his script in Avara's apartment. He flattened it as best he could on the console.

And then he heard a new voice in his head. He jerked and stared around before he recognized it: Avara. "Art!" she cried. "I'm holed up in the scoutship—I got my message out, fled before they could track me, dodged my way back here…Art, the message is out, but it hasn't made any difference. We've got open insurrection. Arklund's Skywatchers are attacking government installations all over the continent." She paused. "And Art, I just found out…the attack force launched hours ago, *before* I broadcast my message. It must be getting close to you. And it's under the control of the Skywatchers. Arklund is piloting the command ship himself.

"None of them even heard what I said. They wouldn't have listened if they had. I can't stop them, Art. It's up to you." A final pause, then a choked, "Good luck."

"Good luck," Art whispered back, though she would never hear it. *Now or never*, he thought. He turned to the microphone, activated the public address system. "Attention, Passengers and Crew," he said, his voice echoing back at him from the ceiling, his pale, strained face gazing out from every idle vidscreen on the bridge. "This is Arthur Randall Stoddard with a special news bulletin, a bulletin Captain Nakos and his Crew have attempted to keep from you by having me arrested and imprisoned.

"Fellow inhabitants of the starship *Mayflower II*, our long voyage is over. We are no longer hurtling blindly through the galaxy, nor have we been for several days. In fact, even as I speak we are orbiting a gas giant. And further starward in this system there is another world. A habitable world. An *inhabited* world." He started a video clip of scenes of life on Peregrine that Avara had provided him. "But that is only part of the story. Here is the rest…"

As he read the script and played the original file that had begun his strange journey of the past two weeks, Art wished he could see, through the camera lens, the faces of all the Passengers watching him. Would they believe him, or would they dismiss his message as some vile plot to undermine the Crew that some of them—like his parents—nearly worshipped?

Avara's message had already gone out to her people, blanketing all of Peregrine. He thought of the Kymbals, and Javik, listening out in the forest and knowing, as Avara spoke, that he was still alive and back on board the *Mayflower II*…

And not knowing what had happened to Lorn. That thought was like a punch to the stomach. His words faltered for an instant but he forced himself to go on. "Captain and Crew have done their jobs—brought us safely across the void to this new world. But now they don't want to give up the power they've gathered to themselves.

Instead, slaves to orders issued on Earth centuries ago, they plan to destroy this world and everyone on it, and launch us once more into the dark, for another thirty years, or forty, or forever—while more systems fail, and Habs die, and our society stagnates.

"That's what will happen unless you prevent it. Right now the control room is in the hands of the Crawlspacers. But we can't hold it forever. Join us! Fill the streets! Surround the 'keeps stations! Show Captain and Crew that the Passengers have had enough—that they want to do what they left Earth to do—build a better world, and a better life!" His die cast, Art reached out and switched off the audio pickup; but he left the image of Peregrine whirling silently on every screen.

Shadow pushed him aside and began calling up images from throughout the ship. "They're coming out!" she cried. "There's a crowd forming around the 'keeps HQ—Service Sector workers are heading to the Hab Twelve tube station—" She opened the channel to the Captain. "Look, Father! The Passengers are joining us. You've lost. Even if you retake the control room, you can't hold the ship!"

The Captain met her gaze steadily, his face sad, the fire and bluster gone. "I wouldn't start celebrating yet, Cynthia. Check the main tracking display."

Shadow raised her eyes to the hologram. Dozens of tiny flecks of light flicked across it like fireflies. "Stoddard, what's going on?" she demanded.

Art's throat had gone dry. "It's the attack fleet," he said. "Avara warned me, just before I spoke…those ships are piloted by Skywatchers. And Arklund is in command."

"What does he intend to do?" Shadow growled. "Stoddard, *what is he doing*?"

Only the Conqueror of Time and Space can threaten his power, Art thought. *He'll destroy everyone on board this ship to be sure that I'm dead—and, now that he has what he wants, so no one else can take my place.*

All his old fears rose to choke him. Once again, he'd done the wrong thing. "He's after me. He wants me dead. He wants all of us dead."

"He's attacking?"

Art nodded numbly.

"Shit!" Shadow strode to the weapons console. "Philip!"

"Yes, Shadow?"

"Arm all warheads."

"No!" Art started reflexively toward her, but Philip spun, raising his rifle.

"No closer!" he snarled.

Art stopped. "Shadow—" he pleaded.

"I meant what I said to my Father," she told him coldly. "I never wanted to be Captain, but that's what I've just made myself. My first responsibility is to this ship. I won't sit here and let the *Mayflower II* be blown out of the sky."

"If you launch those missiles at their planet they'll attack us for sure!"

"If they attack us I'll be sure to launch those missiles. You tell them that."

"If I tell them you're threatening to launch they'll try to destroy the *Mayflower II* before you have the chance!"

"Then tell them this. A ship comes within a thousand kilometres, I launch one missile. A ship comes within five hundred kilometres, I launch five. And if I'm fired on, I launch them all. You tell them if they keep their distance, I won't launch anything."

"They'll think it's a trick. They won't trust you!" Art glared at her bitterly. "Like *I* shouldn't have trusted you!"

"I trusted you, too, Stoddard. Your plan failed."

"Did it?" Art pointed to a nearby vidscreen showing the crowd massing at Peacekeeper Headquarters. "What will you tell *them* if you destroy the planet?"

"I have no choice!" Shadow shouted. "The ship comes first. Now get on the comm. Tell those ships what I said. *Move!*"

Art turned to the console, knowing as he did so that it was useless. The attacking pilots weren't just soldiers, they were

Skywatchers, fanatics, willing to do whatever Arklund had ordered, in the belief they were hastening paradise. They would accept the destruction of all the cities of Peregrine fatalistically, confident that God would build a new world on the ashes of the old.

He stiffened. Confident, because that was what the First Visionary had told them. But the First Visionary had *also* told them that he was the Conqueror of Time and Space! Every Skywatcher knew it, and there was no way Arklund could have repudiated that proclamation without undermining his own power.

So who *truly* spoke for God, in the Skywatchers' creed?

There might be a way out yet! He tapped the touchpad, setting up the board to broadcast on all frequencies. "Ships of the Skywatchers!" he called. "Acknowledge!"

Shadow shot him a suspicious look, and he suddenly remembered that she could not understand the language of Peregrine. She would have no clue what he told the ships.

Great, he thought. *I'm sure that'll make her* much *more likely to trust me.*

Silence, then a voice he knew all too well said, "Hello, Art."

Arklund!

"If you're planning to surrender, don't waste your breath," the First Visionary continued. "Your ship poses a grave danger to Peregrine, and Peregrine is mine—or soon will be."

Art's hands tightened on the edges of the console. He muted the microphone. "How near are they?" he cried to Shadow.

"Ten thousand kilometres and closing fast. Have you told them what I said?"

"Not yet."

"Then do it! Because whether you've warned them or not, when the first ship hits that thousand-kilometre limit I'm launching."

Art ground his teeth and turned quickly back to the console, activating the mike again. "Ships of Peregrine, you're making a grave mistake. You have been misled by the First Visionary."

“I don’t think blasphemy is going to win them over,” Arklund said dryly.

Art ignored him. He boosted the signal strength to full, added the video component, stared into the camera. He didn’t want anyone in the fleet to fail to hear him or see him. “I am the Conqueror of Time and Space!” he cried to the pilots, in the rolling, stentorian tones he had used when Arklund had proclaimed him as such. “You saw me, in the Great Service. But you did not see me again until now, because The First Visionary attempted to imprison me to prevent it. Having used me to secure his power, he did not want me to speak to you again.

“But *I am the Conqueror of Time and Space*, and the First Visionary has no power over me. I have returned to the vessel in which I crossed the great void: this vessel. And still the First Visionary tries to prevent me from talking to you. He has ordered you to destroy this vessel—my vessel. Can you think of a greater sacrilege?

“The First Visionary no longer speaks for God. He has succumbed to the lust for power, and in that lust he is headed for destruction: his destruction, your destruction, and the destruction of your entire planet. Turn back now! Turn against the First Visionary! Save yourselves and your world…or face the full wrath of God, the God whose will Arklund now defies!”

“Ignore him,” Arklund said, but Art thought he could hear fear in the First Visionary’s voice. “I order you to ignore him! He is an imposter! It is he who commits sacrilege, by pretending to be the Conqueror. Continue the attack!”

Art shot a glance at the hologram. The sparks of light marking the Skywatcher fleet continued their steady approach. “Range?” he whispered to Shadow.

She gave him a look of deep suspicion. “Six thousand kilometres. I don’t know what you’re telling them, Stoddard, but you’re running out of time.”

That’s it, Art thought dully. *There’s nothing left to try*.

He stepped back from the console. At least he *had* tried. He took what comfort he could in that as he stood and watched the lights drawing steadily nearer, and waited for the end.

Then he blinked. Some of the sparks were changing direction, falling out of the larger grouping. Others followed, until only one ship was still on an intercept course with the *Mayflower II*. "Look!" he cried.

"I see it," Shadow said. "But it's not good enough."

"But there's only one—"

"One is enough. One hit on the Core and the ship is dead." She glanced down at her board, then back at Art. "Four thousand kilometres."

"Arklund!" Art roared. "Arklund, are you there?"

"Well-played," Arklund said, voice a tight growl. "Perhaps you really *are* the Conqueror of Time and Space. But you're still going to die. 'Lord, I believe. Help thou my unbelief.'"

Art turned desperately toward. "I can't stop him," he told Shadow. "I was told there are smaller missiles. Can't you just fire at him? You don't have to launch—"

"His ship is too fast and too small," Shadow said. "Stop him, Stoddard. Or in a few hours Peregrine is going to be as uninhabitable as the Captain wanted us to think it was." She met his gaze steadily. "Three thousand kilometres."

For a moment Art stood frozen, thoughts spinning furiously but uselessly. One ship—only one ship had defied him. The First Visionary. All the others had believed he was their Conqueror and turned back. But one stubborn man was about to cause the deaths of thousands, maybe millions. One man out of—

Cursing himself for a fool, Art leaped at the comm console. "Skywatchers! Stop The First Visionary! I command it! If you love God, if your faith is strong, if you believe—*stop him*!"

He spun toward the hologram, as Shadow said, "Twenty-five hundred kilometres." She turned to Philip. "Program missile guidance systems."

"Wait!" Art cried. "You have to wait!" He stared hard at the sparks of light marking the Skywatcher ships nearest Arklund.

Was there movement there?

Yes, he was sure of it! Two—no, three ships were still in position to intercept the First Visionary. Seconds passed. They were closing the gap—but so slowly. They wouldn't be in time. "Shadow, look!" he shouted. "Dammit, look at the display! *They're going to stop him*. You don't have to fire…"

But Shadow was only watching her board, and her voice had taken on the military cadence Art had heard before. "Fifteen hundred kilometres. Fourteen hundred. Thirteen hundred." Her hand touched a switch. "Opening missile silo one. Guidance confirmed?"

"Confirmed," Philip replied.

"Firing in five—four—three—"

Art leaped forward. He grabbed her arm. She jerked it free with more strength than he'd realized she'd possess, then backhanded him across the face, knocking him to the deck. Ears ringing, tasting blood in his mouth, he frantically rolled over—only to find her glaring down at him, sidearm in her hand, pointed at his chest.

The end, he thought bitterly as he stared at the unwavering black barrel. *The end of everything*. If he tried to stop her now she would kill him. She'd won, but she'd also lost. They'd all lost. *Hopeless*, he thought. *It was hopeless from the beginning. All for nothing. Lorn died for nothing...*

But then from somewhere inside him rage welled up: rage and a cold, hard determination. *No!* he snarled at himself. *That's the same argument—you can't act because you can't succeed. I've lived with that long enough, I'll be* damned *if I'm going to die with it too—* As Shadow turned her head slightly to reach for the firing button again, he launched himself at her.

The flash of light from her gun seemed to fill the world. The impact of the bullet smashing into his chest twisted him half-around, but momentum carried him into Shadow and they crashed to the floor together. For a moment he lay on his back, his head on her thigh, ears ringing from the sound of the gunshot, staring up at his blood spotting the weapons console vidscreen; then Shadow moved and his head cracked against the floor, and all he could see was a glowtube in the ceiling.

As it faded into darkness, his last thought was that he would soon have lots of company in death.

Chapter Sixteen

Art did not expect to wake. Certainly he did not expect to wake comfortably ensconced in a private room in the Hab Three hospital, with bright daytime light pouring through the windows along with the sweet smell of honeysuckle.

Yet there he was, and there it was—and at the foot of his bed, even more astonishingly, was Avara.

He blinked just-opened eyes at her, swallowed, and whispered, "Let me guess. We're both dead, and this is Skywatcher paradise?"

"Not quite," she replied. She smiled, stood, and came to his bedside. "How do you feel?"

Art considered the question. He was terribly thirsty, the intravenous needle in his left arm itched, and beneath the skinseal liberally encasing his right side there was a faint but definite ache, but actually he felt amazingly well—the more so as recent events reconnected in his mind and he realized what Avara's presence must mean.

"We did it?" he croaked incredulously.

"*You* did it. It was your broadcast to the Skywatchers, as their Conqueror of Time and Space, that defused things. Not just up here, but on Peregrine. News of the First Visionary's death, at the hands of his own followers, spread like wildfire." She smiled. "And I suppose my own broadcast of images of the *Mayflower II* over the PFN helped, too. The jihad collapsed. Most of the Skywatchers just laid down their weapons and vanished back into the woodwork. The government was so busy taking deep breaths and regaining control it quit worrying about the *Mayflower II*...or the PFN. By the time anyone was in any position to give it more thought, your friend Shadow was broadcasting in your place—offering to negotiate peace."

"What?" Art blinked. "But…she was ready to launch. That's how I got shot. I tried to stop her—"

"You did stop her," said a new voice, and Shadow came into the room.

"You missed it," Avara said, and Art suddenly realized she was speaking English, not Peregrine. "He woke up while you went for semicaf."

"Figures," Shadow said. She stood on Art's other side from Avara. "Yeah, you stopped me," she told him. "Long enough. When I turned back around to launch the missiles I saw on the holographic display that Arklund had been blasted out of space by two of his own ships, who were hightailing it away from us."

Art shook his head. In his own way, Arklund had wanted better things for Peregrine, just like the Crawlspacers had wanted better things for the *Mayflower II*.

On the other hand, given that his route to better things had been paved with bloodshed and death, Art couldn't feel very sorry for him.

He looked from Shadow to Avara. "So…you two have met?"

"We've met," Shadow said. She glanced at Avara. "I've reassured her on several important points."

"Indeed, she's been very kind," Avara said.

Shadow turned back to Art. "I've got some other news for you," she said. "That boy you arrived with…"

"Lorn Kymbal?" Art swallowed, the bright light of the skyplate coming through the window seeming suddenly dim. "Did you…recover his body?"

"We recovered him…but he wasn't just a body. He's still alive."

"What?" The day suddenly brightened again. "But…how?"

"He closed his faceplate before he blew the lock. That automedic thing managed to keep him stable while he floated away from the ship. I made a point of looking for him as soon as I had the chance after I…um….”

“Tried to kill me?” Art said.

“That’s such a harsh way of putting it,” Shadow said. “Anyway, thought you’d like to know. Now I’ve got to go. I’m having dinner with my father for the first time in years. I’ll talk to you later.” She gave Avara another look. “Oh, and you have other visitors. I’ll send them in.” She went to the door, said, “He’s awake,” and exited. Avara gave Art a small wave and followed her.

Jonas Woods entered first. That wasn’t completely unexpected. What *was* was the appearance in the doorway behind him of Art’s parents.

His mother pushed past the others to take Shadow’s place at his side. “Arthur,” she said severely. “What have you been up to? You always were a troublemaker.”

Art stared at her for a moment. Her mouth twitched in a smile, and he smiled back, then laughed. “Guess I was, wasn’t I?”

His father joined her. “Yes,” he grunted. “Always.” He stared down at his son for a long moment, studying his face as if he’d never seen it before. Art met his gaze steadily. “Councilor Wood,” his father said abruptly, “Explained some things to us. Things I hadn’t been aware of. About what you did…were trying to do. And why. Set me straight on a few other matters.” He reached out and straightened the edge of Art’s blanket, and suddenly Art remembered another time when he’d been ill, and his mother, too, and his father had looked after both of them, reaching out just like that to tuck his blanket under his chin…he swallowed. “Just wanted to say…I’m proud of you, son. You saved the ship. Saved us all. I’m…proud.” He cleared his throat. “We’ll talk more later. When you’re better.” He turned abruptly. “Come along, dear,” he said, and led his wife out. She glanced back over her shoulder and gave Art a brilliant smile just before she vanished.

Art stared after them, looked back up at Councilor Woods. “You’re some kind of miracle worker.”

“No,” Woods said. “I’m just a hard-drinking man of the

people." He glanced at his watch. "Who is late to a meeting of the new Debarkation Planning Committee, of which he is chair. Just wanted to come by and say get well soon…and thanks." His voice dropped. "Thanks." He, too, turned and went out.

Art stared at the door for a moment longer, half expecting Treena and Peter to walk in hand and hand and proclaim they were engaged to be married and wanted him to be best man… but in fact the only one who came in was Avara.

"So…how did you and Shadow get along?" he asked her cautiously.

Avara grinned. "Things were a little tense at first. I thought she wanted something I wanted. And I could tell she's just like me: we're both used to getting what we go after."

"That's what attracted me to you in the first place," Art said quietly. "I finally figured it out, in between trying to stay alive. You've never let your doubts keep you from at least *trying* to accomplish something. I always have."

Avara raised one eyebrow. "Really? You must give me an example some time. I haven't noticed." Abruptly she leaned over and kissed him on the forehead, then straightened again. "You'd better rest now. You're going to be very busy as soon as you're strong enough to work."

"Work? Work at what?" Art laughed briefly, but stopped because it hurt. "I don't think anyone will want me as an Information Dissemination Specialist anymore."

"No—however, as Conqueror of Time and Space—"

Art winced.

"De facto chief negotiator for the union of ship and planet—"

Art's eyes widened, but Avara hadn't finished yet.

"Not to mention a hero who will be sought for everything from sausage-factory ribbon cuttings to Landing Day parades—"

Art sighed.

"You'll find plenty to keep you busy." She leaned down and kissed him again, this time on the lips, lingeringly. "Rest up," she breathed. "You'll need it." Then she was gone.

Art licked his lips and swallowed hard, then turned his head and looked out the window at the familiar glowing skyplate of a Hab. After all he'd been through, he was back where he started. Home. Avara said he had work to do, and he supposed he did, but there were a few other things he had to do, too—like apologize to Peter, and explain gently to Treena that she was going to have to find someone else. With a whole planet full of men to choose from, he didn't think she'd mind.

As for him…there was Avara to think about.

He wondered what her status was, now. Did the Peregrine government know she was the mastermind behind the PFN? Did they even care, after all this?

What kind of future could they have together?

He didn't know. But at least, now, there *was* a future. It might not be as bright as it seemed…but at least it was there.

For the moment, that was all he needed to know.

The End

Edward Willett is the author of more than 40 books of science fiction, fantasy and non-fiction for adults, young adults and children. Born in New Mexico, he grew up in Weyburn, Saskatchewan, where he began his career as a reporter and eventually news editor of the Weyburn Review. He also spent five years as communications officer for the Saskatchewan Science Centre before becoming a fulltime freelance writer in 1993.

Among his novels: the Aurora Award-winning SF novel Marseguro (DAW Books); the Saskatchewan Book Award-winning YA fantasy Spirit Singer (just re-released by Tyche Books); epic steam-punkish fantasy Magebane (DAW), written as Lee Arthur Chane, and Masks (also DAW), first book in a new fantasy trilogy, written as E.C. Blake. Nonfiction topics include science, history and biography. In addition to writing, Ed is an actor and singer. He lives in Regina with his wife and daughter.

www.edwardwillet.com